OUT OF ABATON

THE WOODEN PRINCE

BOOK 1

JOHN CLAUDE BEMIS

DISNEP • HYPERION

LOS ANGELES   NEW YORK

First Edition, March 2016

10 9 8 7 6 5 4 3 2 1

FAC-020093-15349

Printed in the United States of America

Reinforced binding

Library of Congress Cataloging-in-Publication Data

Bemis, John Claude.

The wooden prince / John Claude Bemis.—First edition.

pages cm.—(Out of Abaton ; book 1)

Summary: Desperate to save her father, Princess Lazuli, the daughter of the ruler of a magical kingdom called Abaton, enlists the help of the automa Pinocchio and his master, wanted criminal and alchemist Geppetto, who are trying to discover why Pinocchio seems to be changing from a wooden servant into a living, human boy.

ISBN 978-1-4847-0727-2—ISBN 1-4847-0727-3

[1. Fantasy. 2. Characters in literature—Fiction.] I. Title.

PZ7.B4237Wq 2016

[Fic]—dc23   2014049772

Visit www.DisneyBooks.com

SUSTAINABLE FORESTRY INITIATIVE   Certified Sourcing
www.sfiprogram.org
SFI-00993

THIS LABEL APPLIES TO TEXT STOCK

For my father, whose greatest gift was his unconditional love

PART ONE

THE

AUTOMA

1.

The Elongated Nose

By the time Pinocchio arrived in the village of San Baldovino, he was bursting with impatience to get free. Being locked in a trunk shouldn't have bothered him. He was an automa, after all. Back in the palace where he came from, Pinocchio had been locked in closets and stored away in cupboards with the other mechanical servants all the time. It had never bothered him before.

But since he'd been locked in this trunk, he was changing.

Pinocchio shouted and tried again to kick the inside of the trunk, but with his wooden knees pressed into his wooden chest, he was too cramped to make much of a kick. He wriggled and twisted, tangling his smock shirt and tearing his leggings, until he became aware of muffled voices outside the trunk.

"Let me out!" he cried.

A moment later came the sound of squealing nails being pried from the lid. Then the trunk was opened. Pinocchio stretched out his legs and sat up with a puff of relief.

Two figures stared at him. The closest was an automa butler with chipped paint on his wooden face, wearing a moth-eaten black suit. The automa butler held the ax that had been used to open the lid. The other was an elderly man with a bright red nose and watery red eyes that struggled to focus on Pinocchio.

"Otto, give us more light," the old man wheezed.

The automa butler tipped back the crown of his head, exposing a gas flame that hissed to life from his skull. The orange light illuminated racks and racks of wine bottles filling a cobweb-draped cellar.

"It's just an automa, Captain Toro," the old man called. "Put down your gun. It's no danger to us."

Pinocchio realized that a third man was in the cellar. He turned to see an imperial airman in dingy armor, great mechanical wings folded against his back. He had a long-barreled musket aimed at Pinocchio.

The airman lowered his gun. "But, Don Antonio, why would someone try to sneak an automa into the village in the dead of night?"

"I have no idea," Don Antonio said, his breath wet and raspy. "You didn't see who they were?"

"Outlaw vermin, most certainly. Why else would they have run when I came after them? Something suspicious is going on with this puppet."

Don Antonio held a goblet of red liquid in his shaky hands. Pinocchio recognized this as wine. He had served it plenty back

4

in the palace, but the guests usually sipped it. They didn't guzzle it the way Don Antonio was doing.

Don Antonio wiped his mouth on his sleeve. "What scoundrels delivered you here, automa?"

As an automa, Pinocchio had to answer people honestly, even if they weren't his master. Unless, of course, his master had given him orders to lie, but that wasn't the case now, so he replied, "I don't know, *signore*. I never saw them."

"Then where is your master?" Don Antonio asked.

"I don't know that either."

Captain Toro gritted his teeth. "Do you even know who your master is?"

"Yes," Pinocchio said with an eager smile, glad to be able to answer this question. "Geppetto is his name."

Don Antonio gasped, sputtering some wine. "Your master is Geppetto? Geppetto Gazza . . . the traitor to the empire!"

"I don't know," Pinocchio said. "I've never actually met him. But before I was locked in the trunk, I was told I was being sent to my new master and that his name was Geppetto."

"Is this Geppetto here in San Baldovino?" Don Antonio asked, his eyes wide.

Pinocchio was feeling a bit overwhelmed by all the questions and the strange faces Don Antonio and Captain Toro kept making. He had never been any good at interpreting human expressions. No automa was—it wasn't part of their design. Otto, thankfully, just stood placidly over by the wine racks with the ax, the flame flickering atop his head.

"I don't know where Master Geppetto is," Pinocchio said. "Please forgive me, *signore*."

"Traitor, eh?" Captain Toro said. "If I'm not mistaken, this Geppetto is our lord doge's high alchemist."

"*Former* high alchemist," Don Antonio corrected. "He's been on the run since his betrayal. You need to better keep up with the news from the capital, Captain Toro."

Captain Toro made one of those strange expressions that Pinocchio was struggling to understand. Did lowering one's eyebrows and gritting one's teeth mean he was glad to get Don Antonio's suggestions? Pinocchio was determined to figure it out.

"I keep up with news from Venice," Captain Toro growled. "And I can assure you, I will get reassigned to our capital and away from this dusty backcountry one of these days."

"I'm sure you will, Captain," Don Antonio said. "Possibly sooner than later. Don't you see? These weren't half-beast outlaws who delivered the automa, not if it's for the traitor Geppetto. They must have been Abatonian spies! And if you foil their attempts, then I suspect our lord doge will be very pleased with you, Captain Toro. Especially if, in fact, the traitor Geppetto turns out to be hiding in our very midst."

Captain Toro jerked upright. "Yes, I should search for him now."

Don Antonio held up a hand. "And risk failure? You are but one airman."

"I can handle one former high alchemist."

Don Antonio shrugged, a gesture that Pinocchio decided he liked. He tested the movement out a few times while Don Antonio spoke.

"Are you sure, Captain Toro? Would it not be more prudent to deliver the news to Venice and return with reinforcements?"

Captain Toro grumbled.

Pinocchio tried to mimic the noise. Both Captain Toro and Don Antonio looked at him with raised eyebrows. He decided to stay quiet.

"What about the automa?" Captain Toro asked.

"I'll hold it here in my cellar," Don Antonio said. "And just to be safe, I'll order the guards to seal the village gates. No one will enter or leave until you get back."

Captain Toro nodded approvingly. "It will take several days to reach Venice and return."

"Then fly swiftly, good captain," Don Antonio said, lifting his now empty goblet.

Captain Toro picked up his musket and hurried up the stairs.

Don Antonio poured another glass of wine. "Well now, my little automa friend, let's see what we can do with you. Come over here so I can get a better look."

Pinocchio climbed out of the trunk. Don Antonio wasn't his master, but there was no reason not to obey his orders. He vaguely remembered that before he was locked in the trunk, back when he served in the palace, he had been given all sorts of orders: *Bring the tray of spiced meats to the ballroom. Fetch the guests' luggage. Wave the feather fan for Her Ladyship.*

Pinocchio stood before Don Antonio. The old man broke into a wet cough that nearly doubled him over. Don Antonio wiped his knuckles across his mouth and wheezed, "Aren't you just a mystery? I've never seen such a finely constructed automa. You're no crude Hungarian model, like my Otto. No, you came from one of the great workshops of Florence or Milan, I'd gamble. Perhaps you are one of Master da Vinci's Vitruvian designs. Just look at your frame."

Something made Pinocchio suspect that Don Antonio wasn't actually asking him to look at himself. But he decided that orders were orders, and held out his hands to inspect them. He'd never really noticed how he was designed before and certainly had no idea what workshop he'd come from.

"Mahogany for strength," Don Antonio said. "And if my eyes don't deceive me, there's holly, too, for lightness. You must be geared inside with the most delicate of machined parts. The alchemist who designed you was a master. And his elementals, who transmuted your wood and metal to flex like muscle and skin . . . Oh, fine work indeed. And such rich clothes. You must be quite expensive, eh?"

Pinocchio shrugged.

Don Antonio gave a laugh that became the sickly cough again. "Funny expressions they've given you! Shrugging your shoulders. Ha! I've never seen an automa do that. Oh, to have an automa like you . . . But alas, there are better things than a princely servant."

Don Antonio was eyeing him up and down in a way that made Pinocchio's gearworks feel strange. He'd never felt this before. In truth, he'd never felt any sensation before his whole ordeal with the prisoner and the trunk. What was going on with him? Whatever it was, at that moment Pinocchio desperately wished he could get away from the old man.

But he was an automa, and automa had to do as they were told.

"Yes, there is a better use for you," Don Antonio said, reaching a gnarled hand toward Pinocchio's chest. "Your fantom. What I would give for that! Let's just open you up and take a look—"

But before the old man could touch his chest panel, Pinocchio's hand shot out and grabbed Don Antonio's wrist. He hadn't meant to do this, and it surprised him completely.

"ARGH!" Don Antonio cried out. "You're crushing my bones! Let go of me, you fiend!"

Pinocchio couldn't let go, no matter how much he wanted to.

Something about Don Antonio reaching for his chest panel had caused him to grab the old man. Watching with horror as Don Antonio struggled to pull free, Pinocchio realized how strong his gearworks made him—so much stronger than a human, especially an old one.

"I'm sorry, *signore*. I don't know why I'm doing this. I can't help it! Really I can't."

His nose began to grow. Little by little it inched out from his face. Pinocchio knew what this meant. Automa weren't supposed to hurt any person, unless their masters ordered it. And the mark of an automa who caused harm or wasn't following orders properly was an elongated nose. Oh, why couldn't he let go? Why couldn't he be an obedient automa?

Don Antonio wailed in agony and dropped to his knees. "Otto, help me!"

The mechanical butler was there in an instant, struggling to pry Pinocchio's grip from his master's wrist. But it was no use. Pinocchio couldn't get free.

"The . . . ax!" Don Antonio managed.

Otto picked up the ax and reared back with it. Pinocchio furiously tried to get his fingers to let go of Don Antonio, but they wouldn't obey.

Otto swung. The ax bit deep into Pinocchio's arm. Naturally it didn't hurt, but as the iron blade lodged into his wood, Pinocchio felt his gearworks go slack and his vision dim. Direct contact with iron—or with lead or any other base metal—disrupted an automa's functions. Pinocchio knew that well enough.

The blow from the ax finally allowed him to release Don Antonio. Pinocchio fell with a clatter on the stone floor. His vision came back into focus. He stared dimly up at the ceiling, past his horrid long nose. All sorts of feelings flooded through him, feelings that he had no name for, feelings that made the wooden surface of his face seem to burn and made his gears feel mangled.

"Are you injured, my master?" Otto asked in his monotone voice.

Don Antonio whimpered. "My arm . . . I think I can move it. Nothing seems broken."

"Very good," Otto said. "What should I do with the automa?"

"Lock that thing back in the trunk," Don Antonio snarled.

Pinocchio wanted more than anything not to go back in that dark, cramped box. But he couldn't disobey. His nose was long enough already.

Movement was beginning to return to his gears, but Pinocchio allowed Otto to place him inside the trunk. As Otto began to hammer the nails back into the lid, Pinocchio heard Don Antonio say, "After you're finished, send for Signore Polendina."

"The shopkeeper?" Otto asked.

"Yes, the *shopkeeper*," Don Antonio said with what almost sounded to Pinocchio like a chuckle. Why would he laugh? That was puzzling. "I've been wondering about our village's new shopkeeper," Don Antonio went on. "If we are properly persuasive, Otto, I suspect Signore Polendina might have much to reveal about the traitor Geppetto's whereabouts."

2.

Traitor to the Empire

Trapped once again in the trunk, Pinocchio wished he could return to his old life. Back when he was a servant in the floating palace, he hadn't had any of the confusing feelings that were churning through his insides now. What he would have given to be back simply following orders and serving the palace guests like a good automa. Not hurting anyone.

Soon muffled voices returned to the cellar. Pinocchio tried to hear what they were saying, but only snatches of words came through the trunk's lid: ". . . Captain Toro found it . . . outside the village gates . . . flown back to Venice for orders . . . returning with airmen . . ."

At last the lid came off. At the sight of Otto and his ax, Pinocchio flinched down as flat as he could in the trunk.

"He looks frightened," a man said.

Pinocchio peered up from the trunk. The man, who must have been the shopkeeper Signore Polendina, was about half the age of Don Antonio. He had a pointed mustache and streaks of silver in his black hair. He wasn't nearly as well dressed as Don Antonio, but Pinocchio liked his face right away. He didn't narrow his eyes or do those funny things with his eyebrows.

"Frightened?" Don Antonio chuckled in his wheezy voice. "Don't be ridiculous, man. An automa can't be frightened."

Pinocchio wondered if in fact that *was* how he was feeling. Frightened.

"Yes, of course." Polendina stroked his mustache. "The automa's nose has extended. What's he done?"

Don Antonio gave a wet cough before saying, "That's why I've brought you here, Signore Polendina. Have you heard what these automa have inside their chests?"

Polendina hesitated half a moment. "I know a little. A fantom, so I've been told? The springwork that the imperial alchemists use to animate these automa."

"Exactly. But did you know that their fantoms can be used as elixirs? They can be turned into potions that extend life." Don Antonio grinned. "What can I say? I was curious. I tried to open the automa's chest to get its fantom."

He gave Pinocchio an accusing frown and held up his bandaged arm. "But when I did, this fiend nearly broke my wrist! Even Otto was not strong enough to break its grip. He had to strike it with an ax to get it to let go of me."

Polendina's eyes searched until he spotted the tear in Pinocchio's sleeve. Pinocchio brought his hand up to the spot, feeling the notch in his wooden arm. For an instant their eyes met, and Polendina gave Pinocchio a tilt of his head.

"I couldn't help it, *signore!*" Pinocchio said all at once. "It wasn't my fault."

"Be silent," Otto said, shaking the ax at him.

As Pinocchio shrank back, Signore Polendina's gaze remained fixed on him.

"I assume you want me to keep quiet to Captain Toro that you've been curious about his captive?" Polendina said.

Don Antonio's voice lowered. "I want more than that of you, Signore Polendina."

"What do you mean?"

"I believe you know who this automa belongs to."

Signore Polendina frowned. "Who?"

"The automa says its master is Geppetto."

Signore Polendina blinked so placidly he might have been an automa. "I don't know any Geppetto."

"I think you do," Don Antonio said with a strange smile. "When I learned that the automa was supposed to be delivered to the traitor and former high alchemist Geppetto Gazza, the pieces fell into place. You see, not many know this, but Geppetto Gazza's wife and son recently lived here. In a fortified villa not far outside our walls. In fact, sadly, Geppetto's family was murdered here, supposedly by a band of half-beast outlaws."

Pinocchio watched, transfixed, struggling to make sense of what Don Antonio was saying. He found that his hands were fidgeting with something in his pocket. A key. Pinocchio vaguely remembered the prisoner giving it to him, but there was no time to wonder about that now.

"No one would have guessed that the fugitive Geppetto would return to his wife's hometown," Don Antonio continued. "Such a man would be better off taking refuge in the false pope's court in France or fleeing into the deepest wilds of the Kongo. Coming here would be the act of a man with nothing left to live for, nothing left to lose. A man simply waiting for his inevitable capture. Still, he came, although none of us were the wiser."

Don Antonio poured himself a glass of wine before continuing. "When you arrived in our village a few months back and set up your shop, Polendina's Abatonian Imports and Refurbishments, I assumed, as any would, that you were simply a dealer in Abatonian magical goods. A nice business. A welcome addition to our little out-of-the-way town. But we don't get many new citizens here. Our town is not the sort of place strangers come to start businesses. Let me speak plainly. You aren't who you claim to be, are you, Signore Polendina?"

"I don't know what you're talking about," Polendina said.

Don Antonio pointed to Polendina's hands. "You always wear gloves indoors, *signore*. Why don't you take them off and show me your fingers?"

Signore Polendina crossed his arms, tucking his gloved hands away.

"Are you afraid to show me your burned fingertips? Afraid to show that you have the marks of an alchemist, *Master Geppetto*?" Don Antonio said.

Pinocchio tried to make sense of this. Was Signore Polendina actually Geppetto? Was that why Don Antonio had brought the man here? A warm feeling surged through Pinocchio's gears at the thought that this might be his new master.

Geppetto or Polendina or whoever he was gave a swift look back at Otto, his face momentarily showing that he was . . . what was the word? *Frightened*? The automa butler stared blankly back at him, the ax held firmly across his chest.

"Don't worry, dear man. I mean you no harm," Don Antonio

said. "Yes, you are in danger, but not from me, I can assure you. Captain Toro will return soon with a whole squadron of imperial airmen, if not Flying Lions. They will want to capture this Geppetto as a traitor to the empire. But it will take days for them to return all the way out here. We have time. We still have time."

"Time for what?"

Don Antonio waved to Pinocchio. "For me to give you what is rightfully yours."

"You have me mistaken for someone else, Don Antonio," Signore Polendina said, walking quickly past Otto and toward the stairs. "I bid you good night."

Don Antonio let him pass before saying, "And what shall I do with the automa? Give it over to Captain Toro? Let them take it back to Venice, where they'll disassemble it to find out why it was sent to the traitor Geppetto?"

"No!" Pinocchio cried, leaping from the trunk.

This was his master! He was sure of it. He couldn't let Master Geppetto go. But Otto reared up with the ax, waiting for Don Antonio's orders. Pinocchio shrank back. "Please don't let them do that to me, Master!"

The shopkeeper froze. He looked back over his shoulder at Pinocchio, his face pinched. "You fear being disassembled?"

"Yes, Master," Pinocchio pleaded. "Don't leave me here."

The man slowly walked back toward Don Antonio. "Am I to believe that you would simply defy an officer of the empire and allow me to escape with this automa?"

Don Antonio smiled. "You are right, *signore*. It is a crime, is it not? But suppose the trunk was smashed open, and suppose I told Captain Toro that the prisoner escaped?"

"That might be believed." The shopkeeper crossed his arms over his chest. "But you would be taking an enormous risk."

"Yes, I would." Don Antonio tapped his whiskery chin thoughtfully. "But suppose you made it a risk I was willing to take?"

"What do you want from me?"

"I am an old man," Don Antonio wheezed. "I am nearing the end of my life. I'm not eager for it to be over. Who is? A few more years would be most welcome. A few more years to enjoy my glasses of Chianti and plates of pasta and roasted boar."

"You want an elixir."

Don Antonio gave him a playful poke in the chest. "My father, rest his soul, dabbled in alchemy. He told me all about how elixirs are made, although he was never able to make one himself. If you, sir, are the fabled alchemist Geppetto Gazza, then you would be able to make an elixir that could extend my life a few more years. Dare I hope even decades?"

"Possibly," he answered. "But to make an elixir, I'll need the fantom of an automa. Where would I get the fantom?"

Don Antonio held a hand toward Pinocchio.

The shopkeeper shook his head. "If I remove his fantom, he'll no longer function. I'd never know why the automa was sent. What good would it be to take the lad if he no longer functioned?"

Pinocchio didn't like how that sounded.

Don Antonio sighed. "I feared that might be the case. But you are quite right. Fortunately, we have another option."

His eyes darted to Otto.

"I can always purchase a new butler," Don Antonio said. "But the opportunity to make an exchange with an alchemist of your talents, Master Geppetto, does not come along often. You may use Otto's fantom."

Slipping off his gloves and exposing his blackened fingertips,

Geppetto stepped toward Otto. The mechanical butler watched him impassively.

"Put down your ax, Otto," Don Antonio ordered.

Otto laid the ax against the wall and faced Geppetto again. Geppetto pushed Otto's cravat out of the way and unbuttoned his shirt, revealing a compartment in the middle of his chest. Geppetto turned the latch and opened the panel. In the hollow square gleamed a golden orb of gears and springs.

Pinocchio had never seen a fantom. In fact, he'd had no idea his kind even had them. He'd never wondered before about how he worked. But now curiosity was burning in him, and he watched eagerly.

Don Antonio seemed eager as well as he hissed, "Yes!" at the sight of the fantom.

Geppetto took Otto's fantom in a firm grip and pulled it loose. Otto's eyes dulled and his head tilted, the flame continuing its flickering from the open crown of his skull.

Pinocchio knew Otto was no longer functioning. An automa wouldn't mind this. Automa didn't mind anything. But something about seeing Otto this way now bothered Pinocchio deeply. It frightened him, and he didn't like this new sensation.

"I have my father's laboratory instruments," Don Antonio said. "Tell me what you need, master alchemist."

"I only need a glass," Geppetto said drily. "A clean one."

Don Antonio hurried back through the wine racks, wheezing noisily, to where he fetched a new wine goblet.

"Just hold on to it," Geppetto said when he returned.

Don Antonio gripped the stem of the goblet, hands trembling terribly. Geppetto took a small leather case from his pocket.

"Is that a salamander's tail?" Don Antonio asked, smiling. "My father had a fine collection of minor elemental creatures—"

"Quiet, so I can concentrate," Geppetto said.

He clutched the case in one hand and cupped his other hand around the fantom, holding it over the shaking goblet. Geppetto closed his eyes, murmuring softly under his breath. Orange molten light grew at the seams of the case.

The hard metal of the fantom dissolved all at once like melted butter, running through his fingers and filling the glass almost to the rim with a golden liquid. Don Antonio held his breath to keep the glass steady.

When the cup was filled, Geppetto opened his hands. Not a drop remained on his palms. The tips of his fingers, however, smoked with the stench of burned flesh and powerful alchemy.

Don Antonio smacked his lips at the shimmering elixir. "Shall I?"

"Drink it," Geppetto said.

Don Antonio raised the glass as if giving a toast and wheezed, "To life!"

Geppetto grunted in reply, his eyes narrowed on the old man.

In greedy gulps, Don Antonio emptied the goblet. The sickly rumbling from his chest quieted. His waxy face took on a healthy glow. And as he opened his eyes, they were clearer than before. He almost looked sober.

"Where is the lad's fealty key?" Geppetto asked.

"I'm afraid I don't have it," Don Antonio said, already pouring himself a glass of wine. "But we have our agreement, so—"

"I have a key in my pocket," Pinocchio said.

"Let me have it," Geppetto said.

As Pinocchio handed it to him, he asked, "Am I coming with you now?"

"Yes," Geppetto replied. "Turn your head so I can get to your fealty lock."

Pinocchio looked to one side. "Will I serve in a court? I did before. I remember a palace. Do you live in a palace?"

"No," Geppetto said.

"That's right," Pinocchio said, feeling the key slide into the lock at the back of his neck. "You're a shopkeeper. Will I work in your shop?"

"I won't be able to keep my shop anymore."

"What will we do?"

"I don't know yet," Geppetto answered. "Do you have a name?"

"Pinocchio."

"Well, Pinocchio, if you are willing to come with me and do as you're told, I can fix your nose."

Pinocchio touched the clumsy rod sticking from his face. "Good. I hate my nose this way. It makes me feel . . . I don't know what the word is."

Geppetto stared at him intently before saying, "Embarrassed?"

"I suppose," Pinocchio said.

Geppetto's mouth opened and closed before he managed to ask, "What automa feels embarrassed?"

Pinocchio shrugged.

Geppetto shook his head. "There is much to figure out, but first this nose of yours." He reached forward to tap Pinocchio's nose.

"No, Master!" Pinocchio shouted.

But it was too late. He had Geppetto by the wrist, squeezing with that terribly strong grip.

Geppetto gritted his teeth. "Release me, Pinocchio! I'm your master. I order you to release me."

"I can't! Really I can't," Pinocchio cried.

"Shall I fetch the ax?" Don Antonio asked.

"Wait," Geppetto grunted. He reached for the fealty key in the back of Pinocchio's neck and gave it a turn.

A wonderful sensation of lightness and freedom came over Pinocchio, like at any moment he might float up to the ceiling.

"Pinocchio, I, Geppetto, am your master now."

Pinocchio felt as if a heavy weight had suddenly been placed on him. His limbs flopped slack, and Geppetto used that instant to jerk his hand free and scuttle back from Pinocchio.

Sitting on the floor as the dizzy feeling passed, Pinocchio crossed his eyes and watched as his nose shrank to its normal proportions.

"Thank you, Master," he sighed. "Thank you. I hope I didn't hurt you."

Geppetto massaged his wrist. "I'm fine. We need to leave now." He snatched the key from Pinocchio's neck and slipped it into a coat pocket.

Don Antonio smiled, his eyes already swimming once more with wine. "Yes. Our dealings have come to a close." He patted the motionless Otto. "I'll tell Captain Toro that the boy destroyed my butler's fantom in his escape. You have nothing to fear from my story."

The look on his master's face as they left made Pinocchio realize there was actually much they needed to fear.

Pinocchio followed his master down the steep, winding streets of San Baldovino. It was still night, and the village was quiet, except for their footsteps on the cobblestones. They reached a shop with the sign POLENDINA'S ABATONIAN IMPORTS AND REFURBISHMENTS hanging over the door.

Geppetto unlocked the door and led Pinocchio inside. The shop was cluttered with shelves of boxes and bottles, rolls of fabrics and old boots. Pinocchio had no idea what they were all for, but he looked around with great interest.

Geppetto pointed to a stool behind the counter that divided the room. "Sit there."

Pinocchio sat.

Geppetto hung up his cloak and stood on the far side of the room, staring absently at Pinocchio.

"Should I light a lamp, Master?"

"No," Geppetto mumbled.

Pinocchio looked up at the darkened rafters. "Do you have pixie bulbs? I could light them if you have a bellows. I know how to do that."

"No," Geppetto said. "It's late."

"Would you like me to—"

"I'm going to bed." Geppetto marched toward a curtain separating his shop from a back room.

Pinocchio wished his master wouldn't leave him all alone. But he said nothing. Automa are fine by themselves, he reminded himself. His master was human and needed sleep.

Geppetto stopped in the curtained doorway. "Just stay there. Until I awaken in the morning."

Pinocchio nodded.

"You'll do as I've asked?"

"Of course, Master," Pinocchio said pleasantly.

Geppetto sighed and disappeared through the curtain.

Pinocchio heard a tiny voice chirp in the other room, "Who's out there? What's happened? You look shaken to your core!"

"I'll explain in the morning," Geppetto whispered. "And Maestro . . ."

"Yes?" the other voice asked softly.

"Listen out. If you hear anything, wake me right away."

"Fiery phoenix, Geppetto! What have you gotten us into?"

A few moments later, a faint song began from behind the curtain. Pinocchio sat on the stool, listening, spellbound. The music was . . . what was the word? *Lovely*? Now that was a notion he'd never considered before!

What was making those lovely, lovely sounds?

Curiosity made his knee gears twitch. He desperately wanted to go over to the curtain. Just a peek. Just to see what sort of windup box or water-clock chime was making those exquisite sounds.

He clamped his hands over his knees. "No," he whispered to his legs. "Master said to stay here."

Pinocchio fought the urge until at last the song came to an end and quiet filled the shop. His knees relaxed, and he stayed on the stool through the long and weary hours of night.

3.

The Missing Fantom

Pinocchio waited on the stool until finally dawn grew golden at the windows. Sounds emerged from the room behind the curtain: Logs fed into a hearth. The clanking of pots. Murmurings between Master Geppetto and the small chirping voice.

Pinocchio couldn't hear them properly until at last Master Geppetto bellowed, "It's too dangerous with all the half-beasts! We can't leave unless we can hire an armed coach. And unfortunately, we have no gold. . . ."

More murmuring. Pinocchio's eyes were glued to the curtain. At last Master Geppetto swept it aside, carrying a bamboo cage, which he placed atop the clutter on the counter. He marched over to open the shade on the door, turned the sign around to BENVENUTO, and headed once again into the back room.

"So you're our new automa?"

Pinocchio looked around before spotting a cricket emerging from the cage. "Who are you?"

"Maestro," the cricket replied, poking his antennae out.

"Are you the device that was playing music last night?"

"I'm no windup toy, you ignoramus!" the cricket chirped. "I'm real. I'll have you know I hatched from an egg in farthest Abaton. I come from a long and prestigious line of musicians who performed for Prester John himself."

Pinocchio had never heard of any Prester John, but then he'd never heard of Abaton, either. The only country Pinocchio could think of was China. As a palace servant, he'd always had to say "Care for a cup of coffee, *signore*, or a tea from China?" So he asked, "Is your homeland near China?"

"Nearer to China than to here," the cricket said. "Where do you come from, or were you never told?"

Pinocchio was eager to show he knew. "I come from a palace."

"Whose palace?" Maestro asked.

Pinocchio thought. He knew it floated high above a magnificent city with streets of water. His master had been the head butler, and even he was a servant of the palace, although not an automa servant. But had his former master ever mentioned whose palace it was . . . ?

"You don't know, do you?" Maestro said, with a playful flicker of his antennae.

"Don't tease him, Maestro," Geppetto said as he came back in, carrying a cup of coffee and a box. The box was etched with designs and speckled with colorful pieces of glass. Set into the

24

lid was a complicated mechanism of gears and brass parts.

"What does it matter?" Maestro chirped. "He's just an automa."

Geppetto gave a grunt and took out some tools to begin working on the box. He tapped out dented gears and heated solder over a gas flame.

"What should I do, Master?" Pinocchio asked.

"Can you repair broken chimera boxes?" Geppetto asked.

"I don't think so."

"Then just sit there."

Geppetto pried at a piece of ruby-red glass on the side. The jewel cracked under the tip of the chisel. "Blast it!" He slammed the tool to the counter. "Maestro, must you just sit there in silence?"

"Not if you ask nicely," the cricket said.

Geppetto smirked at him. "I'll floss my teeth *nicely* with your antennae."

"Incorrigible barbarian," Maestro muttered, before beginning a song.

"What does *incorrigible* mean, Master?" Pinocchio asked.

"It means 'wonderful,'" Geppetto said, a smile poking out beneath his mustache.

Maestro stopped playing and shook his tiny head in exasperation before continuing his song.

Geppetto leaned over the counter to peer cautiously out at the street. A man was pushing a vegetable cart up the cobblestone lane. Others were sweeping away the debris from last night's storm.

Discreetly, from a drawer beneath the counter, he took out the case that Pinocchio remembered contained a salamander's tail, whatever that was. Geppetto held the case in one hand

and touched a blackened fingertip to the broken glass jewel. The glass sizzled and then became whole once more, popping out from the casing and rattling onto the countertop. Geppetto stowed the case back in the drawer. Then he straightened up and took a satisfied sip of his coffee.

"How did you do that, Master?" Pinocchio asked.

"A trick I picked up from an elemental," Geppetto said before resuming his work.

Pinocchio had a vague memory that the alchemist who used to do repairs on the palace automa often worked with a gnome. "Is a gnome an elemental?"

"An earth elemental," Geppetto said absently. "But enough questions. I need to fix this chimera box if we're to earn some gold, and you've already cost me an evening of work."

"I didn't realize I had," Pinocchio said. "Forgive me, Master. I heard you say you needed gold to hire an armed coach. Are we going somewhere?"

Geppetto narrowed his eyes at him but didn't reply. He continued his work, soldering bits of metal to repair portions of the lid. As he worked, his eyes flickered to Pinocchio.

Pinocchio shifted on the stool. "Am I just to sit here, Master? I could do something for you." He saw no feathered fans around to wave, and certainly Master Geppetto didn't need him to carry out any trays of food. "I could hand you your tools."

"I can get them myself." Geppetto squatted to search through drawers under the counter.

"What does a chimera box do?" Pinocchio asked, reaching to open the lid.

"NO!" Maestro shouted.

A horrendous noise rose from the box. Geppetto leaped up

and clapped the lid shut. "Ravage and ruin! How am I supposed to work with you around?"

"I—I only wanted to see what it did," Pinocchio stammered.

"As you can now see," Geppetto said gruffly, "it's an alarm that is supposed to go off only around chimera—or half-beasts, as we call them here in the empire. This one is broken and has been going off around anything remotely animal, including Signora Ferragutti's numerous house cats as well as . . . Maestro."

"I'm sorry, Master. I just wanted to help you with it."

"You can help by keeping your hands to yourself!" Geppetto said. "I have much to sort out. We haven't much time."

"Time before what?" Pinocchio said. "Before we leave?" He was curious to know where Geppetto was planning to take him. He hoped it was somewhere interesting.

Geppetto pointed to a broom. "Take that and go sweep my quarters in the back. You shouldn't be out here in plain view anyway. Can you do that?"

"Of course, Master."

"Then do it."

Pinocchio hopped down from the stool and took the broom back through the curtain, excited to see where Geppetto lived. He was disappointed to find a single room of ancient stone walls and a dusty stone floor. A narrow, unmade bed sat against one wall. A dresser and sagging bookcase stood beside the back door. Otherwise the only furniture was a chair and an oak table, where Geppetto's bowl of half-eaten porridge remained. It was no better than the storage room for the automa servants back in the floating palace!

Pinocchio began to sweep, brushing the dust toward the hearth. Something moved in the cinders of the fireplace. He bent down to get a closer look and spied a fat, wriggling lizard in the fire. The creature's tail looked broken off, and Pinocchio suddenly realized that this must be a salamander.

Geppetto stormed in, and Pinocchio hurriedly began sweeping again.

"Sit down over here," Geppetto commanded, gesturing to the chair.

"You want me to sit again?" Pinocchio flopped down.

Geppetto perched himself on the edge of his bed, rubbing his hands together. "Why are you here?" he asked.

"I don't know what you mean, Master. You took me from Don Antonio's last—"

"Someone sent you to me. I want to know who it was."

"I don't know."

Maestro flew in and landed on the table. Geppetto ran his fingers through his mane of silvery-black hair. "Cursed oblivious automa," he grumbled. "If only we designed you with decent memories . . ."

"But I do, Master."

"Do what?"

"I do remember," Pinocchio said. "At least I remember something. Not really before. But since."

Geppetto sat straighter. "Before and since what?"

"The night the prisoner freed me."

Geppetto's expression changed, as completely as night to day. "Who freed you?"

"He didn't exactly free me," Pinocchio said. "He gave me to you, Master. But he freed me from the palace. And he did something strange to my functions. Before, I hadn't a care for anything except attending to the palace guests like the other automa. But after that night when I delivered a meal to the palace prison, I began to notice things I hadn't before."

"Do you remember the prisoner's name?"

"He never told me," Pinocchio said. He touched the front of his shirt. "For a few moments, I stopped functioning and everything went dark. When I started working again, the prisoner was closing the panel in my chest, and he said, 'Your new master is going to be Geppetto. I'm sending you to him.' Then he said, 'They'll be back any moment. Quickly now. Out the window before they arrive.' So I jumped as he ordered."

That had been such a curious feeling. The falling. That had certainly never happened to him before.

"I sank down to the bottom of the sea," Pinocchio said. "I can't swim, after all, with these heavy gears in me. It was dark down there. Finally hands took hold of me. They put me in that trunk. For such a long time! I banged and shouted and wanted to get free, but I couldn't, until they let me out in Don Antonio's cellar. And now I'm with you here, wherever this is."

Maestro shifted on his cricket legs. "The last refuge of the hopeless."

"Oh," Pinocchio said, having no idea what the cricket meant.

"You're in Tuscany," Geppetto said. "An out-of-the-way corner of the Venetian Empire."

"Oh," Pinocchio said again, no closer to understanding. "But why did the prisoner send me to you, Master?"

"That's what I want to know." Geppetto twisted his mustache. "The prisoner didn't give you instructions?"

"No."

"Are you sure? No message for me? He just sent you to me."

Pinocchio shrugged.

"How anyone knows I am here is troubling, to put it mildly," Geppetto mumbled.

"Maybe there's a message inside with his fantom," Maestro said.

"But whoever placed it there has made sure the automa will protect it," Geppetto said. "He nearly broke my arm last night. He can't allow me to open him."

"I would if I could," Pinocchio said. "You're my master. I don't like when my nose grows. I want to do as you ask."

Geppetto's eyes flashed as if he had just realized something. "Yes! Just maybe . . . Stay still, lad. I want to try something." He walked several strides back from Pinocchio. "Open your shirt."

"All right, Master," Pinocchio said and unbuttoned his shirt.

Geppetto nodded to the polished wood of Pinocchio's chest. "Can you open that panel?"

Maestro crept slowly on his long legs to the edge of the table to get a better view.

"I think so," Pinocchio replied.

"Then try it."

Pinocchio remembered what had happened to Otto last night, and he hesitated. "You won't hurt me, will you, Master?"

"No," Geppetto said gently. "I promise you I won't."

Pinocchio turned the latch and opened the panel door.

Geppetto gasped and took a step forward. Pinocchio's hand shot up protectively, but Geppetto was too far out of reach.

"I'm not going to touch you," Geppetto said, leaning forward. "Just stay where you are. Keep your hands still if you can."

Maestro's wings buzzed with agitation.

Pinocchio struggled to bring his hands to his lap. "What is it, Master?" He mashed his wooden chin as hard against his wooden chest as he could. He could make out something rounded, with barklike spikes. It didn't seem to be golden like Otto's fantom.

"I've never seen anything like this!" Geppetto murmured.

Pinocchio reached for it but then remembered what had happened to Otto and feared causing the fantom to come loose.

"My fantom's not like Otto's," Pinocchio said.

Geppetto paced in a circle. "It's not a fantom at all, as far as I can tell."

"Then what is in my chest?" Panic began to well in him.

"A pinecone, Pinocchio. You have a pinecone where your fantom should be." Geppetto locked eyes with him. "By all logic, you shouldn't even be alive."

4.

Squashed Salamander

Pinocchio didn't know what to make of this strange news. "But I'm not alive. Am I, Master? I'm just an automa."

"You're a very unusual automa," Geppetto said. "But you're right. No, you're not alive. A poor choice of words. Let me ask: When you were at the bottom of the sea, how did you feel?"

Maestro laughed a musical note. "Don't be ridiculous. Automa can't feel."

Geppetto ignored him, waiting for Pinocchio's answer.

Pinocchio wasn't sure what his master was asking. "I suppose I felt frightened. Frightened that I would be stuck there forever."

"Yes," Geppetto mused. "And you might have been. What a dismal existence, to lie forever at the bottom of the sea. Had you ever felt that before? Scared, that is. Frustrated at being stuck somewhere."

"I was frustrated that I couldn't get out of the trunk."

"But before then? Before the prisoner?"

"No, I don't think I felt much of anything before then," Pinocchio said.

Geppetto exchanged a glance with Maestro, but Pinocchio had no idea what they were thinking. "The man in the prison . . . did he do something bad to me?"

Geppetto smiled, the first kind smile Pinocchio had seen him give. "No, my dear Pinocchio, he did nothing bad. In fact, I believe Prester John has done something quite wonderful to you."

Maestro sprang to Geppetto's shoulder. "Prester John! You think *he* sent the automa to you?"

"Who else?" Geppetto said. "Pinocchio, you said you jumped from the window of a palace into the sea. Was the palace hovering in the sky?"

"Yes. Above a city with streets of water."

"Venice!" Maestro exclaimed, his wings fluttering. "He served in the Fortezza Ducale, the doge's floating palace! But why is Prester John there?"

"I can't say," Geppetto said. "But if he's imprisoned, it can't be good. All the more reason I need to finish that chimera box so we can leave and get some answers. Wait here."

Geppetto returned a moment later with the box and a handful of tools. He sat down at the table and continued his work.

"Master, what's happened to me?" Pinocchio asked. He was sorry to interrupt Geppetto, but he needed his own answer now. "And who is this Prester John anyway?"

"Prester John?" Maestro chirped. "The immortal king of Abaton! Don't you—no, of course you don't know."

"That's where you're from, right?" Pinocchio said, pleased that he remembered Maestro mentioning it before. "You're from Abaton."

"But of course," Maestro sighed. "And what I'd give to be back home, performing again in His Immortal Lordship's court, rather than stuck in these savage humanlands . . ."

"But is Abaton here in the Venetian Empire," Pinocchio asked, "or in China?"

"Why do you keep thinking I'm from China?" Maestro chirped. "No, my home is not part of the humanlands."

"Abaton is an island far out in the Indian Ocean," Geppetto said, glancing up from his repairs. "Until the explorer Marco Polo outwitted the sea monster that guards Abaton's shores, no human had ever seen Abaton. But since then, since Prester John opened trade between Abaton and Venice, our human kingdoms have changed dramatically, none more so than the Venetian Empire."

"What do you mean, 'changed'?" Pinocchio asked.

"Well, we certainly had nothing like you before," Geppetto explained. "Automa and all the extraordinary machines our alchemists have designed could never have been created if it weren't for Abaton's magic."

"Geppetto," Maestro interrupted. "If this is true and Prester John has been captured by the doge, then Abaton is in danger."

"I know," Geppetto said, reshaping a bent gear. "He should never have come. It was foolish to think he could negotiate with the doge."

"Who is this doge?" Pinocchio asked. "You said I came from his floating palace. Is he the king?"

"More like the tyrant," Maestro said.

"*Doge* is the title for the ruler of the Venetian Empire," Geppetto said, holding up a gear to inspect his work.

"But doesn't the doge like Prester John?" Pinocchio asked. "Doesn't he like getting magic from Abaton?"

"It's complicated," Geppetto said. "He likes how alchemy has made our empire powerful. But our current doge has a particular dislike for Abatonians—despite the fact that elementals and chimera have lived peacefully with the citizens of our empire since they immigrated to our lands centuries ago. The doge sees them as little more than monsters that have no place in a land meant for humans."

"In other words, the doge wants the magic but not the monsters," Maestro chirped. "And you can't have one without the other."

Pinocchio wasn't positive what this meant, but he thought it must have something to do with why alchemists used elementals like gnomes whenever they repaired him.

Before he could ask, Geppetto continued. "The doge has declared the empire's elementals and half-beasts a slave class. A move that has upset Prester John greatly. The few who have resisted, mostly half-beast runaways . . . well, the doge's soldiers have come after them ruthlessly. Forced into lives as outlaws, and never having been a danger to anyone before, these half-beasts have fought back just as ruthlessly. Which is why our leaving San Baldovino is so difficult. The roads aren't safe.

"It's also why"—Geppetto grimaced as he tried to pry loose a bent gear—"I need to finish this chimera box so we can . . . buy safe passage. We only have three days at the most before Captain Toro will return."

His chisel slipped from the gears, nearly stabbing Geppetto's other hand. "Blast this thing!" he roared. "Why won't it come loose?"

He leaped to his feet and marched back into his workshop

with the chimera box under his arm, mumbling something about where was a good gnome when you needed one. Once he disappeared behind the curtain, there was an abrupt silence, and then Geppetto growled, "GREAT VESUVIUS!"

"What is it?" Maestro asked, bounding through the curtain.

"Airmen!" Geppetto said. "They're already here!"

Pinocchio ran into the shop. Through the front window, he saw a man with massive mechanical wings folded across his back out in the street. An instant later, a second airman landed beside him. Both wore red cloaks over red armor, golden-winged lions emblazoned on their chests. They carried muskets.

The soldiers banged loudly on the door across the street. When an old lady cracked the door, the airmen barged inside.

"But . . . but Captain Toro just left yesterday," Maestro chirped in panic. "You said it would be three days!"

"Well, obviously we weren't that lucky. Captain Toro must have met a squadron of airmen on his way to Venice."

"They'll search our shop at any moment!" the cricket shrieked.

Geppetto looked around in desperation. He dropped the chimera box on the counter and ran to the door, pulling down the shade and turning the sign to CHIUSO.

"Into the back. Now!"

"Closing early will only call attention to us," Maestro said from Geppetto's shoulder.

"What else would you suggest?"

The cricket wagged his antennae. "We have to leave."

"I haven't finished the chimera box! And how far will we get without an armored coach for protection? Besides, even if we snuck over the wall, we wouldn't get a mile out of town before they'd spot us from the air."

"The villa," Maestro said. "If we could make it to the villa, we might be safe."

Geppetto chewed on his mustache as he pondered.

"What villa?" Pinocchio asked.

"Quick! The back door."

The door opened to an alley. Pinocchio began to follow, but Geppetto pushed him back. "They're in the alley!"

"What do we do?" Pinocchio asked.

A loud banging erupted from the front door. "Open in the name of the imperial doge!"

Geppetto's eyes widened. "Hide!"

"Where?" Pinocchio said.

"Anywhere!"

Pinocchio scrambled under the bed as Geppetto and Maestro headed into the shop. Huddled on the dusty floor, Pinocchio could just hear Maestro say, "But they're after *you*, Geppetto."

"They'll only know who I am if they discover the boy. If Don Antonio stuck to his story that Pinocchio escaped on his own, they'll look for the automa. They'll think he went to find his master."

More banging sounded from the door.

"And when they find him?" Maestro said. "When they discover that Prester John sent the automa to you?"

"Prester John is clearly in some danger. I owe it to His Immortal Lordship to protect the boy, although why he sent Pinocchio to me is an utter mystery."

Then Pinocchio heard his master open the door.

The pair of airmen pushed inside. Geppetto didn't recognize the first, an officer wearing gleaming armor adorned with an officer's insignia on his shoulders. But the other—his armor battered and insignia on his shoulders. But the other—his armor battered and dusty, the red faded, and the canvas of his wing tattered at the edges—was known to all in San Baldovino.

Captain Toro.

The airmen's massive folded wings scraped the ceiling beams as they marched past Geppetto. "You're Signore Polendina?" Captain Toro demanded.

"Yes. How can I help you gentlemen?"

They peered around the shop suspiciously. "Why are you closed in the middle of the day?"

"I have a repair to complete," Geppetto said, "and I'm already late. I couldn't get any work done with everyone and their neighbor barging in. And if you don't mind," he waved a hand to the door, "I need to get busy at once."

"We're looking for an automa," said the other airman.

"I don't usually deal in automa," Geppetto said. "However, I could put in an order—"

"We're not purchasing," Captain Toro said. "We're looking for one that escaped from Don Antonio's house."

"Otto?" Geppetto said in surprise. "Has the old chap begun malfunctioning?"

"Not Don Antonio's servant. The escaped automa destroyed Otto as it got away. We believe it's still in the village, as the guards have seen no one leave since last night. We're searching all the buildings. It might have snuck in without your knowledge."

"Oh, I doubt that," Geppetto said. "I have such a small place. Only my shop."

"What's back there?" the officer said, pointing his musket toward the curtain.

"Just my bed. Nowhere to hide that I wouldn't have seen."

"Check it," he ordered Captain Toro.

Toro marched through the curtain, his wings slipping through the fabric. Geppetto considered following him, but the other airman stayed in the shop front, peering behind the counter, tapping the stone floor with the shoulder stock of his musket, listening for hollow hiding places.

What would he do when Captain Toro found Pinocchio? He heard the captain overturning the bookcase. Furniture crashed. Any moment he'd flip over the bed.

Geppetto reached for the chimera box on the counter. Its screeching alarm wouldn't help, but the box was heavy, and a blow to the airman's temple . . .

Captain Toro emerged back through the curtain. "Empty," he reported.

The officer turned and paused, giving the chimera box in Geppetto's hands a quizzical look.

"I—I'd best get back to work," Geppetto chuckled, holding up the box. "Good luck in your search." He hurried to open the door and let them out.

The airmen marched to the bakery next door.

Geppetto locked the door and ran into the bedroom. His books and belongings lay scattered. His bed was flipped completely over.

Maestro hopped from surface to surface. "Where is he?"

Geppetto looked around in confusion. Then a muffled voice sounded from the fireplace. "'M stuck!"

Geppetto spied the salamander in the coals. It was squished, the poor beast. The lizard's eyes had rolled up, and its black tongue dangled out.

"He's up the chimney!" Maestro said.

Geppetto poked his head into the smoky air to peer up the flue. He pulled back from the heat, coughing, and reached up to grasp Pinocchio's ankle. With a tug, he pulled him down. Pinocchio landed again on the salamander, squishing molten innards from the dead creature. Pinocchio leaped off the coals and tumbled to the floor in a cloud of soot.

"My feet!"

Flames ignited across his wooden soles. Geppetto grabbed a bucket of wash water and doused Pinocchio's feet. With a hiss of steam, the flames extinguished, but the charred remains of his toes crumbled away with the water. The gearwork mechanisms beneath lay exposed.

"My poor feet," Pinocchio cried. Although they couldn't hurt, the boy clutched his feet pitifully.

Geppetto knelt before Pinocchio. "You clever boy," he laughed. "You might have burned your feet off—and killed my poor salamander—but they'd have found you for sure if you'd stayed under the bed."

"That's what I realized," Pinocchio whimpered, the corners of his mouth twitching with pride. "Can you fix them?"

"Yes, but we haven't much time," Geppetto said. "When the airmen finish their search and haven't found us, they'll be back for a more thorough sweep. And we need to be gone."

5.

The Mechanipillar

Geppetto rummaged through the shop's shelves until Pinocchio heard him give an "Aha!" and he returned with a pair of tattered boots.

"What are those?" Pinocchio asked.

"Seven-league boots. They've lost their proper enchantment, but you just need feet, so they'll do."

Geppetto set about tinkering with Pinocchio's copper tendons and performed a transmutation that fixed the boots over his burned feet. When he finished, he said, "Try them out."

Pinocchio took an awkward step and then another. The boots were several sizes too big and gave his feet a comical appearance. "Feels funny." But he soon found the right gait to keep them from clopping. He tried a bounce.

"Not bad." He took a few steps and tested a jump, launching

over the table and landing in a crouch. "Did you see that?" he laughed. This was an extraordinary feeling. Almost like he could fly.

"Be careful," Geppetto warned. "They might still have a bit of their old enchantment."

Pinocchio ran toward the table again. "I couldn't jump like this before—" The launch shot him like a cannonball. His head crashed against a ceiling beam, flipping him into a somersault before he landed, splintering the table in two.

"Incorrigible," Maestro sighed.

Geppetto ran to Pinocchio. "Are you all right?"

Pinocchio sat up, blinking with embarrassment. Being made of wood sometimes had its advantages. Stepping on the salamander might have burned his feet off, but the battering-ram blow against the ceiling had injured only his pride.

"Like I said," Geppetto explained, "the boots have a bit of their old spring. You won't manage seven leagues. But they might occasionally send you a bit farther than you intend if you're not careful."

A heavy thud sounded, rattling the furnishings and sending a small shower of dust from the ceiling. Another thud followed, then another.

Maestro and Geppetto hurried to the curtain. Pinocchio ran after them, careful that his new feet didn't launch him into another accident. Out in the street, armored carriages, linked together in a long train, stalked past on dozens of mechanical legs.

Pinocchio grinned at the extraordinary machine. He'd never seen anything like that in the palace. "What is it?"

"A mechanipillar," Geppetto said. "Maestro . . . are you thinking the same as me?"

"I'm thinking it would be complete madness," the cricket said, "but it might be our best chance."

"What's it for?" Pinocchio asked, wishing he could go outside to get a better look at the walking vehicle.

"The mechanipillar carries goods and travelers to the neighboring towns," Geppetto said. "This part of Tuscany has far too many runaway half-beasts for people to travel without the protection of an armored coach. Those who can't afford private transportation take the mechanipillar."

Pinocchio wondered how dangerous these half-beasts really were. Something about them ignited him with curiosity. It would be oh so exciting to see one. He decided not to say this to his master. It was doubtful Geppetto shared his enthusiasm.

"If we're going to leave," Maestro said, "it must be on that mechanipillar."

Geppetto shook his head. "If the airmen think Pinocchio is still in the village, they'll inspect the mechanipillar before it leaves the gates."

"What if you hide him?" Maestro suggested. "You could take off his arms and legs, stuff him in a box, and cover him with other parts. Say you're delivering a repair to someone in another village."

Pinocchio yelped. "What? No, don't pull off my limbs!"

Geppetto waved at him to be silent. "I don't have gold enough to buy passage! Signora Ferragutti's chimera box still isn't finished."

"Then hurry and finish it!"

"There's no time! And besides, they'll search the mechanipillar. Unless . . ." Geppetto narrowed his eyes.

"Unless what?" Pinocchio asked.

"Quiet." Geppetto tapped his fingers on the counter. "If we

got *under* the mechanipillar, we might ride out unnoticed." He looked at Pinocchio now. "Could you support my weight and hold us to the undercarriage?"

"I'm strong, Master," Pinocchio said, grateful his master was considering options besides pulling off his legs.

Geppetto nodded. "I have no doubt you are, lad. But it'll be a bumpy ride."

"I won't drop you. I promise."

Maestro sprang from the counter, a flurry of wings and whirling antennae. "This is lunacy! You can't get under the mechanipillar without everyone in the village seeing you, not to mention those airmen swarming the streets."

"I have an idea," Geppetto said, picking up the chimera box. "It's good that I didn't repair this after all."

"Why?" Pinocchio asked.

"You'll see," Geppetto said. "Maestro, get in your cage. Pinocchio, grab the blanket off my bed. We must be quick."

Geppetto emerged from the alley, pushing the wheelbarrow he used for deliveries. On the top was Maestro's cage, covered with a silk cloth. Beneath the cricket was the chimera box, the lid closed to keep its alarm from sounding. Below, covered by a blanket, huddled Pinocchio.

Geppetto maneuvered the load down the cobblestone lane toward the gates.

"What if you're stopped, and they look under that blanket?" Maestro chirped from inside his cage.

"It's a risk we have to take," Geppetto whispered.

"But if they do?"

Geppetto nodded hello to a passing neighbor before whispering to Maestro, "Then we get to see Venice again."

"You mean the doge's prison," the cricket said. "If you're lucky! More likely you'll face the gallows."

"Hush."

As expected, the mechanipillar was stopped at the gates while airmen searched it. Groups of villagers stood around, impatient to board. The town's guards—battered hulking automa sentries—waited for orders to open the gates.

Geppetto gave a jolt.

Above the town gate was an imperial warship, hovering overhead like a black storm cloud. Geppetto's anxiety worsened. This was no ordinary patrol. That was an onyx-class military warship, most certainly equipped with Flying Lions. Peering down from the ship's bow was General Maximian, the doge's personal guard and commander of Venice's imperial airmen. Of all the soldiers here, this one alone might recognize Geppetto.

Geppetto pulled his hood over his head and wheeled onward. The airmen took no notice as they rustled through the few travelers' trunks and pulled open crates of vegetables bound for neighboring markets.

Near the gates were the piles of garbage the villagers left for the automa guards to remove to burn outside the village. Geppetto set Maestro's cage on the stinking heap.

"Is this what the renowned musician Maestro of Abaton has come to?" the cricket complained. "Rummaging through filth. Disgraceful! My grandfather would pluck off his antennae in shame if could see me."

"Remember what I said," Geppetto whispered, as he placed the chimera box next to Maestro. "Give us time to get on the other side of the mechanipillar."

"If you get caught," Maestro said, "I'm not coming with you."

Geppetto loosened the lid on the chimera box. "Then I

wish you the best and hope that the bird that eats you doesn't get indigestion."

"Incorrigible," the cricket mumbled.

Geppetto adjusted his gloves and stole a glance at General Maximian. The officer was watching the airmen finish their final inspections. Passengers began boarding, a few calling last good-byes to family members. Geppetto kept his gaze low as he made a wide swath with the wheelbarrow, pushing it through the crowd to the other side of the mechanipillar.

"Signore Polendina," a voice rang out.

He pushed faster.

"Oh, Signore Polendina, dear!" An elderly woman made her way from the crowd, her cane clanking on the cobblestones as she hurried to catch him.

Geppetto stopped and turned with a brittle smile. "Signora Ferragutti, I was just coming to see you."

Captain Toro, standing by one of the mechanipillar's legs, glanced over his shoulder at them. Geppetto didn't meet his eye as he took Signora Ferragutti's arm to steady her.

"Have you finished my box? I haven't slept a night without it. You promised it would be ready."

Captain Toro narrowed his eyes on the wheelbarrow behind Geppetto.

"Yes, soon," Geppetto said, desperate to escape Toro's attention. But the airman was already coming his way. "It's nearly finished. It's just . . . I've run into a snag . . . and . . ."

Signora Ferragutti frowned. "What sort of snag?"

An earsplitting shriek rose from the other side of the mechanipillar. The villagers scrambled as if under attack. Toro and the other airmen on the ground began shouting at one another, searching wildly for the source of the sound. General Maximian leaped from the hovering warship, throwing his wings wide, and landed atop the mechanipillar. Signora Ferragutti wobbled in alarm. Geppetto steadied her before turning to snatch the blanket from Pinocchio.

"Now!" he said.

Pinocchio wanted nothing more than to stay hidden. The voices screaming in panic and the piercing wail of the chimera box scared him. But Geppetto pulled him sharply to his feet. All eyes were, for the moment, on the far side of the mechanipillar. They had a clear run for a gap in the mechanipillar's legs, but it would lead them behind Captain Toro. There was nothing to do but hope he didn't turn around.

Pinocchio stumbled on his new feet, trying to get them to work properly. As they passed Captain Toro, the airman's wings snapped open, the blow knocking Geppetto to the cobblestones. Captain Toro sprang to the top of the mechanipillar.

"Master!" Pinocchio cried.

They had only seconds before someone might notice them. Pinocchio awkwardly tried to help Geppetto up. A trickle of something red ran along Geppetto's temple, and his eyes looked dazed. Pinocchio glanced around. The others were all still startled by the noise.

Grabbing his master tightly around the waist, Pinocchio sprang for an opening between the mechanipillar's massive legs. The seven-league boots fired him straight through, landing him with a skid on his back. Pinocchio found a grip underneath the mechanipillar and held Geppetto to his chest as he kicked his feet up over a metal rod.

"Are you all right, Master?" he asked, settling into his perch and noticing the red liquid on Geppetto's forehead. "I didn't know you had wine inside you."

Geppetto blinked away the dizziness and swiped a hand to his temple. "That's blood. But I'm fine. Have you got us?"

"I think so."

"Then stay quiet."

Pinocchio felt a welling of pride. He had saved his master. But the proud moment vanished as musket fire erupted and the crowd surrounding the mechanipillar yelled in panic.

"Hold your fire!" an airman shouted. At once, the shrieking chimera box went quiet. Pinocchio and Geppetto looked at each other as they listened.

"It's just some alchemied alarm someone threw in the trash. Return to your posts, men."

The villagers calmed, but there was an anxious edge to their conversations. Captain Toro dropped back down to the street. From under the mechanipillar, Geppetto and Pinocchio could only see his boots pacing back and forth. Another soldier strode up to the captain.

"Should we hold the mechanipillar, General Maximian?" Captain Toro asked.

"No, it seems to have just been an accident," the general replied, before shouting, "Open the gates!"

The creak of turning gears sounded as the village automa began cranking open the gates.

Geppetto exhaled with relief. Captain Toro followed the general away, when a woman with a clanking cane caught up to him.

"Captain Toro? Was that a chimera box causing that commotion?"

"So it seems," the captain replied, still walking. "No need to worry, Signora Ferragutti. You can go—"

"I think that might have been mine. Signore Polendina was repairing it, but surely he wouldn't have thrown it into the trash."

Captain Toro stopped. "Wasn't he here just a moment ago?"

"Right beside me," she said, "before that commotion broke out. Look, there's his cart."

"What do we do, Master?" Pinocchio whispered.

Stay quiet, Geppetto mouthed.

The mechanipillar took its first earthshaking step.

"General Maximian!" Captain Toro called. "Signora Ferragutti here seems to be the owner of the box that was causing all that noise."

"Then she can explain why she set off that uproar," the general said, walking along beside the mechanipillar's stomping feet.

Captain Toro hurried to keep up with him. "Sir, you don't understand. The man who was repairing that box was just here and now he's gone."

"Half the village scattered at that noise, captain."

"But he might have—"

"I don't have time for an old lady's trinkets, Captain, much less a bumbling frontier patrolman such as yourself second-guessing my orders. The mechanipillar is inspected. We will resume our search of the village before that automa and his traitorous master find a way out. Get to your rounds."

Pinocchio watched Geppetto's face as the mechanipillar marched through the gates, leaving the village behind.

"Are we safe, Master?" he asked. "Did we escape?"

"We escaped," Geppetto said, "but we are far from being safe."

6.

The Tomb of Alberto

An automa has no muscles to tire, so Pinocchio held Geppetto securely underneath the mechanipillar as it stamped along the road. He soon grew bored, however.

"How long do we have to hang here?" Then he added, "Where are we going, anyway? And what happened to Maestro? Is he all right?"

The corner of Geppetto's mouth twitched. "We are going to my wife's villa. We're almost there. Maestro will meet us. He's exceptionally skilled at finding his way. You know, you're quite impatient for an automa."

Pinocchio thought about that as they continued. Was impatience bad? He decided to stay silent.

Geppetto soon said, "Get ready. When I tell you, let go, but don't roll to the side or you might wind up crushed by the feet."

The mechanipillar was climbing a steep, winding road, and the sunlight dimmed as they entered a wood.

"Now," Geppetto ordered.

Pinocchio let go. He landed in the dust. Geppetto grunted as he smacked Pinocchio's hard wooden chest. "Stay still," Geppetto said.

When the last carriage of the mechanipillar had marched over them, Geppetto said, "Quick, into the trees."

Pinocchio dashed after Geppetto. His feet did not completely cooperate, causing him to take one half step and another that bounced him sideways. When they were in the woods, Geppetto said, "I'll have to repair your feet properly."

"Thank you, Master," Pinocchio said. "That would be . . . incorrigible."

Geppetto chuckled. "I'll explain to you later what that word really means."

The mechanipillar disappeared around a bend. "Come," he said. "We should go. But listen out! We don't want to encounter any airmen or half-beasts."

Geppetto led them through the woods. When they reached the edge, Pinocchio gasped at the commanding view of the countryside. Golden-umber hills rose and fell, spiked occasionally by dark cypress trees and dotted with olive groves. He had never seen anything quite so lovely.

Pinocchio spied a dozen or more distant houses spread around the landscape. "Do people live out here?"

"Yes," Geppetto said, marching with long-legged steps. "Farmers, mostly."

"Don't they fear the half-beasts?"

"To live out here, one guards his estate with automa. Not little servants like you, but large sentry automa like the ones that protect San Baldovino. Come along."

Pinocchio stumbled in the seven-league boots but managed to keep up.

"Look at that one!" He pointed down the hill toward an elegant villa surrounded by high stone walls.

"That's where we're headed," Geppetto said.

"Is that your wife's house?"

Geppetto nodded.

"Why don't you live with her?"

"She was killed," Geppetto said, his hand reflexively touching a jeweled pin on his shirt. "Along with my son."

"Oh," Pinocchio said. "Is that what happened to Don Antonio's automa?"

Geppetto frowned. "I did not kill Otto. Automa cannot die. They only stop functioning."

"But didn't your wife and son stop functioning when they were killed?"

"It's not the same," Geppetto said. "My family was once living. Otto was never truly alive."

As Pinocchio puzzled over this while they walked, he noticed Geppetto watching him. Pinocchio gave him a smile.

Geppetto sighed. "I've never had such a conversation with an automa. I can see this is hard for you to understand, Pinocchio. Whatever Prester John has done to you, it must make you feel like you're alive. But you were constructed, just like Otto and the sentries of those estates out there. No matter how curiously you function, you aren't alive."

"But what was the potion you made for Don Antonio?" Pinocchio asked, shuffling to keep step with his master. "He said it would give him more life. You made that from Otto's fantom, didn't you?"

Geppetto began chuckling. "You're perceptive, lad. I'll give you that. The fantom is one of alchemy's great discoveries. It can be transmuted into an elixir, and that elixir can extend life for a human. *Extend*, mind you. It cannot create life. Nor can it resurrect the dead or offer immortality. Only Prester John is blessed with eternal youth. A fantom, you see, does not make an automa living, any more than the donkey that pulls the cart makes the cart alive."

Pinocchio scratched his head. He'd seen his master do this before and liked how it looked. Maybe it would help him think better.

"Let me explain it this way," Geppetto said. "Alchemy, in its simplest form, is the ability to transform one thing into another. To transmute, as it's called. It all has to do with macrocosmic and microcosmic correspondences and the manipulation of elemental forces—"

Pinocchio's eyes began to lose focus.

Geppetto gave a pondering stroke to his mustache as he walked, and Pinocchio wished he had a mustache too.

"I'll see if I can make it simpler," Geppetto said. "The elemental races of Abaton possess magic that can manipulate the forces of this world. Gnomes have power over earth, stone, and metal, sylphs over air, djinn over fire. And undines over water. We human alchemists don't have true magical powers of our own. But unlike elementals, we are capable of integrating the different powers of elementals into alchemical inventions and wondrous technology. This is what makes alchemy different from Abatonian magic.

"If an alchemist wanted metal that was as light as a feather— say, for an airman's armor—he would work with a gnome and a sylph. By integrating their elemental powers over metal and air, using *transmutation*, as we alchemists call it, armor could be created that's essentially weightless. It's not quite that easy, but that's the basic idea. A gnome and sylph could not make that armor without a human alchemist. Nor could they make a miraculous device like you, Pinocchio.

"But you see, there is one thing that alchemists can't transmute. Ourselves. The living are different, Pinocchio. We are not wood and metal. We have flesh. Flesh is the transmutation of the spirit into physical form. It makes us special. It makes life special and, above all things, precious and valuable. Not something to be taken lightly."

Pinocchio nodded, though he wasn't at all certain he understood. What Geppetto said seemed true enough. Humans—and animals, even—weren't made of any earthly material. They were different. But he couldn't help feeling that he was not a device. He was something more, wasn't he?

They reached the walls of the estate. Weeds grew thick, although clearly it had been a grand place at one time. Geppetto led them to a gate, where a sentry, as big as a boulder, lay scorched in the courtyard, its armor torn open like it was nothing more than tin.

"Did half-beasts do this?" Pinocchio asked.

"Certainly not," Geppetto said. "It would take imperial Flying Lions to bring down a sentry that size. Now stay quiet until we know we're safe."

He walked past the fallen sentry and looked around the overgrown courtyard before cautiously approaching the doorway of the villa. It was open, hanging on its hinges. Musket-ball pits speckled the plaster around the frame.

A creak came from inside. Geppetto crouched. Not knowing what to do when one was about to be ambushed by half-beast outlaws, Pinocchio stood perfectly still, his eyes wide. He realized this reaction probably wasn't the best defense.

A small coppery-black form shot out from the doorway and landed on Geppetto's arm.

"Maestro," Geppetto exhaled.

"It's empty," the cricket said. "But vandals have taken all the finery."

"It's of no consequence," Geppetto said. "Let's get inside."

The interior of the villa was in worse shape than the outside. Chunks of plaster had fallen from the walls. What little furniture remained had been broken. A rug that was blackened with blood lay pushed into a corner.

"Master, I don't understand," Pinocchio said. "Who killed your family?"

A dark expression grew over Geppetto's face. "The doge had them murdered, along with all the servants." He stared, his jaw tense. "I . . . haven't been back here since I first arrived in San Baldovino."

"I thought you said life was valuable. Why would the doge do this to them?" Pinocchio felt a strange tingling through his gears, sending little prickles down to his feet. He badly wanted to start walking anywhere, as long as it was away from the villa. "I don't like this place, Master. Why are we here?"

"I need to repair your burned-off toes, lad. And to see if there is any gold still hidden. We'll need it, if we are to get to Venice."

"Venice!" Maestro chirped. "Why would we want to go there?"

"To rescue Prester John," Geppetto said. "He must have sent Pinocchio to tell me he'd been captured. We have to help him. I owe him that much."

"Impossible!" Maestro said.

"It is if we don't try," Geppetto said. "Besides, we'll never be safe staying in the empire. Don't you want to go back to Abaton?"

"Of course!"

Geppetto started up the stairs. "Then our only hope lies in Prester John."

The villa was much bigger than Don Antonio's mansion and full of room after room that surely had been grand before being sacked. In the back of a library on the top floor—books seemed to be one of the few things the vandals hadn't taken—Geppetto took down a thick volume and blew off the dust. He plucked a hair from his head, placed it inside the book, and stuck it back on the shelf.

The bookcase swung open, revealing a room hidden behind.

Pinocchio smiled with wonderment.

"You're easy to impress," Maestro said, fluttering from Geppetto's shoulder into the dark.

Geppetto found matches in a drawer and lit a candelabrum. The secret room had tables covered with curious brass devices and strangely shaped crucibles and flasks. Shelves were lined with glass jars, racks of tools, elaborate sets of scales, and other scientific instruments.

"What is this place?" Pinocchio asked.

"My laboratory," Geppetto said, opening the front of a small furnace that sat in the middle of the room. A salamander wriggled from the ashes and snapped its jaws at Geppetto.

"Somebody's hungry," Maestro said.

"Pinocchio, fetch some of the furniture," Geppetto ordered. "We'll need it broken up in bite-size portions."

When Pinocchio returned with an armload of chair legs, he

found Geppetto tearing pages out of one of his books and feeding them to the salamander, which was already glowing fiery red. Pinocchio began breaking the chair legs, the springwork in his arms winding noisily as he splintered the hard wood into smaller and smaller pieces.

"Is this where you worked?" he asked, handing Geppetto a few chunks of wood.

"When I was home, which wasn't very often." Geppetto tossed a piece of wood to the salamander. As the creature ate, flames erupted along its back. "When I was appointed as the doge's high alchemist, Cornelia decided to move from Venice back here to her parents' estate. On my infrequent returns home, I found it hard to leave my work behind."

His mind seemed to wander, until the salamander snapped at his finger. "I spent too many hours in this room. Too many hours I should have spent with them."

Pinocchio looked at Maestro, perched on the stem of a beaker. The cricket's antennae drooped.

"Why should you have spent more time with them?" Pinocchio asked.

Geppetto blinked. "Because I loved them. They were more important than any foolish experiments. But I didn't see that then. I was ambitious. I was proud of my post. It took the loss of what I truly loved to teach me that."

"But, Master, I still don't understand why the doge would kill your family."

Maestro rattled his black wings against his shell. "Can't you hush your incessant questioning?"

"It's all right, Maestro. The wood," Geppetto reminded Pinocchio.

Pinocchio quickly snapped off a few more pieces.

As Geppetto fed the salamander, he said, "The doge's only son, Prince Ignazio, was killed driving out a band of half-beasts that were threatening Rome. With Ignazio dead and the half-beast outlaws wreaking havoc, the doge feared his empire would not be safe after his eventual death. The doge wanted his son back. He loved Ignazio, of course, but more so, he needed his son to rule. He knew of only one way."

Geppetto paused, lost in thought, and Pinocchio struggled to not be impatient.

"Prester John of Abaton possesses many wonders. Venice would not be the mighty empire it is today if it weren't for the gifts and magic he's shared with the world. But Prester John has many Abatonian wonders that the humanlands have never seen. Wondrous and mysterious objects. Among them is the Ancientmost Pearl."

"What is that?" Pinocchio asked.

"Even we Abatonians don't know for sure," Maestro said. "No Abatonians have ever seen the Ancientmost Pearl, except for maybe the prester's wives and his children."

"Whatever the Ancientmost Pearl is," Geppetto continued, "all agree it is the source of Prester John's immortality, for he has been alive for centuries. And some say the Pearl has the power of resurrection. That is why the doge ordered me to steal it."

"You?" Pinocchio's eyes widened. "Did you?"

"No," Geppetto said. "But I was in a difficult position, Pinocchio. Prester John wanted to end the enslavement of his people living in the Venetian Empire, so he urged the doge to send an ambassador to Abaton to discuss a solution. He had not allowed a human visitor for many years—decades, even. The doge was not going to pass up this opportunity. He gave me explicit instructions to appease Prester John and do whatever it took to steal the prester's Pearl of Immortality."

"So what did you do?" Pinocchio asked, then worried he was being impatient.

Geppetto was so lost in his story, he didn't seem to notice. "Only Prester John can guide a ship past the sea monster that guards Abaton, so I met him in Arabia and we made the long voyage aboard one of his vessels. When we at last arrived, and I saw his glorious garden palace, the Moonlit Court . . . what a wonder! I thought I was in Eden—"

Maestro groaned.

Geppetto gave a wave of apology to the cricket before turning back to Pinocchio. "The prester was like no one I've ever met. Eyes like golden sunshine. He is like a living god among his people. The races of Abaton consider him their father."

"Is he really their father?" Pinocchio said.

"Obviously not mine," Maestro said. "His Immortal Lordship does have children of his own. But remember: He's lived an eternity. He's had countless wives and fathered countless children."

"Whom he's had to watch grow old and die over the years," Geppetto said. "I think it is hard for him. Prester John is a being both ancient and powerful. But he is not able to share his gift of immortality with any of his family. Because of this, I don't think he's very close to his children. He loves them, as he loves all his subjects. As a good king should. But most of all, he loves Abaton."

Geppetto absently fed the salamander more wood. "Abaton is the most remarkable place in the world, Pinocchio. I realized right away how I admired the prester for being willing to share the magic of his land with humans. I couldn't allow Abaton to be corrupted by the doge. So I confessed to Prester John what the doge had asked of me, how I had come as nothing better than a common thief. I half expected to be imprisoned. To my surprise, Prester John was not angry with me."

"That's good," Maestro said. "His Immortal Lordship can be a bit . . . intimidating at times."

"No, in fact, Prester John seemed quite moved by the tragic news of the doge's son," Geppetto continued. "Maybe it was because Prince Ignazio died at the hands of chimera—even Venetian half-beasts are of Abatonian descent, after all. Or maybe it was because the prester had seen so many of his own children die. Prester John wouldn't give me the Ancientmost Pearl, of course, but he didn't want to send me to the doge empty-handed. He believed the doge would be reasonable."

"Insanity," Maestro grumbled.

Geppetto nodded. "So he sent me back to Venice bearing three gifts—gifts that he hoped would pave the way for negotiations by easing the doge's grief over his dead son."

Maestro flicked his antennae. "That's how I wound up in this wasteland."

"You were one of the gifts?" Pinocchio asked.

"Maestro, as you know, was Prester John's official court musician," Geppetto said.

"It was supposed to be a great honor that Prester John was giving me to that tone-deaf imbecile," Maestro chirped.

"The other gifts were equally generous," Geppetto said. "I brought back a gilded sword to lay as a blessing on Prince Ignazio's tomb, and an enchantment for the dogaressa that would allow her to bear a son. But the doge was not satisfied. I had failed to bring him the Pearl. He flew into a rage."

"I'm sure he would have squashed me flat if you hadn't attacked him with that sword," Maestro said.

"You attacked the doge?" Pinocchio gasped. He hadn't taken his master for a warrior.

"I had little choice," Geppetto said.

"He cut off the doge's hand," Maestro added, with a flick of his antennae.

Pinocchio stared in disbelief at Geppetto.

"It was my only hope of escape," Geppetto said. "I managed to get out of the Fortezza, and with the help of some of my elemental assistants, I escaped from Venice."

Geppetto touched the pin on his shirt. Pinocchio hadn't paid much attention to the pin before, but he now saw that it was a jeweled rose. Absently, Geppetto's fingers traced the edges as he whispered, "I knew I would eventually have to face the doge's retribution, but I never imagined that he would exact his revenge on my poor Cornelia and Alberto...."

Pinocchio wondered if the jeweled pin had belonged to Geppetto's wife. He could see the pain in Geppetto's face, and it sent a strange prickling through his gears. He wished there were a way to fix his master, a way to take the hurt from his chiseled face.

"Come on, Pinocchio," Maestro said. "We need to let Geppetto work if he is to make new feet for you."

Geppetto sat, lost in thought a moment, before blinking at them. "Yes," he said, taking down a bellows from the wall. "It shouldn't take long. Don't go far."

Pinocchio reluctantly followed Maestro from the laboratory. As they wandered down the hallway, Pinocchio said, "Maestro, isn't there a way to help Master feel better?"

Maestro fluttered from wall to doorknob. "It's a terrible tragedy. But all living creatures feel pain at the loss of those they love. It can't be helped, Pinocchio. It's part of life."

Pinocchio stumbled on his boots. "Then I'm glad I'm not alive."

They wandered through room after room, but anything of interest had long been taken. At last they sat by a window on the fourth floor, looking down on an overgrown garden. The roses had turned spindly and lost their flowers. There was a brick walkway in the shape of a circular labyrinth, now overtaken by dandelions. At the far end of the garden, against the outer wall, Pinocchio spied two broken rectangular slabs.

"Maestro, what are those stones back there?"

The cricket crawled up the windowpane to look. "Oh," he said. "Those are the tombs for Geppetto's wife and son. Looks like the vandals even broke open their graves looking for treasures. Monsters!"

"Would Master be upset if he saw them like that?"

"He won't go back there," Maestro replied. "But don't tell him about it."

"So, yes?" Pinocchio asked, wondering why crickets and people couldn't just answer questions properly.

"Yes," Maestro said. "He wouldn't want to see them like that."

"I'm going down there." He headed for the door. "Are you coming?"

"No," Maestro said, tucking his wings and antennae back. "You go explore. I'll sleep right here. That was a long journey from San Baldovino."

Pinocchio went down to the garden. The shadows had grown long with late afternoon. Starlings swooped across the tops of the wall, catching insects. He thought the birds might have had something to do with why Maestro had not joined him.

As he reached the pair of tombs, he saw writing on the shifted slabs. He couldn't read the words, but he could tell from the carved figures which tomb contained Geppetto's wife and which held his son. He knelt by them and traced his fingers over the images. In the carvings, they looked as if they were sleeping. Was that what death was? Like when humans slept?

Where the slabs had been slid aside, he saw dark openings. He had come to put the slabs back in place, but curiosity crept over him. The carvings were so nondescript they could have been anyone. What did Geppetto's wife and son really look like?

He peered into the shadows. The light was such that all he saw were vague lumps down in the holes. He cast a glance back at the villa. Geppetto wouldn't be finished yet. He slid the slab from over Alberto's tomb a little more to let the light in. The boy below was wrapped in a shroud. Pinocchio reached into the tomb, but couldn't take hold of the fabric.

It wasn't very far down. He could climb in and still get back out easily enough. Pinocchio lowered himself into the grave. Kneeling by Alberto's side, he pulled back the shroud.

He had been expecting to see a sleeping boy, like the one carved on the tomb. What he saw was something else. Something horrific.

Pinocchio yelped, standing up so suddenly that the seven-league boots shot him against the portion of the slab still covering the tomb. He frantically scrambled out. With all the strength of his gears, he shoved the slabs back into place over Alberto and Cornelia.

He sat back against the tomb, feeling something awful in his gearworks. Was *that* what happened when humans died? No wonder life was valuable. If what he had seen was death, that was a horrible way to be, worse than being locked in a trunk or made to sit on a stool for a thousand nights.

He couldn't stop thinking about poor Alberto. Then he spied an apple tree that grew in the corner of the garden, and he went over to break off a thick limb. He tore at the bark and smaller branches, getting it down to a piece that could have been made into his own leg.

With his fingertips, he shaved the wood, working and shaping it. He didn't know how long it took, but when he finished, the sun had set and the sky was turning a purple-blue. He sat admiring the wooden sword.

"What are you doing out here?"

Pinocchio shot up. Geppetto stood over him.

"Where's Maestro?" his master asked.

"Resting inside, I suppose," Pinocchio said, holding the sword behind his back.

Geppetto grimaced, his face weary from his work. "What are you up to? Show me what you're hiding."

Pinocchio hesitated before holding up the sword. It didn't look as nice as he had hoped. The handle was crooked, and the sides were far from symmetrical.

"Planning to fight off any half-beasts who set upon us tonight?" Geppetto asked.

"It's for your son, Alberto," Pinocchio said, suddenly worrying that Geppetto might be angry with him. "It's . . . well, you said Prester John sent a sword for Prince Ignazio's tomb. I know it's not as fine as that sword, but I thought that maybe Alberto . . ."

Geppetto blinked, his eyes dark in the dimming light.

"I wanted to put it on his tomb," Pinocchio said. "As a blessing."

Geppetto stared at him. Then he reached for the sword. He held it, running his fingers along the blade.

"You made this?" he whispered.

"Yes."

"How?"

Pinocchio held up his hand. "Just carved it. I think I cracked

64

one of my fingers. I'm sorry, Master. I know it's not good enough for—"

Geppetto threw his arm around Pinocchio's shoulders and pulled him against his side. "You incorrigibly wonderful little scamp! It's finer than any treasure from Abaton." He handed the sword back to Pinocchio. "Go ahead. Put it on his grave."

Pinocchio smiled and laid the wooden sword on the chest of Alberto's carving. Then he stood by Geppetto's side and looked up at him. His master's face was no longer pinched with anguish, but Pinocchio couldn't quite figure out Geppetto's strange expression. His eyes seemed to glisten with moisture.

"Are you all right, Master?"

"Yes." Geppetto took a shuddering breath and lifted Pinocchio's hand. "Come, my boy. I can fix that finger before I put your new feet on."

7.

New Feet

ack in the laboratory, Pinocchio sat beside Maestro on the table while Geppetto repaired the crack using alchemical compounds he had simmered in a series of glass beakers over a flaming salamander's tail. Finished, Geppetto removed the jeweler's glass from his eye and wiped his hands on his leather apron. "Should be good as new, if you don't go poking at anything tonight while it dries."

"Yes, Master."

"Now for the feet."

As Geppetto removed the seven-league boots, Pinocchio glanced over at the new pair of feet lying on the table. Although made from a darker wood, they were almost identical to the ones he'd had before, if not better. He was admiring how each toe was articulated, with nearly seamless joints, when Geppetto gasped and dropped the boot to the floor.

"What is it, Master?"

Geppetto hurried to undo the laces on the other boot. Pinocchio stretched out his bare foot. It was no longer burned. In fact, it had an odd leathery quality. He flexed it around, wiggling his toes.

"What happened to it?" Pinocchio said in horror.

Geppetto wrenched off the other boot. "Great Vesuvius! It's healed as well."

"Healed, Master? You mean fixed."

"Fixed!" Geppetto shouted. "Who could have fixed you? This is a transmutation beyond what any elemental could have achieved! And what's this material?"

He grabbed Pinocchio's foot, twisting it side to side. Pinocchio had to clutch the table so he wouldn't fall off.

Maestro leaped out of the way. "It looks like hide."

Geppetto squeezed Pinocchio's foot. "It's hard as wood. And I still see some grains, but it does look like . . ."

"Like what, Master?" Pinocchio asked.

"Flesh," Geppetto whispered.

Pinocchio winced. "Why would seven-league boots turn my poor feet into flesh?"

"They shouldn't. They couldn't." Geppetto wrinkled his brow half a dozen ways before saying, "No, it wasn't the boots."

"Then what?" Maestro asked.

Geppetto reached for Pinocchio's chest. Pinocchio's hand shot out, crushing Geppetto's knuckles.

Geppetto grimaced, digging the fealty key from his pocket. "Let . . . go!"

Pinocchio couldn't until Geppetto jammed the key into the back of his neck. "I'm sorry, Master! I'm so sorry. Why did you do that? You know I can't help it!"

Geppetto staggered away, clutching his hand to his stomach. "What's happening to you?"

"I don't know, Master." Pinocchio curled his feet up under him, trying to hide them with his hands. "It's that pinecone, isn't it? I haven't felt right since Prester John stole my fantom and put that dreadful pinecone in me. He did this to me!"

"But what exactly has His Immortal Lordship done?" Maestro asked.

Geppetto looked dazed. "Prester John is in danger," he muttered. "All I can assume is that he performed some spell on you, so you could help me rescue him. Although why would you be turning to flesh?"

He pulled down jars from the shelves, scattering their contents on the benches.

Pinocchio slid from the table and quickly put the seven-league boots back on to cover his feet. What was happening? Geppetto had told him flesh was the one material that no alchemy could make. This was impossible. And yet, here he was, transmuting from wood into flesh. He looked over at Maestro, but the cricket's distant black eyes gave him no assurances.

"Here!" Geppetto jingled a bag of coins. "I knew I had tucked some away. Montalcino is two days' walk. Once we get there, we can buy passage on a coach to bring us to Venice." He stuffed the coins into his coat pocket.

"But you haven't slept," Maestro said.

"I can't sleep now anyway," Geppetto said, untying his apron and shouldering his cloak before marching toward the door. "Let's leave this place."

They walked through the night. Despite his anxiety about his transformed feet, Pinocchio found that they worked much better in the seven-league boots than his old feet. He wasn't making unexpected bounces anymore. By dawn, however, all the walking made his new feet ache, and Pinocchio wanted nothing more than to stop and give them a rest.

He had never needed to rest his body before. An automa could work tirelessly. Pinocchio gave a little grumble under his breath. Yet another reason to dislike Prester John and his meddling!

Fortunately for Pinocchio, Geppetto was beginning to stumble with weariness by the time the sun was coming up. They found a grove of trees hidden from the road where his master could sleep.

Geppetto lay in the leaves, rolling his cloak into a pillow. "Listen out, Pinocchio. And watch the skies for airmen. Wake me if you sense danger."

"Master?"

"Yes," Geppetto mumbled, not opening his eyes.

"Are you upset with me? Because . . . because I've taken you from your old life at the shop and caused all this trouble?"

"No, lad. It's not your doing. You've done nothing wrong."

Maestro landed on Pinocchio's shoulder. "Let him sleep," he whispered.

Pinocchio walked to the edge of the grove, where he could see the orange sunlight play across the hills. In the distance, a floating barge made its way across the dawn sky, sails flapping from the sides like the fins of a great fish. The faint voices of the half-beast slave crew called in unison as they cranked the wheel on deck. Pinocchio watched until it disappeared over the horizon.

"Maestro," Pinocchio whispered.

The cricket hopped to a log beside him. "What is it?"

"Will you play that song for me?"

"Which song?" Maestro said, a little irritably.

"The one I heard you play back at Master Geppetto's shop when he was going to bed."

"I can't remember what song I was playing then," Maestro said. "My musical knowledge is immense, the number of songs in my repertoire countless. It could have been a nocturne or a sonata or an aria. Not that I'd expect you to know the difference."

"It had a slow beginning, just a few notes you kept repeating." Pinocchio closed his eyes to remember. "Then the pace picked up, and you did this little thing—I'm not sure if you use your mouth or your legs—"

"My wings, actually."

"Well, it sounded almost like—I'm not sure how to describe it—like a voice in the distance, calling a lonely traveler. And it sounded like the traveler was calling back. It was amazing how you were able to make all those different sounds. The music was like a painting in my mind. Or more like a story, because I imagined that the lonely traveler was about to reach the other voice, and he was getting quite excited, when . . ." Pinocchio opened his eyes and chuckled. "Well, then Master gave a snore and you stopped playing."

Maestro stared at Pinocchio with his black droplet eyes.

"Do you know what song it is now?" Pinocchio asked.

Maestro was dead silent another moment before he said, "'Orpheus.' The song is called 'Orpheus.'"

The cricket was talking so breathlessly, as if he was in a trance, without any of his usual high-and-mighty tone. It gave Pinocchio the creeps. "What's the matter with you?"

"You . . . did you really imagine all that from my playing?"

"Why? Was that all wrong?" Pinocchio was waiting for Maestro to chastise him as a hopeless automa.

"No!" Maestro said, brightening up. "That was it precisely. It's just . . . I've never performed a piece where anyone actually saw the imagery and felt the emotion I was trying to express. You really felt all that?"

"Of course I did," Pinocchio said. "Will you play the song for me so I can hear how it ends?"

"Why, yes! I'd be delighted, my boy." Maestro circled around on his six legs until he found a good spot from which to deliver his performance. "Are you ready?"

Pinocchio laced his fingers behind his head and leaned against a tree trunk. "Oh, yes. Very ready." Soon he forgot all about his aching feet and their troubles. He was lost in Maestro's quiet, lovely music.

Later that morning, as they set off, Maestro rode on Pinocchio's shoulder, chattering away happily to him about this song and that, explaining how he could rub his wings together to produce certain sounds and pitches. Pinocchio listened with polite interest, but found Maestro's music much more appealing than his explanations of it.

Geppetto gave Maestro a curious cock of his eyebrow. "Looks like you two are getting along."

"*He* appreciates my music," Maestro announced with a haughty flick of his antennae. "Unlike the rest of you Venetian brutes."

"Is that what we are?" Geppetto chuckled. "Little better than barbarians to you dignified Abatonians?"

"Most certainly," Maestro said. "Look at what contact with humans did to my people. Abaton is peaceful. Prester John makes sure of that. But here my people have been forced to become either slaves or wretched outlaws. Not the Abatonian way at all."

"I feel sorry for them," Pinocchio said. "These half-beast outlaws."

"Do you now?" Geppetto said. To Pinocchio's surprise, his master looked almost pleased.

"Well, they just want to be treated fairly," Pinocchio said, hoping he was saying the right thing.

"Yes, I pity their treatment too, but attacking villages?" Maestro chirped indignantly. "Robbing and killing? No, I have no wish to meet any of these runaway chimera. Sounds like they've become perfect savages. I wouldn't be surprised if they ate me as a snack, without a care for the calamity my absence would cause the musical world."

"Don't worry, Maestro," Pinocchio said. "I won't let any half-beasts eat you."

"Thank you, lad," the cricket said soberly. "It would be nearly as criminal to lose someone with your refined musical tastes."

Pinocchio smiled brightly.

Geppetto shook his head. "I've got to give it to you, Maestro. You've got an unshakable sense of self-importance."

"And why shouldn't I?" Maestro said.

Geppetto led them to a farm, where he hoped to purchase a meal. While Geppetto was negotiating with a farmhand, Pinocchio stared at the massive automa sentry that guarded the front gate. Surely the mere sight of such an intimidating armored giant would keep away any half-beast outlaws.

"Go on," Maestro urged. "Ask him."

"I will, I will," Pinocchio said, then called up to the automa sentry, "Excuse me, sir, but have you seen many half-beasts in these parts?"

The automa cast his blank gaze down at him. "Yes," he replied.

"He has," Pinocchio whispered excitedly to Maestro. He

couldn't help but think it would be thrilling to see some half-beasts—from a safe distance, at least.

Maestro crept deeper into the recesses of Pinocchio's collar. "I wonder if they're still in the vicinity."

"I'll ask." Pinocchio called up again. "Sorry to bother you, sir, but when was the most recent sighting?"

"Recent?" the colossal automa said.

"Yes, when was the last time you saw any?"

"I do not recall," he replied. "Time. I do not pay attention to such things. I just do my job." With that, the gears in his neck clicked until his gaze returned to scanning the countryside.

Before Pinocchio could ask more, Geppetto returned with a bundle of food. "Let's go."

They soon reached the edge of a steep gorge. Geppetto pointed beyond the trees on the far side to a towering hill town in the distance. "Montalcino," he said.

Maestro chirped a glad tune. "Thank goodness! We've almost made it."

"Don't relax yet," Geppetto said. "We still have to hire a coach and get away without any airmen spotting us. Montalcino is larger than San Baldovino. They have full-time human guards in addition to their automa sentries. Captain Toro's men might have sent word about a man traveling with an automa."

Maestro sighed, his antennae sagging.

Pinocchio surveyed the gorge and the river far below. "How will we get across?"

"Down is too treacherous," Geppetto said. "Maestro, fly out and see if there's a better crossing."

When the cricket returned, he said, "There's an aqueduct to the west that spans the gorge. We can cross there."

They followed the bluff until the aqueduct came into view. It was a massive stone expanse, rising from the depths of the gorge in a series of Roman arches. Pinocchio had never seen such a thing, and when they reached the aqueduct, he realized it wasn't a bridge for people, but for water. A trough ran down the middle, but they could cross by walking on one of the edges.

"Come, Master," Pinocchio urged, eager to get to Montalcino.

He scampered onto the narrow rim of the aqueduct. As he traversed, he looked back to see Geppetto warily starting to follow. He was standing sideways with his arms out like a bird, inching his feet side to side.

"What's the matter, Master? Why are you walking like that?"

Geppetto grumbled, and Maestro said, "He's not as foolhardy as you! If you fell, you might damage a few parts, but going over the side could kill him. And if he falls in the trough, he'll be swept away by the water and—"

"Can you please be quiet, Maestro?" Geppetto snarled, slowly facing forward and taking measured steps, one foot in front of the other.

This was yet another strange thing about humans, Pinocchio decided. Geppetto had been so brave when they were sneaking past the airmen in San Baldovino, but here his master was frightened by the simple act of walking on a bridge.

Pinocchio watched until Geppetto had nearly caught up to him. "Keep going," Geppetto said, waving a hand.

"But I'm worried for you, Master. I don't want you to fall."

"Then please quit distracting me."

Pinocchio felt the tug of the orders threatening to lengthen his nose, so he took a few more steps before reaching back a hand. "Let me help you, Master. That's why I was sent to you. Prester John wanted me to help you. Please take my hand. I don't want to lose you."

Geppetto froze. His face went white. "What did you say?"

Maestro buzzed down to land on the aqueduct. "What's wrong, Geppetto?"

Geppetto knelt to keep his balance, his eyes fixed on Pinocchio. "It's just . . . when I left Abaton, when Prester John sent me back with the three gifts for the doge . . . Your words reminded me of something he said. 'Don't be angry with the doge for asking you to steal my Ancientmost Pearl. There is nothing that grieves a parent more than losing his child.'"

Pinocchio tilted his head curiously. "Is he right, Master?"

"Of course he's right," Geppetto said. "And Prester John must have heard what happened to my family. How his gifts provoked the doge's anger against me . . . against them."

Maestro wiggled his antennae. "I'm not understanding what you're saying, Geppetto."

"The boy." Geppetto nodded to Pinocchio. "Prester John sent him to me."

"Yes, we know," Maestro said.

"To be my son."

"What?" Maestro and Pinocchio said together.

"When Prester John heard what happened to my son, he sent his own gift to ease my grief. He sent me Pinocchio, an automa who is becoming a boy."

"I'm meant to be your son?" Pinocchio murmured. Something warm and strange and wonderful was welling in his gearworks.

A gentle smile gathered on Geppetto's face. "I believe you are. And I—"

Over the tree-topped hill behind them, a figure rose in the air, long wings stretching from his back, red armor glittering in the sunlight. The happiness drained from Pinocchio.

"Airman!" he gasped.

8.

The Death of Captain Toro

Geppetto nearly lost his balance. "Go, Pinocchio!" he shouted. "Get to the other side."

The airman hovered high in the air, his gaze locking on the aqueduct. With a dive, he came for them. Geppetto began walking faster, a dance of steps with his arms outstretched and flailing.

Pinocchio didn't want to leave his master, but Geppetto had given him an order. He reluctantly headed for the other side. The airman swept across the aqueduct, a shot booming from his musket. A chunk of rock exploded near Pinocchio's feet.

He froze. The airman was coming around in a tight arc, his mechanical wings beating the air.

"Hurry, Master!" Pinocchio shouted.

Geppetto was hurrying as best he could, but the airman landed on the aqueduct between them. He aimed his weapon at Pinocchio. "Stay where you are!"

This was not an order Pinocchio had to follow. The airman was not his master. But Pinocchio wasn't going to leave Geppetto to be captured.

"*Signore Polendina,*" the airman barked.

Pinocchio realized with a jolt who this was. Captain Toro.

"Or are you, in fact, Geppetto Gazza, traitor to the empire?" Captain Toro said. "We'll soon find out. Order your automa to stay where it is while I secure you."

Geppetto narrowed his eyes. "Pinocchio," he said. "Continue to the other side. Get away."

Captain Toro reloaded his musket and trained it on Pinocchio. "I can shoot it. An automa is not so easily repaired after having its chest splintered by a musket ball."

"You won't," Geppetto said. "The doge wouldn't want you to do that."

Captain Toro turned the musket on Geppetto. "You seem the brave sort, *signore.* Let's test it. Order the automa to stay where it is or I'll shoot you instead."

"You won't do that, either," Geppetto said.

Captain Toro leveled his musket. Pinocchio hesitated, not sure enough about how people worked to know the difference between a threat and a warning.

"Go!" Geppetto shouted at Pinocchio.

At once, the musket blasted in a cloud of smoke.

"NO!" Pinocchio shouted, running for Captain Toro. The seven-league boots gave him a surprising burst of speed, and he tackled Captain Toro, rocketing the two of them out over the river. As he did, Pinocchio realized that Captain Toro's shot had been aimed high. Geppetto was still standing on the aqueduct, unharmed.

But it was too late. He and Captain Toro were falling.

One of Captain Toro's wings opened, but Pinocchio had the other one pinned. They sailed around in a spiral, Captain Toro sputtering and trying to pry loose Pinocchio's powerful hold.

Pinocchio's nose grew as they fell. Geppetto had ordered him to go, and he had defied his master. What else was he supposed to have done? But it was too late to worry about that now.

They splashed into the river. The swift current immediately swept them away. Pinocchio held tight to Captain Toro, fearing that if he let go, the airman would fly back up and capture Geppetto. They sank to the bottom, the current dragging them by Captain Toro's lone wing.

Captain Toro fought and struggled. His musket was lost. With one hand he beat at Pinocchio. With the other he clawed at the river bottom. Pinocchio clung to his back in the racing current. Captain Toro's fight began to fade, and soon he was no longer moving. Reluctantly, Pinocchio loosened his hold. The captain drifted limply in the water.

Pinocchio turned him over. Captain Toro's eyes were wide, but he didn't see Pinocchio. Pinocchio tapped at the captain's cheek. He didn't respond.

He gave the captain a shove. *Wake up!*

But the captain wasn't sleeping. He had stopped functioning. And when humans stopped functioning . . .

"No!" Pinocchio roared, his voice dulled by the water.

He had to get Captain Toro out of the river. Maybe then he would come alive again. He grabbed the captain's arm and pulled, fighting the current to walk toward the bank. As he brought the captain onto the shore, Pinocchio broke off the mechanical wings so he could lay the airman on his back.

He patted Captain Toro's face. "Just function again," he murmured. "Please don't be dead. I forgot you could die. I didn't mean to do it. Just start working again."

There was a terrible burning in Pinocchio's gears, beginning from his feet and working its way up to his chest. Was this what Geppetto felt every time he thought about his wife and son? Pinocchio rested his hands on Captain Toro's stomach, feeling shame and despair at what he had done. Something burning hot flooded down his arms into his fingertips.

Captain Toro sputtered, and Pinocchio shot to his feet. Then, with another sputter, a fountain of water spewed from Toro's mouth. The captain coughed brutally, rolling onto his side.

Pinocchio fell back, drained. His head felt as if it were filling with thick mist. "Captain?" he whispered. "Are you alive?"

Captain Toro opened his dark-rimmed eyes. His helmet was gone, and strings of wet hair were plastered to his face. "You drowned me," he gasped.

"I didn't mean to," Pinocchio said.

"But . . ." He breathed heavily. "You . . . saved me."

"I suppose I did mean to do that."

"Why?" Captain Toro said weakly.

Pinocchio's thoughts weren't so clear anymore. The mist that seemed to fill his head was making it hard to think. "My master told me human life is valuable," he said. "You will live, then?"

The captain nodded.

"Good." Pinocchio ran into the trees, scrambling up the embankment to get away. His thoughts were so muddled by whatever he'd just done to Captain Toro, he forgot why he was even out here in this forest. His automa impulses, however, were working better than ever. He was an automa who had lost his master. He simply had to find him again.

After he had run some distance, he noticed something in his field of view. He touched the long nose sticking from his face. He couldn't remember now why his nose had grown long. What had he done? It didn't matter. He just had to find his master. Master could fix it.

"Master!" he shouted.

But where was his master? He vaguely remembered his master had been on a sort of bridge that carried water. Yes, an aqueduct.

He continued up the gorge, running into the base of a cliff, where he simply kept going by pulling himself hand over hand up the sheer face. When he reached the top, he scanned the ravine. No aqueduct.

"Which way is it?" he said to himself.

A voice answered behind him. "Which way is what?"

Pinocchio turned to see five swords pointed at his chest. Five swords floating in the air.

Even this didn't surprise Pinocchio. He stared blankly until he realized that the swords were being held by five nearly invisible figures. They wore cloaks covered in leaves and bark that perfectly camouflaged them.

"Look what we've got here, Rampino," one called.

A bush rustled, becoming a sixth cloaked figure. Rampino chuckled and drew a sword. "You lost, automa?"

"Yes," Pinocchio said. "I am lost and looking for my master."

"Are you now?" Rampino smiled, showing crooked yellow teeth. "Looking for your master, or run off from him?"

Pinocchio tried to understand why the men were holding

swords on him. "I assure you, I am no danger to you. You can put away your swords."

A round of laughter burst from the men.

"Hear that, boys?" Rampino chuckled. "We can put away our swords."

For some reason none of the men put away their swords.

Pinocchio's fealty lock was buzzing at him to get back to his master as soon as possible. He was a good automa. A loyal automa. He should not be wandering around the woods on his own.

"Can you help me find my master? He was—"

"That's what we're here for, automa," Rampino interrupted. "We're going to help you find your master."

"That is good," Pinocchio said.

"A *new* master, that is," Rampino clarified. "Get him in the cart."

New master? He did not want a new master. He had to get back to his.

A man came forward, and as he reached for Pinocchio, his hand came too close to Pinocchio's chest. With a flash of movement, Pinocchio grabbed the man's wrist. He yowled in pain.

"Let go of him, you blasted puppet!" Rampino growled, swinging his sword.

Pinocchio held up an arm to block the blow. The sword gave a *thunk* as it stuck in his forearm. The effects of the sword's iron were instantaneous. His knees buckled, and he collapsed, motionless, to the ground.

"Get him in the cage, boys," Rampino said.

The men had an automa donkey cart hidden over behind some trees. Like the mechanipillar, it walked on metal legs, but it had only four, one at each corner of the wagon. The wooden donkey's head, sprouting from the wagon front, peered around to look placidly at Pinocchio. Fixed atop the donkey cart's wagon was a large metal cage.

Pinocchio was hoisted inside. He struggled to sit up before the barred door was locked, but he was too slow. "*Signori*, you do not understand. I must return to my master. He is nearby. He will be looking for me."

"Hear that?" Rampino called. "Better hurry."

The donkey brayed like a warped piston. The wagon jerked forward and began to sway as it walked over roots and stones through the forest. The men marched beside the donkey cart.

Rampino sheathed his sword with a laugh. "A fine catch! Did you see that fight in him? He'll earn us a nice bag of gold. Just you see."

The one man was whimpering, clutching his arm tight to his chest, but the others smiled at their leader, hardly a mouthful of teeth between them.

"And I know just who'll pay nicely for an automa like this," Rampino said.

"Al Mi'raj?" another replied.

Rampino chuckled. "That's just the fire-eating djinni I was thinking of."

9.

Flight of the Blue Fairy

Lazuli was hiding in a tree. She'd been hiding a lot lately, and, as a princess of Abaton, this was not something she was used to. It seemed that ever since she'd arrived in this cursed Venetian Empire, it had been one near escape after another. And now . . .

A musket blast echoed up from the ravine.

It had to be imperial airmen. She'd seen her share of them, although fortunately, so far, from a safe distance.

Something was happening over in the ravine, but from her hiding spot up in the tree, she hadn't been able to tell what was going on. Clearly the airmen were pursuing someone. Maybe it was some poor enslaved chimera—or "half-beast," as they were called here in the empire. She'd heard that the slaves who ran away from their human masters were hunted down. Who knew what horrible things they did to them? These Venetians really were savages.

While the calls of airmen seemed to remain down in the ravine, someone was coming her way. Hurried footsteps were crunching on leaves on the forest floor below. Lazuli came out a little farther on the branch to see who it was.

It was a human, and given his attire, not an imperial soldier. He bent over, his hands on his knees, catching his breath. Lazuli guessed he was the one the airmen were looking for. So they hunted their own kind as well. Did their savagery have no end?

"Are we safe?"

The voice was so chirping and light, Lazuli couldn't imagine that it belonged to the man. But there didn't seem to be anyone else with him.

"Not in the slightest," the man said. "Give me a moment and we'll keep going."

"But where?" the chirping voice asked. "We don't know where Pinocchio's gone."

"The lad can't drown. And automa are too heavy to float. He could be stuck on the river bottom. Ten to one he's already managed to drag himself ashore. But where's he hiding?"

The man stood and gave a great stretch of his arms. Lazuli glimpsed his face now. That pointy mustache, that mane of silver-black hair. She knew this man! He was the only human she'd ever seen, at least before she'd arrived here with her father in this vile humanland empire.

He was Geppetto, the high alchemist of Venice. Or least he had been the high alchemist. Her father's spies had said that Geppetto had barely escaped with his life from the doge's fortress after returning from his visit to Abaton.

And now she could see that a cricket was clinging to his shoulder. Could that be Maestro?

Lazuli cupped a hand to her mouth and called lightly, "Are you Master Geppetto?"

Geppetto spun this way and that, peering around at the forest but not looking up. "Who's there?" he hissed.

"I don't like this," Maestro chirped anxiously.

"I'm up here," Lazuli said.

Geppetto looked up and gave a start when he spied her. "Great Vesuvius, girl! How did you get stuck in that tree?"

"I'm not stuck," Lazuli said, stepping easily along the branch back to the trunk.

Geppetto waved his hands in alarm. "Stop!" he cried. "You're going to fall!"

Lazuli walked down the trunk, her feet flat against the bark and her body perfectly horizontal to the earth. When she landed without a sound on the forest floor, she pulled back her hood to reveal her bright blue hair.

"You're a sylph," Geppetto gasped.

"That's not just any sylph!" Maestro piped. "That's Princess Lazuli, Prester John's daughter!"

"And you, Master Cricket, are Maestro, the renowned musician of the Moonlit Court," Lazuli said, flourishing a hand.

"Why . . . yes, Your Highness," Maestro said, bowing his antennae repeatedly. "I'm . . . I'm honored you remember me."

Geppetto frowned. "But what are you doing here?"

"Searching for my father," Lazuli said. "He's been captured."

"Yes, I know," Geppetto said. "But you shouldn't be here, child. You're in terrible danger!"

"I'm no child, Master Geppetto." Lazuli cocked a hand to her hip. She resented being seen as a little girl. She might have been the youngest of her father's children—and the only one still living—but she would be old enough to marry in a few years, although that was a dreadful thought.

"I accompanied my father on his voyage to Venice," Lazuli said. "We had just reached the lagoon near the city when our ship was attacked. . . ." Her throat went tight at the memory of that terrible night, of the fiery missiles that rained down from the doge's floating warships, of her father hurling her from the side of their ship just before the explosion, of having to run across the surface of the water to get away.

Tears of bitter shame threatened to form. She had run away and left her father to be captured. But what else was there to do? She'd only have been caught as well, or worse.

Geppetto's expression softened. "You don't have to—"

Lazuli cleared her throat and jutted her chin. "I was able to get away in time. I hid under a piece of wreckage. My mother is a sylph, so I can't sink on water. And my father, being who he is, wasn't harmed by the explosion, although the others . . ."

She closed her eyes to compose herself. It wasn't proper to show this sort of emotion. Geppetto put his hand gently to her shoulder.

Lazuli opened her eyes and continued. "Father was carried away by some sort of alchemy contraptions in the form of winged cats."

"Flying Lions," Geppetto said.

"Be glad they didn't find you, Your Highness," Maestro assured her.

"I wish they had," Lazuli said fiercely. "I'd tear every single one of them into a million pieces."

Geppetto blinked with surprise.

Lazuli composed herself. "You're an alchemist, Master Geppetto. What I don't understand is how the doge could capture my father. What terrible alchemy devices could do that?"

"Your father might be immortal," Geppetto said, "but he's not omnipotent. He could survive that attack, but there's a weakness all Abatonians share, a weakness that I now realize even your father has. It's no device or alchemical creation. It's a simple substance. Lead."

"Lead?" Lazuli said. "What's lead?"

"A metal found in the humanlands, but not in Abaton. Lead—like iron, or any other base metal—disrupts anything magical. It would only take a simple touch of lead for any Abatonian—or automa for that matter, since alchemical technology operates on Abatonian magic—to become completely helpless."

"So the doge is using lead to hold my father—" Lazuli began.

At that moment, a trio of airmen came soaring over the treetops.

"Get back!" Geppetto growled, pushing Lazuli behind a tree. They flattened themselves against the trunk. Lazuli drew a sword from under her cloak.

"Do you know how to use that, Princess?" Geppetto said.

"Most certainly," she said. "The master of ceremonies in my father's court gave me lessons—"

"It won't do us any good against them," Geppetto said, pointing up. He shook his head and mumbled, "I can barely take care of myself. And now I have the daughter of Prester John to worry about."

"You don't have to worry about me, Master Geppetto," Lazuli said, scowling before she could stop herself. "I'm quite capable, I'll have you know."

Geppetto gave an apologetic look. "I'm sure you are, Your Highness. It's just that your being here multiplies our danger."

"Danger from those airmen?" she said. "Are they pursuing you?"

"One of them, Captain Toro, nearly captured us before he fell into the ravine with my automa," Geppetto said. "If they fished Toro out, he'll have told them we're nearby."

"Can those airmen even get down into this forest with those ungainly wings?" Lazuli asked.

"Not easily," Geppetto said, scanning the tree canopy for the airmen.

"But their Lions can," Maestro said, his voice trembling.

"They have Flying Lions?" Lazuli asked. Her bravado from before was not holding up against the prospect of confronting actual mechanical lions.

Overhead a roar erupted. It was an unnerving sound, equal parts mechanical and monstrous, and it sent a chill through Lazuli's core.

"Master Geppetto?" she said, unable to stop the annoying note of worry that made its way into her voice.

"Be calm," Geppetto said.

"I'm calm!" she snapped.

He sighed. "We just need to wait for—"

Branches cracked up in the leaf canopy some ways off. Something heavy and wooden exploded. Lazuli realized with sudden, icy certainty that this was the sound of one of those terrible Lions barreling through a tree trunk. Blessed shores of Abaton, that thing was huge!

Geppetto hoisted Lazuli to her feet.

"We can't outrun them!" Maestro chirped.

The series of exploding trees grew louder.

"We've got to find somewhere to hide!" Geppetto growled. "Now!"

They ran. Lazuli's weightless steps barely rustled the tops of fallen leaves, but Geppetto sounded like a hippogriff as he raced through the underbrush after her.

An airman overhead shouted, "They're down here!" He dove into the treetops, snagging on branches and cursing as he descended. Another airman was trying to follow him, but they were having trouble breaking through the canopy.

Lazuli spun around, desperately searching for a way to go, but they were cut off.

"There they are!" one of the airmen shouted.

They had to find a place to hide. She had an idea. It wasn't the safest of options, but what else were they to do? Closing her eyes, she focused all her elemental powers.

A cyclone-force wind rushed through the forest, whipping up leaves and rustling the branches. Geppetto put an arm across his face, trying to block the dirt and debris battering him. Lazuli pushed him flat on his stomach, and he gave a gasp. She dropped across his back.

"What are—" Geppetto began.

But Lazuli was drawing the air like a funnel into the ground beneath them. The earth gave way. Geppetto sucked in a surprised breath before submerging into the crumbling sinkhole. She hoped he was good at holding his breath. An instant later, they were covered by dirt, with only the glow of her eyes casting any light. It trickled in Lazuli's ears and sifted unpleasantly through her hair. She'd never actually tried this before and decided she never wanted to again. But for now, it was their best hope.

Even buried, she could hear faint voices shouting at first and then talking to one another in puzzlement, though their words were masked by the mass of earth overhead until the airmen came closer to their hiding place.

".. . how'd they get away?" she heard one airman say.

".. . Toro said the automa leaped at him like a bird. . . . Maybe they flew?"

There was muffled laughter. ". . . flying automa! The man's gone mad."

".. . they can't have gone too far. . . . where's the Lion off to?"

Geppetto grunted and wriggled.

"Be calm," she whispered.

The voices above faded away. Lazuli waited. A few moments more, just to make sure they didn't come back. Soon Geppetto began to grunt more urgently, and she knew they had to risk getting out before he suffocated.

She blew a long breath, and the dirt loosened around them. Geppetto pushed up with his arms, forcing her to the surface. He gulped for air.

"Wait," she whispered. "They might still be here."

Partially hidden by dirt and leaves, she glanced around and listened. The voices were faint now, more distant. Then she heard the cracking of branches, as the airmen and the Flying Lion broke through the treetops and were gone.

Lazuli stood from the hole with ease. Geppetto, however, had to pry himself up, spitting and brushing dirt from his face and hair. He staggered to his feet, clumps of earth peeling away from his filthy clothes.

Lazuli's clothes were spotless. She was glad to be a sylph. She brushed back her hood, letting her long blue hair fall about her shoulders.

"That was madness," Geppetto panted.

"We didn't get caught, did we?" Lazuli said. "I told you I was quite capable."

"Yes, so I see," Geppetto said. "Next time you're feeling capable, please don't smother me."

Lazuli smiled. She hoped this had proved to Geppetto that she didn't need to be treated like a child.

Maestro came down from wherever he'd been hiding and landed on Geppetto's sleeve. "Your Highness!" he chirped. "Are you all right? Are you injured?"

"I'm perfectly fine, Master Cricket."

"I'm fine as well," Geppetto grumbled. "I appreciate your concern."

"Well, of course you are, you indestructible old goat," Maestro snapped. "But we have to protect Princess Lazuli."

Lazuli narrowed her eyes, trying to stay composed as she'd been taught. She might not like being treated like a helpless princess, but Maestro was one of her subjects. She was used to her subjects being annoyingly overprotective.

"Shall we continue the search for my father?" Lazuli asked.

"You're searching in the wrong place," Geppetto said, shaking out his cloak. "He's imprisoned in Venice. How did you wind up way out here, anyway?"

"I'm not searching in the wrong place," Lazuli said, fishing the Hunter's Glass out from beneath her collar. The glass globe was attached to a necklace, and she held it out for Geppetto to see.

"What is that?" Geppetto asked.

"Your Highness," Maestro reprimanded him. "You should address the princess of Abaton as Your Highness."

"Forgive me, Your Highness," Geppetto said.

Lazuli waved her hand. "It's not necessary, Master Geppetto. This is a Hunter's Glass. My father gave it to me for my last birthday. And fortunately, I brought it with me on our voyage, because it's now leading me to him. You see that light that just formed on the side? That means that Father is that way." She pointed into the thick of the forest.

"But why would he be out here in Tuscany?" Maestro asked Geppetto.

"The doge might be moving him," Geppetto replied. "If that's the case, we have a better chance of rescuing him. How far away is he, Your Highness?"

"Unfortunately, the Hunter's Glass doesn't show how far," she said. "Just that he's in that direction."

"So he could be in Siena or Lapland for all we know?" Geppetto said.

"I don't know where either of those places is," Lazuli said, "but I think we can assume he's being moved somewhere here in the Venetian Empire. In fact, the light has been growing brighter lately, which makes me think I might be getting close."

Geppetto twisted his mustache as he thought for a moment. "I agree we need to find His Immortal Lordship, but first we need to find Pinocchio. He's lost and surely searching for me. I . . . we'll need him."

"Who is Pinocchio?" Lazuli asked.

"My automa."

"Are automa those bizarre humanlike contraptions you alchemists make?" Lazuli asked.

"Pinocchio is not bizarre!" Maestro said, and then, seeming to remember who he was speaking to, began bowing his antennae. "That is, he's not bizarre, *Your Highness*. Well, maybe a little, but Pinocchio's not like the rest of those empty-headed automa."

Lazuli was surprised that one of her fellow Abatonians would defend an automa. *"He?"* she asked. "You refer to this automa device as a *he?"*

"If you'd only met Pinocchio, Your Highness, you'd understand," Maestro said. "He's . . . well, he's wonderful."

"Your father has done something to Pinocchio," Geppetto said.

"My father?" Why would her father tinker with some alchemy contraption?

"Yes, he sent Pinocchio to me," Geppetto said, "from his prison cell in the Fortezza Ducale. The boy is changing somehow. He's more aware than a normal automa. More perceptive and sensitive."

"And he has exquisite musical tastes," Maestro added.

Lazuli felt there was something else Geppetto was not telling her about this automa. She realized he must be able to see her skepticism. She tried to master her expression.

"Why would my father send you this automa?"

"For one, to help rescue him," Geppetto said.

"For one?" she asked. "Why else?"

Geppetto hesitated.

Maestro piped up instead. "Your Highness, Pinocchio seems to be turning into a real human boy."

"What?" Lazuli gasped. "Impossible!"

"Not for His Immortal Lordship," the cricket said. "Your father is capable of the most extraordinary things."

Lazuli tried not to grimace. It was true. Her father was powerful, the commander of untold magic, and the immortal king and protector of Abaton. But it was ordinary things—like being an attentive father—that he seemed incapable of handling. Besides the occasional royal dinner or passing in the halls of the Moonlit Court, the most time she'd ever spent with her father was on their voyage to the Venetian Empire. She was just another of his countless mortal children who would one day grow old and die while His Immortal Lordship remained Abaton's eternal ruler.

But she supposed Maestro was right. If anyone could enchant an automa to seem like a real human boy, her father could.

"You see, Your Highness," Maestro continued gingerly, "Geppetto's family was murdered by the doge."

Lazuli winced. She struggled for how to respond to this, and only managed "I'm so sorry, Master Geppetto."

Geppetto gave a gentle smile, tinted with sadness. "His Immortal Lordship, given how many of his own children have died over the centuries, would be particularly sensitive to the loss of a child. Look at how he showed compassion even to the doge after Prince Ignazio died. I believe your father intends for Pinocchio not only to help me rescue him, but also . . . to be my son."

All manner of thoughts and emotions ran through Lazuli. This was certainly not a side of her father she had ever seen. But it was a side she wanted to discover. If only she could rescue him.

"What about the Hunter's Glass?" Maestro squeaked. "Could it lead us to Pinocchio, Your Highness?"

"Yes," Geppetto said. "Good thinking, Maestro!"

"It might," Lazuli said. The automa was really more an object than a person, despite whatever charms her father had put on it. She slipped the Hunter's Glass from around her neck and handed it to Geppetto. "Just visualize your automa."

Geppetto cupped his hand around the Hunter's Glass and closed his eyes. An instant later, a light formed on the side of the glass.

"That way," Lazuli said, peering into the thick of the forest. "And fortunately, my father seems to be held somewhere in that direction as well. Master Geppetto, the airmen said your automa could fly. Is that true?"

"He's wearing seven-league boots. Poorly functioning ones, but enough that Toro imagined he could fly."

"Well, we have that in our favor," Lazuli said. "If they're looking for a man traveling with a flying automa, we hopefully won't look so conspicuous. Shall we go?"

"Yes," Geppetto said. "But we still need to avoid being spotted. I only hope we find Pinocchio before anyone else does."

PART TWO

THE

MAGPIE

10.

The Djinni

Since saving Captain Toro from the river, Pinocchio wasn't thinking clearly. He wasn't really thinking at all. The encounter had left him as close to a normal mindless automa as he had been since Prester John gave him the pinecone.

He sat on the floor of the donkey cart, staring blankly at the forest passing by. He barely noticed when a patrol of airmen soared overhead, prompting Rampino's men to hide beneath their cloaks. The next day, Pinocchio faintly noticed when Rampino's men left the forest for the open countryside. Their cloaks transformed, the green foliage on the fabric becoming dusty brown grass, not unlike the grass rolling across the hills all around.

Pinocchio sat in the jostling cart. The unrelenting pull of the fealty charm made him desperate to find his master again. The more ground Rampino covered, the farther Pinocchio got from

Geppetto, the worse the fealty charm pulled on him. It focused his dull thoughts on his master.

As the cart bumped over a rocky patch of road, a memory bubbled its way through the thick mist filling his thoughts. Pinocchio suddenly recalled the last thing he had asked his master: *I'm meant to be your son?*

Geppetto wasn't just his master. He was going to be his father.

In that instant, melodic bird sounds, loud and riotous, filled his ears. He felt the warm wind brush his cheeks. Pinocchio sat bolt upright with a gasp.

"Master Geppetto!" he murmured. "Father . . . where are you?"

"Quiet," Rampino growled, threatening to poke him with the sword.

Pinocchio stared and stared, hoping to see his father, and knowing they had gone hopelessly far.

When they reached the walls of Siena, the guards waved them through cheerfully. "Light load, Rampino," one called, nodding to Pinocchio.

Rampino smiled his crooked-toothed smile. "Yes, but we've got a fine one for the fire eater this time."

The donkey cart stopped in a square with flapping banners showing, oddly enough, a snail. Rampino deposited his men at a stable and unlocked the cage to let Pinocchio out.

"Follow me," he growled. "And no funny business or you'll feel my sword's iron."

Pinocchio stepped down, his right foot giving a little spring that caused him to stumble. He was better at controlling the seven-league boots, but after all the riding, he had to remember how to steady the boots' tendency to bounce.

Rampino marched him through the crowded streets of neighborhoods with banners showing a panther, and deeper in the city, past banners with an eagle, until they came to an empty sliver of an alleyway. Pinocchio's captor rolled aside a barrel and they descended a hidden set of stairs. At the bottom, Rampino rapped at a cellar door. The loud clanking of hammers on metal sounded from somewhere deep inside. Finally, a small panel in the door opened and a dark eye peered out.

"I've got a new actor for Al Mi'raj's theater," Rampino said.

As the panel closed and a series of locks began to click, Pinocchio desperately wanted to run, but before he could get up the nerve, the door opened. A boy in tattered leggings and a loose shirt stood before them.

No, not a boy, or at least not a human one. He was covered in fine, tawny fur and had long ears poking from the sides of his head, and was that a tail? This boy was a half-beast! He wasn't so terrifying. But Pinocchio had no time to stare before Rampino shoved him forward.

The room at the end of the long hall ahead glowed like an oven. Rampino opened his cloak and wiped his forehead. They entered a workshop filled with half a dozen open pits of burning salamanders. Tiny bearded workers, who looked more like molded clumps of earth than men, were busy with hammers and tools. Gnomes, Pinocchio realized.

A massive creature sat at a table in the workshop's center. He was bright yellow with black spots speckling his skin. A curved horn sprouted from one side of his head. The other horn was broken off behind his ear. He carved at a flaming salamander on his plate, forking bites into his fang-filled maw.

Pinocchio had never seen one before, but he knew this must be a djinni, a fire elemental.

"Greetings, Al Mi'raj," Rampino said.

Al Mi'raj looked up from his meal, taking a sip of a thick black liquid in a goblet. A thin flame shimmered on the drink's surface. The djinni's eyes were as yellow as his skin, with a reptilian shard of black bisecting the middle.

"Just one?" Al Mi'raj's voice rumbled like a volcano.

Rampino shrugged. "Farmers are keeping their automa off the roads lately."

"You'll have to venture out to new territory next time," Al Mi'raj said, slicing the head off the salamander and crunching down on it with his jumble of teeth. He chewed disgustingly as he eyed Pinocchio. "He looks small. How much do you want for him?"

"Look closer," Rampino said. "Very fine craftsmanship. He looks like a lad, but he's strong. We saw him scale a cliff with his hands. Fought like a tiger when we tried to cage him."

Al Mi'raj grunted, unimpressed. "How did he get the nose?"

"Probably a malfunction. They get that way when they're not properly maintained. Your gnomes—er, your gnome will get him tip-top."

Al Mi'raj surveyed Pinocchio. "He doesn't look like a farmhand. They make these boy models as parlor-room servants. I can't afford to have some don recognize his missing houseboy. Not interested."

"Ninety ducats," Rampino said. "That's half what I sold you the last automa for."

"Twenty," Al Mi'raj said, reaching for a box on the table and counting out the golden coins.

Rampino spat. "I could get more than that if we sold him for parts."

Pinocchio decided that was enough. He was not going to be disassembled into spare parts. Although he should have tried to get away when he was still outside, maybe he could make it to the door.

He shoved Rampino and turned to run, but Rampino regained his balance and swung the flat edge of his sword against Pinocchio's back. His gears froze and everything went black as he collapsed to the floor.

When Pinocchio was able to open his eyes, he found Al Mi'raj standing over him. The creature was massive. Terrifying. Worse than anything Pinocchio had imagined any monster could be.

The djinni smiled. "Yes, he has spirit, doesn't he? That'll make for a good show. I'll give you the ninety ducats. Find me more like this one, Rampino."

Rampino stammered as Al Mi'raj deposited the coins in his hand. "Yes—thank you—I will." He bowed before hurrying out the door.

"Bulbin," Al Mi'raj called. "Set up our new performer."

The group of gnomes around the workshop hurried over. As they approached, they collided into one another like they were made of mud. They merged together until they formed one slightly larger gnome, although Bulbin—or was it Bulbins?—still wasn't quite tall enough to reach Pinocchio's waist.

"My master will come for me," Pinocchio warned Al Mi'raj. "He'll be angry when he knows what you've done."

"He's not your master anymore," Al Mi'raj said.

Bulbin took a ring of keys off his belt and began sorting through them, holding one up at a time and comparing the key against Pinocchio. "Vitruvian Moppet? A squint too tall to be that one." Bulbin took another key. "Vitruvian Boymunculus? No. Vitruvian Pandroid? Close. Ah, here 'tis. Vitruvian Manikin. Palace servant, eh?"

"That's not my fealty key," Pinocchio said, scooting away from the creature. "My master has mine. And he's an alchemist, mind you. Only he can control me."

Bulbin snickered and then broke apart into about a dozen smaller versions of himself. Each one clambered onto the others' shoulders until they made a wobbling tower of Bulbins that reached Pinocchio's shoulders. The one on top tried to slip the key into the back of Pinocchio's neck, but Pinocchio twisted his head side to side irritably.

Al Mi'raj smirked. "Stay still for Bulbin. You'll want to stay on his good side, manikin. Unless you want him to rearrange you into a donkey cart. Or worse."

Pinocchio remembered Rampino's donkey cart and wondered if that had once been an automa. "What could be worse?"

"How'd a talking chamber pot suit you, Al Mi'raj?" Bulbin asked.

Pinocchio froze.

The gnome laughed as he got the key in the lock and the tumblers clicked. He turned the key, and a strange sensation came over Pinocchio's body. A feeling that he was weightless, that he could just float away.

Then Bulbin said, "Al Mi'raj is your master now."

It was as if lead anchors had snapped onto his limbs. He felt temporarily crushed. He fought against it, trying to think of Geppetto. He was his real master. Not this revolting djinni. But as Pinocchio felt his nose return to its normal size, he knew he had to obey Al Mi'raj.

The tower of gnomes toppled and collapsed into the larger version of Bulbin. "Done," the gnome said with a satisfied clap of his hands.

Pinocchio stood, glaring at them. "So what do you want me to do?"

"Your fellow actors will explain. Wiq! Come show our newest member to his quarters." Al Mi'raj strolled back to the table to finish his meal. Pinocchio eyed the smoking, half-eaten carcass with disgust. Fire eater, eh? Well, he hoped Al Mi'raj choked on the salamander's tail!

The half-beast boy who had answered the door appeared. "Follow me."

Wiq didn't seem very friendly. In fact he seemed angry, although Pinocchio couldn't guess why.

"Doesn't Al Mi'raj have a master?" Pinocchio asked once they were down the hall.

Wiq didn't answer. Pinocchio thought that maybe the grumpy boy didn't understand why he was asking. "It's just I've heard that elementals like him serve alchemists—"

"Al Mi'raj and Bulbin don't work in a normal workshop," Wiq said, his tail swatting side to side. "They run the theater for the lord mayor of Siena. They serve him, as the mayor serves the empire. Good, obedient servants. You know all about that, don't you, puppet?"

"My name's not Puppet. My name's Pinocchio."

"Be quiet, puppet." Wiq kept marching him down the twisting hallways.

"Look, did I say something wrong?" Pinocchio felt he must have offended the boy. "I'm sorry if—"

"I said don't talk to me, automa. I don't like your kind."

Pinocchio frowned. "Well, it's a funny place to work, then, don't you think?"

"You think I choose to work here?" Wiq growled. He touched

his hands to a metal collar around his neck. "I might be a slave, but I'm no puppet like you!"

Wiq opened a door, gave Pinocchio an abrupt shove through, and slammed it behind him.

The room was a large, vaulted cellar lit by pixie bulbs that were hovering up above like oversize soap bubbles. Wardrobes and chests lined the walls, along with racks of costumes and heaps of fabric. The room was crowded with dozens of automa.

They all stopped what they were doing and turned to stare at him. Some had been sewing costumes. Others were sparring with wooden swords. Another was painting a mask of what looked like a hysterical rabbit. The closest automa seemed like he had been rehearsing some sort of speech, and he stopped midsentence with a hand flung up dramatically, before facing Pinocchio.

"How now, cousin?" he bellowed. "Good greetings. 'Twas fortune that brought thee to us, and fortune that will guide thee in our midst."

"Uh, what?" Pinocchio said.

He'd never heard an automa—or a person, for that matter—talk like this. And what a strangely shaped automa! His belly had been designed to look like an enormous ball, and his face was painted bright red. He wore a tight-fitting black-and-white-checkered costume.

The automa flung an arm around Pinocchio's shoulder and gestured to the others. "Welcome . . . to Al Mi'raj's Grand Marionette Theater!"

The other automa placidly went back to what they were doing.

"Oh," Pinocchio said. "Thanks."

"I am Pulcinella. Thou mayst call me Punch."

"Are you the chief butler?"

"No, lad, no," Punch replied. "Methinks thou art confused. Speak I with the common tongue of an automa servant? Can thou not hear how the ingenious master gnome Bulbin has bestowed me with the vocalizing of a grand orator?"

"Is that why you talk like that?" Pinocchio said. "He won't do that to me, will he?"

"Nay," Punch said. "Thou wilt be a performer. Through thy gestures and acting, thou wilt assist thy fellow performers in creating theatrical productions of high drama."

"I wilt? I mean, I will?" Pinocchio said. "How will I know what to do?"

Punch motioned across the room. "Our star, Harlequin, shall instruct thee."

Another automa was approaching. Unlike Punch, Harlequin was tall and nimble. His wooden face was painted midnight black, and he wore a costume of bright blue, red, yellow, and green diamonds.

He did a series of cartwheels, stopping next to Pinocchio. He produced a wooden bat from behind his arm. With a swing, he knocked Pinocchio in the back of the head.

"Hey!" Pinocchio said, stumbling forward.

Harlequin leaped over Pinocchio and, when he landed, bashed him in the waist, forcing Pinocchio into a bow. With an acrobatic twirl, Harlequin swiped Pinocchio's knees, spilling him flat to the floor.

Punch applauded approvingly.

Pinocchio stood up, grumbling, "What was that all for?"

"Entertainment, lad. Entertainment."

Pinocchio frowned at Harlequin, but the automa simply stared back impassively.

"Is he going to just knock me around onstage?" Pinocchio asked.

"Most assuredly," Punch said. "Tomorrow at evenfall, we perform. Thou wilt lend thy talents to our show."

"What do I have to do?" Pinocchio asked. "Speak lines?"

"Nay. That would be most dull. Thou wilt fight."

Pinocchio eyed the other performers. A female automa was touching up the paint on her eyebrows in front of a mirror. An automa with a comically sad expression carved on his face was stitching up holes in his floppy white sleeves. An automa wearing a black jaguar's mask practiced elaborate moves with a poleax. The blade on the end wasn't wooden. It was metal.

"Fight?" Pinocchio gave a shiver.

"How be thy skills sparring with a sword?" Punch asked.

"I've never tried."

"Can thou swing thy arm?"

"Yes," Pinocchio said.

"Marvelous!" Punch exclaimed. "Do so dramatically. Harlequin will rehearse with thee."

Pinocchio glanced warily over at Harlequin, who handed Pinocchio a wooden sword.

Punch called out to the automa who was painting her face. "Columbine, wouldst thou assist . . . um . . ." He looked at Pinocchio. "I beseech thee, what is thy name?"

"Pinocchio."

Punch waved to Columbine. "Locate a costume for fair Pinocchio."

She applied a final touch of red to her wooden puckered lips, then put down her paintbrush to head toward the racks of clothes.

Punch walked away, calling over his shoulder, "Prepare thyself, Pinocchio, for tomorrow we entertain all the good folk of Siena."

With a flourishing sweep, Harlequin cracked his bat against Pinocchio's head one last time.

II.

The Grand Marionette Theater

Columbine chose for Pinocchio a black cloak tipped in vibrant blue and white feathers, as well as a black helmet with a long beak. Apparently, he was supposed to be some sort of bird. A magpie, she explained. When she handed him a pair of black slippers, he remembered with a start. He couldn't let the others see how his feet had become that strange fleshy material.

"May I keep on my boots?" Pinocchio asked. "I think they look more . . . uh, dramatic."

"If you wish." Columbine batted her eyes with automa indifference. "You'll play the part of one of the half-beasts, led by Scaramouch. Just follow what the others do. Fight off Harlequin's troupe, playing humans. Harlequin always wins, so you'll have to be defeated in the end. Just don't let them hack you up too soon. The audience is here to watch us battle."

"Hack me up?" Pinocchio said. "We won't really damage each other, will we?"

Columbine handed him a curved scimitar. He was relieved to see that it was bronze, so it wouldn't disrupt his gearworks. But when Pinocchio touched the edge of the blade, it nicked a small chip of wood from his finger.

"It's sharp!" he said.

Columbine pulled up her sleeve. Her arm was crisscrossed by cracks and cuts, as if her arm had been severed many times. "The gnome is skilled. He will glue you back together afterward."

A valve in Pinocchio's innards gave an anxious whine.

While the others went about their preparations, Pinocchio decided he had to escape. The gnome's hammering had been silent for hours, so hopefully it was late in the night by now. The other automa weren't watching him, so he tried the door. To his surprise, it opened. Didn't Al Mi'raj lock them in? Was he so used to automa just doing as they were ordered that he never expected any of them to try to escape? Pinocchio didn't much care.

With a rush of excitement, he dashed upstairs and down a hallway and found he had no idea how to get out. This place was a maze! If he could only find the end of the hallway without accidentally barging into Al Mi'raj's bedroom.

He finally came to an end and tugged at the handle, but this door was locked. So the fire eater did lock them in. Pinocchio peered back down the hallway, listening, hoping everyone was sleeping soundly.

He was strong. A swift kick with his seven-league boots should take the door off its hinges. Pinocchio got a running start. He sprang out horizontal, throwing his full weight into the leap, but when his feet met the door, his knees buckled, and the seven-league boots fired him back at an odd angle with a crash.

The nearest door opened. He froze, wondering what terrible thing Al Mi'raj was going to turn him into. But it wasn't the djinni who appeared. It was Wiq.

"What are you doing out here?"

Pinocchio scrambled to his feet. "Nothing. Just . . . uh, looking around."

Wiq rubbed his eyes. "You woke me. Were you trying to escape?"

Pinocchio touched his nose and was relieved to find it hadn't grown. Fortunately, Al Mi'raj hadn't told him explicitly not to try to escape.

Wiq gave him a funny look. "You were, weren't you? Well, you can't get out. We're all prisoners here, of the lord mayor of Siena, and of the empire. Even Al Mi'raj. These doors are reinforced with lead. The mayor has me lock them every night—"

"You've got the keys!" Pinocchio said. "Well, why don't you leave?"

Wiq scowled and touched the metal collar around his neck. "It's sort of like the fealty charm that keeps you from disobeying. If I tried to escape, it would tighten. I'd strangle."

"Could you unlock the door for me?"

Wiq shook his head. "I can only open it to let visitors in." He narrowed his eyes at Pinocchio. "You're a strange automa, you know that?"

Pinocchio shrugged.

"I've never seen one of your kind try to escape."

"My master—my real master, Geppetto—is looking for me," Pinocchio said. "I want to go back to him."

"But why?" Wiq asked, his long ears swishing. "Why do you care about him?"

"Because," Pinocchio said, "he's good. He's kind. He wants me to be his—" But he stopped, realizing he probably shouldn't say any more.

Wiq brushed him away. "Go back to the others before you wake Al Mi'raj and get us both in trouble. I don't know what's malfunctioning with you, but if you know what's best, you'll forget your old master and obey Al Mi'raj."

Pinocchio's shoulders sagged, and he slumped back down to the cellar. For the rest of the night, he sat in a corner while the others prepared for the coming show.

He'd never forget Master Geppetto! He wanted so badly to be with Geppetto again. He longed to hear Maestro's songs and to hear more of Geppetto's stories and to have his master just talk to him in that way no person had ever talked to Pinocchio before—the way he imagined a father would talk to a son. A father and son . . . Would he ever get to really be Geppetto's son?

His insides burned. Something seemed to want to come out from the corners of his eyes, but there was no way for the pressure or steam or whatever it was to escape from the sealed sockets.

As he brought his hands to his eyes, he saw something strange happening to his fingertips. The fine lines of wood were disappearing, replaced by something smoother, softer. Out of his fingers, oval-shaped fingernails of shiny pink had formed.

Flesh!

He held his hands out, gasping in alarm. Had any of the other automa seen? No, they were too busy. The skin extended down his fingers, crossing his knuckles and palms. Once it got to his wrist hinges, it stopped. First his feet, and now his hands! He ran over to the trunks of costumes and began furiously rummaging through them.

"Can I help you find something?" Columbine asked.

Pinocchio hid his hands beneath the piles of scarves and shirts. "Gloves," he said. "Just looking for gloves."

"Over in that cabinet," she said, barely glancing at Pinocchio.

Pinocchio slammed the trunk shut but didn't pull one of his hands out fast enough. He stifled a yelp. His thumb got pinched. A trickle of reddish liquid formed. He had seen this substance before, when Master Geppetto had been injured at the mechanipillar. This greasy, thin liquid wasn't as bright, but Pinocchio knew what it was.

Blood.

Pinocchio tucked his hands under his shirt and made sure the other automa weren't watching before he opened the cabinet, found a pair of black leather gloves, and pulled them on.

As if he needed another reason to worry about getting his hands or feet hacked off in tomorrow's performance. What would Al Mi'raj do if he saw his automa bleed?

"Prithee!" Punch called out the following afternoon. "'Tis time for the performance, majestic marionettes. Gather your props. The show is at hand."

Pinocchio reluctantly followed the other actors down the hall. Scaramouch's troupe of fifteen or so were dressed as half-beasts. They wore an assortment of masks—wolves, baboons, mice, lizards—and carried all manner of bronze weapons. Scaramouch, in his jaguar mask, made a lazy windmill twirl with his poleax.

Harlequin stood beside Columbine and about a dozen other automa without masks, who were playing humans. Each carried a bronze sword. Not nearly as menacing as the arsenal Scaramouch's side had, but if these swordsmen and women fought the way Harlequin did, Pinocchio wondered if being turned into a chamber pot would really be so bad.

When they reached the shadowed courtyard, Pinocchio heard the noise of the crowd outside. Al Mi'raj was standing beside a grumpy-looking Wiq.

"Pulcinella, if you're ready," Al Mi'raj said.

"Down to my fantom, Your Worship," Punch replied before strolling out into the piazza.

Trumpets blared and the crowd cheered as Punch waved to them. Pinocchio pushed his way through the other automa to get a better look at what lay outside. He found himself next to Wiq, who ignored him.

Punch climbed a tall podium that rose from the middle of the wide piazza. The whole arena was illuminated by large pixie bulbs hovering about twenty feet above the brickwork.

"Lord Mayor! Most esteemed dons and donnas," Punch's voice echoed, magnified, Pinocchio guessed, by the gnome's handiwork. "If music be the food of love, I beg you take your leave. But if high comedy and exhilarating combat be your nourishment—hark!—you will be fulfilled."

The crowd roared. Stands had been erected around the outside of the seashell-shaped piazza. Above the stands, finely dressed groups of people watched from balconies. And to one side rose the biggest building, a crenellated hall with a tall clock tower.

"That's the Palazzo Pubblico," Wiq whispered, "where the lord mayor and his council watch."

Pinocchio looked at the boy, surprised that he was speaking to him.

Wiq continued, "Make sure the lord mayor can see you when you get hacked apart. Al Mi'raj doesn't like getting complaints that the mayor's guests couldn't see the show properly."

Pinocchio wilted.

From the podium, Punch boomed, "On this eve, we introduce you to a ferocious band of half-beast rebels."

Scaramouch marched into the piazza with his chest puffed out, followed by his half-beast band. The audience booed and hissed. Wiq had to give Pinocchio a shove. "Get out there!"

Pinocchio scampered to catch up, trying to be as inconspicuous as possible. Peering through the eye holes of his mask, he spied the lord mayor and his council laughing raucously. Pinocchio could only guess why. Automa butchering one another seemed to pass for high comedy in Siena.

"Defending the empire against yond beasts be your champions." Punch waved a dramatic arm. "Harlequin and his spellbinding swashbucklers!"

Harlequin bounded across the piazza in a series of somersaults that made Pinocchio dizzy. Harlequin's troupe raced after him and drew their swords in unison, the metallic chime echoing around the arena.

"Let the performance begin!" Punch cried. The cheers of the audience swelled into a deafening roar. Pinocchio's knees threatened to quit.

The two sides charged each other, leaving Pinocchio momentarily behind. He raised his scimitar feebly and ran after the others. Maybe he could just stick to the back.

At first it seemed an all-out barrage of automa doing their fiercest to hack one another to pieces. But as Pinocchio scuttled around behind Scaramouch's masked troops, he noticed little performances occurring among the battle.

The lovely Columbine was surrounded by a trio of automa wearing jackal, lizard, and parrot masks. Pinocchio thought she was about to be chopped to pieces. She cried for help, and Harlequin burst onto the scene like a slashing tornado. In a series of motions too fast to see, Harlequin scattered all three of Columbine's attackers to the cobblestones in mock deaths and severed pieces. Harlequin gathered Columbine in his arms, and she planted a kiss on his cheek. The top of his head popped open, and a little whistle of steam erupted.

The audience roared with delight. Pinocchio found it bizarre.

He found himself so caught up in watching, he nearly forgot where he was. Until he noticed automa charging at him. Lots of them.

As one of Harlequin's swashbucklers reared back with his sword, Pinocchio panicked and leaped straight up. The seven-league boots propelled him above the automa's swing, all the way up into one of the pixie bulbs hovering over the piazza. It shattered and glass tinkled down. The tiny incandescent creatures inside scattered like stardust into the sky.

When Pinocchio landed, he saw one of Harlequin's swordsmen rushing at him. Before Pinocchio could leap for safety, the automa swung his sword directly for Pinocchio's chest.

Something happened.

Pinocchio wasn't sure where it came from. It was like the uncontrollable instinct that caused him to grab a person's hand if it came too near his chest. Lightning fast, Pinocchio twirled his scimitar to defend himself against the blow. He stared in surprise as his blade blocked the automa's sword.

The shock only lasted a moment.

Pinocchio found himself parrying and blocking with unbelievable precision. This was amazing! With an acrobatic spring, he jumped to avoid the next blow. As he landed, his scimitar chopped clean through the arms of an automa. Pinocchio winced.

A chant was rising from the crowd: "Magpie! Magpie!"

They were cheering for him. He was the one the audience was watching.

And he had discovered his role to play. Harlequin was the acrobatic clown hero. Scaramouch was the prowling villain. Columbine was dainty but lethal.

And Pinocchio was the soaring magpie.

He might have been smaller than the others, but he was swift. With his seven-league boots, he could leap. He could bound. He was practically flying! All the time, he fought with a ferocity he hadn't known he had.

The audience loved this. "Magpie! Magpie!" they cried.

Pinocchio smiled as he fought his way through one cluster of Harlequin's swordsmen after another. He soon discovered that, aside from the jaguar-masked Scaramouch, he was the only one of their troupe still left fighting. He had no time to marvel at his good fortune. The entire horde of Harlequin's swashbucklers surrounded him.

He sprang high in the air, his magpie cloak flapping out like wings, and landed on top of a hovering pixie bulb, this time managing not to break it. The automa below helplessly swung their swords, too far out of reach.

"Come now," one of the automa called up to him. "You cannot hide up there. Jump down and get killed like the others."

Pinocchio decided to ignore this suggestion. He pretended to be caught up watching Scaramouch and Harlequin, who were in the thick of combat. Poor Columbine lay sprawled on the ground, fortunately with all her limbs still intact.

Pinocchio discovered that Al Mi'raj, over in the courtyard, was glaring furiously at him. Pinocchio knew he was in big trouble. Al Mi'raj pointed directly at him, then pointed to the ground where the armed mass of swashbucklers waited. Al Mi'raj drew his finger across his neck. Pinocchio had no doubt what the djinni was saying.

He tried to pretend he hadn't seen Al Mi'raj's order. But too late. His nose began to grow.

A collective gasp rose from the crowd, and Pinocchio saw that Scaramouch had knocked Harlequin onto his back. Scaramouch pressed one foot to Harlequin's chest and roared a surprisingly realistic jaguar howl. He reared up with his poleax, preparing to make the final blow.

"Ha, Harlequin," Scaramouch said in his flat automa voice, "what do you have to say to that?"

Harlequin cocked his head. "I say: *look behind you.*"

Scaramouch turned. Columbine came to life, springing like a wildcat and landing on Scaramouch, cleaving a pair of hand axes into his chest.

"Oh, I am dead," Scaramouch said, and collapsed to the ground.

Columbine embraced Harlequin, and he swept her up in his arms, kissing her and sending another jet of steam from the top of his head.

The applause was thin this time. Most of the audience was grumbling.

"Well now," Punch said, looking pointedly at Pinocchio. "'Twould appear that all the half-beasts are not yet dispatched."

It wasn't just Punch looking at him. The entire city of Siena was staring. So was the mob of automa, even the fallen ones. Worst of all, Al Mi'raj was giving Pinocchio a look like he wanted to set Pinocchio's head on fire and eat it.

His nose grew a few inches longer, mashing into the end of the beak of his mask. His automa impulses told him to obey Al Mi'raj. But if he did, he was doomed!

"Get down," Columbine scolded.

Pinocchio looked below. There were far too many to fight off, especially with Harlequin among them. He'd be splinters in an instant, he knew it.

"Prithee, young magpie," Punch said. "Thy chase is up. All battles must come to an end."

"Halt!" All eyes went to the top of the Palazzo Pubblico. The lord mayor was standing. He spoke hurriedly to one of his attendants. The man nodded and disappeared down the stairs.

Pinocchio gulped. This was bad. The lord mayor, frustrated with Pinocchio's lousy performance, was surely sending orders for some dramatic, gruesome punishment.

Al Mi'raj marched into the middle of the square as the lord mayor's man hurried out from the front gates of the Palazzo Pubblico.

The djinni hunched submissively. "Signore Enrico, please give the lord mayor my deepest apologies. The automa is new. It's clearly malfunctioning. I beg the lord mayor's forgiveness. I'll have it destroyed at once."

Pinocchio winced.

"No! No!" Signore Enrico waved his hands. "Please don't destroy the Magpie. The lord mayor is quite taken with his performance."

"He is?" Al Mi'raj's voice dripped with disbelief.

"Why, yes!" Signore Enrico laughed. "A magpie. What a perfect choice for his role! The way he flew across the others as he fought. And when he landed atop the pixie bulb like a bird in a nest! Most amusing. I thought Harlequin was masterful, but that one . . . that Magpie . . . the way he wields a sword! Well, he's tremendous."

"Yes, he is, isn't he?" Al Mi'raj looked like he'd just eaten a rancid salamander.

"The lord mayor gives you his compliments and requests that you not allow such a magnificent performer to be mangled by these second-rate automa. It would ruin the day."

"It would?" Al Mi'raj mumbled.

Pinocchio's eyes grew wide in the mask. This was an excellent turn of events!

"The lord mayor requests that you call off your swashbucklers and allow the Magpie to display his full talents in single combat with Harlequin."

Pinocchio's smile fell.

"Yes, of course, *signore*." Al Mi'raj bowed.

Signore Enrico swept his cape around his arms and returned to the Palazzo.

Al Mi'raj growled at Punch, "Clear the stage." Then he pointed at Pinocchio. "I want you down here at once."

"Yes, Master," Pinocchio mumbled. If his nose grew any longer, it would break the mask. He slid from the pixie bulb and landed on the cobblestones.

Al Mi'raj clamped a hand around Pinocchio's beak. "You will fight. No hiding on pixie bulbs. Fight! Do you understand, Magpie?"

Pinocchio tried to nod, but Al Mi'raj's furious grip made it impossible.

"You will please the lord mayor, or you will find that Bulbin can turn you into worse things than a chamber pot."

As Al Mi'raj left, a chant rose from the crowd—just a few

voices at first, but it grew, until there was a thunderous "Magpie! Magpie! Magpie! MAGPIE!"

"Well," Pinocchio said as Harlequin approached. "I suppose the lord mayor wants to see me beat you."

Harlequin ran a finger along the blade of his sword, leaving behind a curly wood shaving.

Pinocchio tried again. "Didn't you get that impression from him?"

Harlequin swung the sword so fast it was as if it had burst from a catapult. The tip of the beak disappeared from the front of Pinocchio's mask. Fortunately, he didn't lose any of his nose.

"Oh!" Pinocchio forced a laugh. "Good thinking. Best give them a show first." He tried to find a sturdy hold on the scimitar, but nothing felt right. His fleshy fingers felt weak and slippery.

Harlequin somersaulted backward. When he landed, he began a dramatic series of twirls with his sword. Pinocchio wanted to run. Preferably all the way out the gates of Siena. The dashing Magpie! That's what they'd call him. Of course, that sort of dashing wasn't the kind of show Al Mi'raj and the lord mayor had in mind.

Harlequin launched at Pinocchio. Pinocchio dodged, but Harlequin's sword clipped his collar, chunking out a splinter of wood.

The blow was enough to ignite the protective impulse around his fantom panel. Pinocchio felt a surge of strength run down his arms. His eyes focused into unbreakable concentration. With quick back-and-forth slices, Pinocchio drove at Harlequin.

"Magpie! Magpie!" the audience chanted.

Harlequin never seemed to be where he struck. He was just

too fast, too agile. No, he had to find a different way to beat this perfect performer. *Think! Think!*

Harlequin came down on him in a flurry of blows. Pinocchio leaped, but not quickly enough. Harlequin stabbed his sword deep into the wood of Pinocchio's back.

Before Harlequin could pull the sword back out, Pinocchio circled out of reach. Harlequin was weaponless. But quickly he picked up a double-bladed ax that had been left on the ground. Pinocchio gulped. Great Vesuvius, that ax was big!

As Harlequin charged, the crowd cheered. Were they turning against him? He needed to think fast.

Evading Harlequin's heavy blows, Pinocchio realized what he could do that Harlequin couldn't. *Think.* Harlequin wasn't smart at all. He was just an ordinary automa who had been designed to perform amazing flips and feats. Pinocchio, on the other hand, was strategizing. That certainly wasn't something he'd done before Prester John shoved that pinecone in him.

So how could he outsmart Harlequin?

After a series of jabs and parries, an idea struck Pinocchio. If this went wrong—and there were so many ways it could—he'd be chopped into about a dozen pieces. He set his jaw, ready to attempt this final insane plan.

Pinocchio feigned dropping his scimitar. As he bent down to retrieve it, he prepared himself for the inevitable. Sure enough, Harlequin's ax bit deep in the wood of his back next to the lodged sword. Pinocchio gave a quick twist, and Harlequin lost his grip on the ax.

Pinocchio sprang several strides away, the ax still lodged in his back. He had to wait. There were no other weapons around. Let Harlequin come for the ax. That's what he'd do. He wasn't considering trickery. He was just performing as he'd been designed.

"Come on, you show-off," Pinocchio muttered, bending his knees for a seven-league jump.

Harlequin did a double flip and reached for the handle of the ax.

But the ax wasn't there.

Neither was Pinocchio.

He was ten feet in the air. Down he came with the scimitar, taking off Harlequin's hands. Then he spun around, cleaving the blade into Harlequin's wooden skull. The force of the blow caused the lid to pop open on his head. Steam whistled out.

The audience exploded to their feet, howling, "MAGPIE!"

Pinocchio backed away, not sure what to do if Harlequin continued the attack. But Columbine and Punch were running to him. Harlequin didn't seem to know how to perform a dramatic death. He just stood there, looking up at the scimitar stuck in his forehead.

Punch flourished his hands to the audience and then to the lord mayor. "Our dazzling Magpie hast claimed victory!"

Columbine planted a wooden kiss on Pinocchio's cheek.

The crowd whistled. The lord mayor was standing with his party atop the Palazzo Pubblico, with a smile on his face that Pinocchio couldn't miss.

Pinocchio grinned and took a dramatic bow, the sword and the ax still lodged side by side in his back. An automa could get used to theater life, he thought. This wasn't so bad. Not bad at all.

Later that night, Pinocchio sat with the other automa down in the cellar, trying to repair the holes in his feathered cloak. Bulbin had removed the sword and the ax from his back and filled the notches in his wood.

Pinocchio felt relief wash over him. Relief that he'd survived the battle and that his secret was safe. He was replaying the exciting moments of the day in his head when Wiq came in.

"Come on," Wiq said. "Be quick. There's something I want to show you."

Pinocchio put down his needle and cloak and followed him out the door. "What is it?"

"You'll see. Just follow me. But be quiet so Al Mi'raj doesn't hear us."

Wiq led him up a narrow circular staircase to a rooftop terrace. A misty moon drifted overhead, and Siena was cloaked in quiet. The huge piazza below was empty. The stands had been taken down, and shuttered market stalls stood in their place.

"Over here," Wiq said from the other side of the terrace. He pointed down to a narrow street. "Can you see what's painted on that wall?"

It was hard to make out in the dimness, but a pixie bulb outside a shop cast enough light for him to see that someone had painted a black-and-white bird on the side of a building.

"What is it?" Pinocchio asked.

"Can't you tell?" Wiq said with a flick of his floppy ears. "It's you. The Magpie. You're famous!"

"I am?"

Wiq relaxed an elbow against the railing. "I heard Al Mi'raj say all Siena is abuzz over the dazzling swordsman who beat Harlequin."

Pinocchio smiled. He was famous! He was lost in thoughts of glory when he noticed Wiq giving him an odd look.

"What?" he asked.

"I wondered what you would do when I showed you that banner."

Pinocchio tilted his head curiously. "What I'd do?"

"You look . . . proud," Wiq said.

Pinocchio shrugged, feeling—yes—proud.

Wiq pointed at his face. "That! There! What are you doing?"

"I don't know," Pinocchio said, feeling his mouth.

"You're smiling. What automa smiles, at least smiles for real? You're not acting. You're really smiling."

"I suppose," Pinocchio said.

"There's something different about you, automa." Wiq shook his head. "You're strange."

Pinocchio frowned and felt the wood of his face turn hot. "I'm not strange!"

"Sure you are," Wiq said with a laugh. "Automa follow orders. They do what they're told. But you didn't leap off that pixie bulb to get hacked apart when Al Mi'raj ordered you to. That's strange for an automa."

If that was strange, then Pinocchio was glad he was strange. He preferred being intact.

"But Wiq, you're not an automa," Pinocchio said, "and you do what you're told."

Wiq's eyes flashed angrily. "Being a slave and being an automa are not the same thing!"

Pinocchio wished he could take back his words, wished he hadn't gotten Wiq mad at him just when the boy was starting to act friendly.

Wiq turned his stormy gaze out across the city. "My father once told me, 'We might be slaves, but we're not puppets of the empire. Think for yourself. Trust your own instincts, and they'll reward you in turn.' So yes, I do what I'm told, because that's how a slave survives. But it doesn't make me a puppet."

"Is that why you hate my kind so much?" Pinocchio asked tentatively. "Because you think automa are just puppets serving the empire?"

"I hate automa because if it weren't for automa, I wouldn't be a slave, nor would any of the rest of my family."

"It's not the automa's fault," Pinocchio said.

"No, but Venice needs chimera slaves like my parents to assemble alchemy contraptions like you, working until they are worked to death, all to help make the empire more powerful. So do I hate your kind? Yes, I do! I hate automa. I hate alchemy. I hate Venice."

Pinocchio felt something catch deep in his gears. "Your parents are dead?"

Wiq's furry chin was trembling as he gave a quick nod. His narrowed eyes glistened in the moonlight, sharp with sorrow and hatred.

"I'm sorry that happened to your family, Wiq," Pinocchio said. "And I'm sorry you hate me. I can understand why." He turned for the stairs.

Wiq called to him, "Wait, Pinocchio." He gave a sigh. "I don't hate you. That's what I'm trying to say."

"You don't?"

"No. I watched you out there today. You weren't fighting mindlessly like the other automa. You figured out how to beat Harlequin by tricking him, by thinking for yourself. See?"

"You mean I wasn't acting like a puppet?"

"Exactly!"

"But what did your father mean about following your instincts?" Pinocchio asked. "How do I do that?"

Wiq let his hands flop to his sides. "Just listen to your gut."

"What's a gut?"

"Gut," Wiq said. "It's like your stomach."

Pinocchio touched his shirt. "I don't think I have a stomach."

Wiq laughed. "It means to listen to that voice deep down

inside you that tells you the right thing to do. Do you ever hear a voice like that?"

Pinocchio wasn't sure. "Maybe," he said. "The right thing to me seems to be to find my master." Yes, he heard that call, and at times like this, it was so urgent it made him feel like his spring-work was too tight. "I want more than anything to be with my master."

Wiq gave him a curious look. "When you talk about your master, your real master . . . it's almost like . . . you love him. That would be very strange for an automa. How could an automa do that?" He shook his head in disbelief.

Pinocchio wasn't sure what to say. Part of him was tempted to pull off his gloves, to show Wiq how he was changing, to show how he was even less like a normal automa than Wiq could possibly imagine. But he didn't know if he should trust him. What if Wiq saw how his body was turning into flesh and he was horrified? What if he told Al Mi'raj and Bulbin?

Pinocchio tucked his gloved hands behind his back.

Wiq rubbed his eyes. "We should probably go back down and get to bed. Oh—well, I guess I should get to bed. You don't sleep."

"No," Pinocchio said. "But it's funny, I do feel tired." He found his mouth opening wide for some reason. He snapped it shut.

"Did you just yawn?" Wiq laughed.

"I don't know," Pinocchio said. "Is that what that was? I couldn't stop myself. Strange."

"Yes, very strange indeed." Wiq smiled again at Pinocchio before leading him back down to the cellar.

12.

Deception

The village of Carbone was little more than a dusty ring of buildings on a hilltop, much too small to afford an automa sentry. Hardly the sort of place that even needed one, especially since half the town's inhabitants were half-beast slaves working in the local factory that assembled automa and imperial war machines.

By the time Lazuli and Geppetto reached Carbone's gates, they were starving. It had been a frustrating several days, mostly spent hiding in the woods from the swarms of airmen scouring the countryside. And the Hunter's Glass, which initially had shown them the direction Pinocchio had gone, suddenly stopped working whenever Geppetto tried to use it. This filled the alchemist with mustache-chewing worry. The Hunter's Glass did, however, continue to point toward Prester John. And little by little, from one hiding spot to another, Lazuli led them north until their stomachs couldn't stand another wild root for dinner.

They hesitated at the gates, where an elderly chimera guard snored at his post. An impressive stream of drool was running down the guard's curly chin whiskers. He had a goat's head, with horns so heavy it seemed he might not be able to even lift his head off his chest.

"Should we just go in?" Lazuli asked. "Or should we wake him?"

"We should find out if there are airmen around," Geppetto said.

"I'd be surprised if that old beast can put two words together," Maestro chirped.

Geppetto gave a forceful cough. The guard's eyes sprang open, and he got stiffly to his hooves, clanking the end of his pike on the ground.

"Who goes there?" he bleated.

"Travelers," Geppetto said.

The guard plopped back down on his seat.

Geppetto leaned forward and spoke quietly. "We're looking for a safe place to get a meal. Are there . . . any imperial soldiers in this village?"

The old goat gave Geppetto a suspicious look, then started chewing on something that may have already been in his mouth or might have just been regurgitated.

He gave a limp wave with the pike. "There's a tavern across from the well. The gate is open during daylight hours. Ye can come and go as ye please. Move on."

Geppetto sighed and nodded to Lazuli. "We'll just have to risk it."

Lazuli didn't like this idea, and didn't much like being

ignored by the guard. "He didn't answer your question. Let me handle this."

"I'm not sure that's best, Princess," Geppetto whispered.

She approached the guard anyway. "Kinsman, my companion asked you a simple question. We're having to travel discreetly. Could you be so kind as to tell us if there are any airmen in this village?"

"No," the guard said.

"No there aren't or no you can't tell me?"

The guard stopped chewing. "No," he repeated more slowly, to emphasize his irritation.

Geppetto took Lazuli's arm, but she shrugged him off. "Kinsman, I'm a fellow Abatonian, as you can plainly see. Is it too much to ask for a little courtesy?"

"I'm not your kin, lassie," the guard said. "I don't know ye nor what business yer mixed up in. Maybe yer part of some outlaw gang." He cut an eye at Geppetto. "Maybe yer a spy for the airmen. My orders are to watch the gate, not to answer questions."

Lazuli scowled imperiously at the guard. "Whatever happened to Abatonian hospitality?"

"We're not in Abaton," the guard said. "This is the Venetian Empire. There's no hospitality to be found for our kind. Move on, before ye get us both in trouble."

Geppetto pulled her away. "Let's find a hot meal." Lazuli reluctantly followed him into the village.

It wasn't hard to find the tavern. There was only one well in the whole village, and every building was across from it.

Before they entered, Geppetto said, "Maestro, check inside."

The cricket hopped over to a window. "No soldiers in there. Looks safe enough."

Geppetto pulled his hood over his head. "If anyone asks, you're my elemental servant."

"Servant?" Lazuli scoffed.

"We don't have any fealty papers to show you belong to me, so we'll have to hope nobody asks for them. Give me your sword to hold."

After reluctantly handing it over, Lazuli followed Geppetto inside to a table at the back corner. The few other patrons, all human, gathered at the bar. Two chimera—an ape and a frog—were clearing dishes and mopping the floor.

Geppetto ordered bowls of polenta for them and cups of watery red wine. The innkeeper and the other patrons paid them little mind. They were busy discussing a performer named the Magpie. Apparently half the countryside was journeying to Siena to see his next show.

Lazuli was still fuming. "I can't understand why he wouldn't let us know whether there were soldiers here or not."

Geppetto gave a wry smile. "Your people here live under very different conditions than in Abaton."

"A real Abatonian would never stand for that sort of rudeness," she said. "If that old goat had only known who I was. Father risked everything coming here to try to help free his kind."

"For his kind, Abaton is an utter mystery," Geppetto said. "His ancestors immigrated to Venice so long ago, they've forgotten their Abatonian ways. And any hope of ever being free, of ever returning to their homeland, seems impossible."

Lazuli frowned and picked at her food. Someone at the bar made a joke, and another gave a laugh that sounded more like a croak. The frog chimera, clearly. Why had Father ever thought he could rescue them? Why had he been so foolish as to come here?

Maestro said, "Your Highness, share more news from Abaton. I miss the Moonlit Court. Are the gardens still in bloom?"

"The butterfly orchids were just releasing their blossoms when I left," she said wistfully.

"Oh," Maestro moaned with pleasure. "Such a sight to behold. I composed a piece about them last season. Are the flowers fluttering all over the palace?"

"And getting into everything." She smiled. "Naughty little things."

Lazuli described the snaking starflowers that grew up vines all day, reaching higher than the palace walls, only to burst at nightfall into shimmering pyrotechnic displays. The fountains that seemed to defy all logic, water trickling up and collecting on canopies and then falling in cooling mists.

As the group at the bar laughed, argued, and gossiped, Lazuli found herself pleasantly lost in talking about Abaton, and was grateful to have a few moments to not worry about hiding and searching for food and avoiding airmen.

The moment didn't last. Just as Lazuli was describing the plans for the coming summer solstice processional, an airman burst through the door.

The tavern fell silent. Lazuli had to clutch the table to keep from floating up.

"Captain Toro," Maestro whispered before disappearing under Geppetto's cloak.

As Geppetto adjusted his hood over his head, Lazuli realized that they were fortunate Geppetto was sitting with his back to the airman. Unfortunately, there was no easy way out the door without walking right past the captain.

Lazuli kept her head down but her eyes on the airman. His

wings—which, along with his shiny helmet, looked much newer than the rest of his battered attire—were folded against his back, and his armor creaked as he approached the bar and rested his musket against the wood.

There was something scary about this Captain Toro. Something in his eyes, in the set of his jaw. Geppetto had told her how he had twice escaped from Captain Toro. She wondered if it was shame or desperation that gave the airman that volatile look.

"Captain Toro," the innkeeper said in greeting, wiping a cup with his apron before setting it on the bar. "Haven't seen you in these parts in quite a time. What brings you back?"

"Just making the rounds," Captain Toro said, his voice strained.

The men at the bar quietly sipped their drinks, seeming to sense the captain's dangerous demeanor. The pair of chimera shifted nervously, making a bigger show of cleaning up.

Geppetto swirled his food absently with his spoon, but Lazuli couldn't miss his palpable tension.

The innkeeper poured Captain Toro a glass of wine. "Staying long enough for a bite?"

Captain Toro gave a gruff nod.

"Coming up." The innkeeper disappeared into the back.

Captain Toro lifted his cup and surveyed the room. The frog chimera mopped the same spot over and over, but the airman ignored him.

One of the men at the bar cleared his throat before saying, "Heard there have been Flying Lions patrolling our parts lately. That true, Captain?"

"We're looking for a man traveling with an automa," Toro said in a low, gravelly voice.

"Seen no automa around here," the man said with a nervous chuckle.

Lazuli wondered if they might be able to get up and just walk out, but Geppetto seemed to read her eagerness and made a small wave with his hand over the table.

The innkeeper returned with a plate of food for the captain. He watched him eat a few moments before saying, "The men say the fire eater in Siena has a good show going on. A high-flying performer."

"I don't go to the theater," Captain Toro said between bites.

"I suppose you don't," the innkeeper said. "Busy man like you."

One of the men said, "Captain, you think there's a way to fly without wings? You ever hear of any alchemy like that?"

"No," Captain Toro said, uninterested.

Another of the men said, "Maybe it's like the imperial warships. The ones that float."

"Or the doge's fortress," said another.

"Yeah, like that. How do you think the alchemists do that?"

"Well . . ." Captain Toro paused to take another bite.

The men sat in rapt attention, an anxious silence brought on by the quiet, scary way Captain Toro spoke.

Captain Toro swallowed his food. "All alchemical technology has its origins in the elemental magic of Abaton. So lighter-than-air inventions like floating masonry and my armor"—he clapped a hand to his lion-emblazoned breastplate—"all come from blue-fairy magic."

Geppetto's eyes met Lazuli's across the table.

"Fairies," Captain Toro continued, his words slow and stilted, "being elemental creatures of the air, are capable of manipulating the weight of otherwise heavy materials." He paused before adding, "Isn't that right, fairy?"

The men at the bar looked perplexed. Captain Toro took a sip of wine.

"What's that, Captain?" the innkeeper asked.

"I was asking the fairy lass over there." He turned slowly toward Lazuli. "Am I correct?"

The innkeeper and the men all looked at her. Lazuli tried to master her expression. The captain couldn't know who she really was. She could pretend to be an elemental servant. Of course she could. There was no reason to fear the captain, except that she didn't have fealty papers. What was most important was to distract Captain Toro from Geppetto.

She rose lightly from her seat. Geppetto gave a little shake of his head to stop her, but she ignored him. She could handle this.

"For the most part, you are correct, sir."

Captain Toro's stool barked against the wooden floor as he stood. "Explain."

Lazuli approached the bar. "I can't make *you* lighter than air. I can't transform the living. That's why you have to wear alchemied armor in order to fly. But—"

She walked around Captain Toro, drawing his attention away from Geppetto. All eyes followed her. She picked up Captain Toro's wine cup with a smile.

"If I wanted to make your wine float . . ."

A breeze whirled around the bar, tousling their hair. Beads of bloodred wine rose from the cup. The men laughed with surprise, all except Captain Toro.

"Are some objects easier to levitate than others?" the innkeeper asked.

"That's it exactly," Lazuli said. "I chose the wine and not the entire mug, because wine is relatively insubstantial. It's a liquid.

It's easy to infuse with air. Solid objects are harder. This is why alchemists can do it much better in their laboratories."

"Very interesting, fairy," Captain Toro said. He cleared his throat with a dry cough. "Your fealty papers, please."

A jolt of panic ran through Lazuli.

"Oh," she said, pretending to search inside her cloak. "Yes. Of course."

"This area," Captain Toro said, tapping the bar, "is notorious as a hideout for ungrateful outlaw vermin."

The frog croaked, his throat swelling like it might pop, and smoothed out his fealty papers onto a table as if saying he was grateful he wasn't vermin. It sickened Lazuli. These so-called outlaws only wanted to be free, only wanted to stand up to a corrupt empire.

"Do you work in this village, fairy? Is that your master over there?"

"Um, no," Lazuli said, continuing to search her pockets. "That's my uncle. Our alchemist master is . . . at the show in Siena. He sent us with a package to deliver here—"

"I'll need to see your uncle's papers too," Captain Toro said.

Lazuli wished she hadn't given Geppetto her sword. The master of ceremonies in her father's court had told her she was the best he'd ever taught, although she'd never displayed her talents in any real combat. She hoped Geppetto wasn't planning on doing something stupid and brave with her sword.

As Lazuli fumbled through her cloak, Captain Toro snatched up his musket. The innkeeper and the men drew back from the bar. The frog and the ape chimera scrambled under a table.

"Here they are," Lazuli said with a laugh, holding up folded papers.

The innkeeper exhaled with relief. The men chuckled nervously as they settled back to their stools.

"Wish I were going to the fire eater's show, like your master," the innkeeper said to Lazuli. "It's all anyone's been talking about around these parts."

Captain Toro took the papers from Lazuli's fingers.

"The Magpie," one of the men chuckled. "The automa who flies. The swordsman who beat—"

"What did you say?" Captain Toro hissed.

"W-what?" the man asked nervously.

"Did you say a *flying* automa?" Captain Toro asked.

The realization hit Lazuli like a thunderbolt. She tried to mask her surprise. The flying automa. Was it Geppetto's automa?

"The M-Magpie," the man stammered. "That's why we were asking you if an automa could fly without wings."

Captain Toro looked crazed. "You never said anything about an automa!"

"All the fire eater's performers are puppets," the innkeeper said. "Haven't you seen them?"

"And he's got an automa that can fly?"

"Not fly, exactly. But I hear it can leap. Huge leaps. Almost like flying."

"The fire eater is in Siena?" Captain Toro demanded.

"Of course, haven't you ever—"

Captain Toro was already headed out the door, his wings snapping open in the sunlight. Geppetto spun in his seat, looking from the door back to Lazuli with astonishment.

"What was that about?" the innkeeper said as the crowd broke into noisy discussion.

Lazuli smiled at Geppetto and pretended to wipe the sweat

from her brow. As she headed back to her seat, the innkeeper picked up the papers from the bar.

"Don't forget your fealty papers." The sheets unfolded as he held them out, and his eyes widened. "These aren't fealty papers. . . . Hey! What's this? Are you . . . outlaws?"

The men at the bar got to their feet. They glared menacingly at Lazuli.

Geppetto stood. "Gentlemen, we're plainly not outlaws." He pulled back his hood. "As you'll see, I'm not a sylph or any other elemental or half-beast."

The innkeeper jabbed a finger. "Then why did she tell Captain Toro you were?"

Geppetto looked at Lazuli and murmured, "I did think that was a risky thing to tell him."

Lazuli shrugged. "You weren't exactly coming up with any brilliant ideas."

"Outlaws or not," the innkeeper said, producing a blunderbuss from beneath the bar, "you thought you outsmarted Captain Toro. Thought you could lie to a soldier of the doge. We're good citizens of the empire. Aren't we, boys?"

"Yes," the frog chimera croaked. Even he and the ape chimera looked ready to spring into action against them.

"Hands away from your sword," the innkeeper said, nodding to the hilt sticking out from under Geppetto's cloak.

Lazuli and Geppetto raised their hands before the innkeeper's blunderbuss.

"Gentlemen," Geppetto said, "this is a misunderstanding."

A cup flew from the bar and smashed against the bridge of the innkeeper's nose. He howled and dropped the gun as he cupped his hands over his face. Lazuli snatched the blunderbuss.

Wind whipped through the bar. More cups, plates, and wine bottles rose into the air.

The men and the chimera stared at the hovering objects.

"But—but you said you couldn't lift solid objects," one of the men stammered.

"I lied," Lazuli said, aiming the gun.

The men trembled, panicked eyes locked on the weapon.

"We're leaving," Geppetto said, pushing the barrel of the blunderbuss toward the floor. "And unless any of the rest of you wants a bottle to the head, you'll let us walk out of here."

The innkeeper glared at them with watering eyes. Blood and powdery bits of the broken cup smeared his face.

Backing to the door with Lazuli, Geppetto said, "You've all acted loyally to the empire. There's nothing more you could have done. We bid you good day."

They stared as Geppetto and Lazuli hurried out the door.

As soon as they were outside, Maestro sprang from under Geppetto's cloak and chirped angrily at Lazuli, "Are you *insane*? I mean, are you insane, *Your Highness*? What were you doing back there?"

"Saving our necks," Lazuli said.

Geppetto smiled. "Well done, Princess Lazuli. You continue to surprise me. Now let's get out of here. If that flying automa is Pinocchio, we have to hurry. Toro will reach Siena first, but maybe there's still a way to rescue the lad."

13.

The Fox and the Cat

Pinocchio and Wiq had been sneaking up to the rooftop balcony every evening to see how many new Magpie paintings were showing up on the sides of buildings around the theater.

The Magpie's popularity was growing. Pinocchio had defeated Harlequin in the last three performances and had even been promoted to Scaramouch's position as the head of the half-beasts. He and Wiq stayed up until nearly dawn, reliving the exciting parts of the show and even acting them out with wooden sticks for swords.

When they tired of that, Wiq made up a game of tossing loops made from the jasmine vines that grew up the side of Al Mi'raj's theater. They would try to catch the loops with the wooden sticks. Wiq was much better at it than Pinocchio, since

Pinocchio threw it a bit too hard, and his loops kept flying over the side of the balcony.

As Wiq fashioned a new loop for Pinocchio, he said, "I wish I could run away."

"Where would you go?" Pinocchio asked.

"I don't know," Wiq replied. "Maybe to High Persia. I hear my people are treated better in the other human kingdoms. Although I'd really want to go to Abaton."

"Would you be a slave in Abaton?"

Wiq lowered the loop of jasmine. "Of course not, you goof. There are no slaves in Abaton."

Pinocchio felt his face get warm, and he tried not to be a goof. "Why did your family come to the Venetian Empire, then?"

"They didn't," Wiq said, continuing to weave the jasmine vines together. "It was my ancestors, way way back. Prester John sent them here, along with loads of other chimera and elementals. I guess he thought he was spreading goodwill and helpful Abatonian magic and all that." He gave a snort and shook his head.

"Do you think we could ever run away?" Pinocchio asked. "I mean do you think there's a way to escape from Al Mi'raj's theater?"

"Not with this on me." Wiq touched the collar on his neck. "And not with your fealty lock." He sat up a little straighter. "But let's promise that if we ever find a way, we'll escape. Together. Do you promise?"

"Of course!" Maybe Wiq could help him find Geppetto. Maybe his father could help take care of Wiq, too.

Wiq slipped the jasmine on Pinocchio's wrist like a bracelet. "This is our promise. And I'll wear one too." He put the other loop on his furry wrist, and held out his hand to take Pinocchio's. "Promise?"

"I promise," Pinocchio said, smiling.

Still clutching Pinocchio's hand, Wiq said, "Your hand feels squishy." He let go and pulled up Pinocchio's sleeve. "What's with your arm? It doesn't look like wood."

Pinocchio jerked it back. He was tempted to lie or to find an excuse to leave, but Wiq was his friend. They were going to run away together. He had kept this secret from Wiq for long enough.

"Wiq, I'm going to tell you something, but you have to swear you'll never tell anyone."

"I swear," Wiq said.

Pinocchio's gears felt knotted. He was terrified Wiq was going to hate him again if he knew the truth. But that voice inside him, his instinct, told him he could trust Wiq.

"You know how I'm different from other automa," Pinocchio said. "There's a reason. Do you remember how I told you about my master? Well, he's a friend of Prester John's."

"His Immortal Lordship!" Wiq sputtered.

"And Prester John turned me this way." When Pinocchio had finished explaining how he was becoming . . . what, exactly? Flesh? Human? Real? Wiq wasn't horrified. He was wild with excitement.

"And if Geppetto is able to rescue Prester John," Wiq said, "he might take us to Abaton. Oh, Pinocchio! We *have* to find a way to escape."

Over the following days, try as they might, the boys couldn't come up with a reasonable plan to get away. And each day, Pinocchio was changing a bit more. Every performance put him more at risk of being injured—or worse, discovered by Bulbin and Al Mi'raj.

"Couldn't Harlequin and I . . . uh, be on the same side?" Pinocchio asked Punch one afternoon.

"Nay. 'Tis the lord mayor's continued wish to see you defeat Harlequin in new and dramatic feats."

"But . . ." Pinocchio searched for a way out of this. "Wouldn't the audience prefer to see half-beasts lose and humans win?"

"The lord mayor prefereth that the performance stoke anger against the half-beasts and remind his citizenry of their threat. Adieu, Magpie."

Pinocchio sighed as Punch waddled away.

As Pinocchio waited that night for Wiq, he never came. How late was it? The clanking hammers from Bulbin's workshop had been quiet for some time now, so he decided to look for Wiq. He tiptoed down the hall toward Wiq's bedroom. As he rounded a corner, he bumped into someone.

A feline face with a patch over one eye snarled at him, exposing gleaming fangs. Pinocchio stumbled backward in alarm.

A half-beast!

The hallway outside Al Mi'raj's workshop was filled with half-beasts. And not ones like Wiq. These half-beasts were monstrous, with animal heads on human bodies, all claws and fangs and ferocious demeanors.

Was this an attack? Were these outlaws trying to rob Al Mi'raj?

The cat half-beast was shackled at the wrists. So were the others. A few glanced at Pinocchio: a fox, a burly half-beast with the head of a bear, even a crocodile.

Pinocchio stared at the one-eyed cat he'd bumped into. He had long black-and-white fur, even on his humanlike hands. A bushy tail swished from the back of his coat. He was a little fat in the belly, now that Pinocchio was noticing, but this half-beast looked fierce.

"Planning to paint my portrait, puppet?" the cat growled. "Keep staring. I'll show you my best side."

He snapped his teeth at Pinocchio, but the chain connecting him to the next half-beast clanked tight and stopped the cat from reaching him.

The fox half-beast chuckled. "Be sweet to the puppet, Sop." The fox's voice definitely had a feminine quality, even though she was dressed in men's clothing: a leather jerkin, leather pants, and tall boots. "After all, you might be fighting it tomorrow."

"Quiet back there," a voice called. An imperial airman began pushing his way down the line. For half a moment, Pinocchio was frightened that it might be Captain Toro, but fortunately it wasn't.

Farther down the hall, raised voices came from Al Mi'raj's workshop. The djinni was saying, "General Maximian, I run a theater, not a gladiator pit!"

"These orders come from our lord doge," a voice replied. "I suggest you remember your place, fire eater. . . ."

The airman finally made his way back. "What are you doing here, automa?" He whacked Pinocchio against his head. "Go!"

Pinocchio ran back to the cellar. He tried to tell Punch about the half-beasts, but the automa didn't seem to care. Pinocchio sat the rest of the night next to Columbine, watching her sew. Where was Wiq? He was desperate for his friend to explain what was happening.

But Wiq never appeared.

Al Mi'raj appeared later instead and spoke quietly with Punch. Deep lines pinched the djinni's yellow brow, as if he was troubled.

When he left, Punch clapped his hands to get their attention. "Majestic marionettes! The slightest of changes to our performance. A gang of half-beast rogues hast been captured by the doge's airmen. The lord mayor wishes to have them join our performance. Naturally, they shall play half-beasts. All of you, with the exception of our star the Magpie, will join with Harlequin's swordsmen. You shall be the victors. No longer will Magpie be the leader of the half-beasts, but a turncoat who assists Harlequin in defeating the rogues."

Fight the half-beasts! Pinocchio clutched his hands together nervously. How could they beat half-beasts? These weren't actors. They were real warriors.

Harlequin did a double flip, spinning a pair of blades when he landed.

Pinocchio sighed. At least he'd be on the same side as Harlequin.

The next afternoon, to Pinocchio's immense horror, Al Mi'raj collected him without a word and delivered him to the squad of airmen, who marched him, along with the half-beasts, out into the middle of the piazza.

The piazza was empty except for workers setting up stands for the evening's performance. A metal pen had been erected, and once Pinocchio and the half-beasts were led inside, it was locked.

Pinocchio eyed the half-beasts cautiously. There were about two dozen in all, mostly with the heads of animals and fur-covered humanoid bodies, although he spotted a few like Wiq, with human faces and some animal features, like ears and tails. One looked completely human until it came near, and Pinocchio saw that the half-beast was covered in tan scales. It hissed a forked tongue at him.

They looked like a vicious lot, no mistake about it. If he played the witless automa, maybe they'd leave him alone. Pinocchio found a spot toward the center and stood as still as he could.

The cat with the patch over his eye approached him. "And why have they put you in here with us, puppet?" His voice was rough and full of spittle.

Pinocchio shrugged. Then, remembering too late that automa didn't make those kinds of gestures, he said, in as flat a voice as he could manage, "I do not know."

Pinocchio was already in his costume, but he held his mask in his hands. The cat ran a finger along the beak. When it reached the end, a retractable claw opened, scratching the paint.

"I like birds," he purred. "They're tasty."

The fox sauntered over, the hint of a smile curling on her snout. She was tall and slim, although quite muscular beneath her orange fur and sleeveless jerkin. One of her arms was bandaged, and Pinocchio wondered if she had been injured by the airmen.

"Quit teasing the automa, Sop, old darling. I doubt his sort is designed to appreciate your twisted sense of humor."

"It looks so real." Sop tapped a claw on Pinocchio's cheek. "More real than most of the humans' toys. Don't you think, Mezmer?"

Pinocchio tried to keep looking straight ahead, but noticed out of the corner of his eye how the fox was inspecting the airmen up at their posts atop the piazza's buildings and testing the bars of the pen. Pinocchio guessed she was clever, this Mezmer. A strategist. She was thinking of a plan for escape.

"This one's an expensive model, that's why," Mezmer said, turning back to Pinocchio.

"An expensive scratching post," Sop chuckled. The cat extended his claws, bringing them to the top of Pinocchio's shirt, as if to shred his costume.

Pinocchio dropped his mask to the ground. His hands

instinctively shot out and grabbed the cat's wrists. Sop hissed, his whiskers and ears flattened ferociously. He twisted his hands free and backed away.

Mezmer laughed. "You can't scare these automa, old friend. Leave him alone. We have plans to make."

As the two walked away, Pinocchio realized how easily the cat had escaped his grip. He looked at his own gloved hands. They weren't as strong as they once were. The transformation was more than just on the outside. His gearworks must be changing too.

As the sun set and the crowds began filing in to take their seats, airmen guards opened the pen so a troop of Bulbins could push a wagon piled with weapons inside. The half-beasts shoved one another to get the best weapons. They spread out in the pen, getting the feel for whatever bronze ax, sword, or spiked mace they had chosen. While Sop grabbed a sword, Mezmer chose a spear, giving it a deft twirl to test the weight.

Pinocchio put on his magpie mask and touched his sword nervously. It was nearly time. Where were the automa? Punch and Al Mi'raj waited in the courtyard. And there was Wiq, too. Pinocchio had to stop himself from waving to him.

He wished they were together on the rooftop again. Wiq could have bolstered his courage, maybe even helped him plan a strategy to beat these half-beast warriors. He ran a finger along the jasmine vines around his wrist.

The cheering of the crowd broke his thoughts. Punch took his place atop the tall podium in the middle of the piazza.

"O humble citizens of Siena," he announced. "Welcome dons and donnas, and lord mayor, but especially our most illustrious guest . . . the doge of Venice."

A wave of gasps swept over the audience. They craned their

necks to look to the top of the Palazzo Pubblico. Beside the lord mayor sat another man, crowned and wearing robes of deep scarlet. He stood. The entire crowd bowed in reverence.

Pinocchio could not help but stare, openmouthed. The doge! And there were mechanical Lions on either side of him, sparkling bloodred from their armored manes to their folded wings. Once the doge took his seat, Punch continued.

"Lord Doge, we have something quite special for thee this eve. Thou wilt not only be entertained by the marvelous marionettes of Al Mi'raj's theater company. Thy pleasure shall be multiplied by the introduction of new performers . . . recent captives from a vicious nest of half-beast ingrates."

The audience rumbled with boos.

The half-beasts snarled and circled in the enclosure. They were tough brutes, Pinocchio had no doubt. He wasn't eager to fight them when it came his time in the show to turn sides.

"Siena, welcome your champions," Punch bellowed. "Harlequin and his shimmering swashbucklers!"

Harlequin and the automa swordsmen and swordswomen marched lockstep out into the piazza. They wore glittering bronze armor. Their wood was plenty tough already, but maybe Al Mi'raj wanted to make sure his mechanical performers had additional protection against the half-beast warriors.

The metal enclosure lifted into the air, but the half-beasts didn't charge out. They stayed clustered together. Pinocchio was trapped in the thick of the growling, sweaty mob. He heard Mezmer say, "Steady, darlings. Let's wait to see what they have planned."

The automa raised their swords and charged the half-beasts.

"Looks like they plan to massacre us," Sop said, lashing his bristly cat tail.

The half-beasts drew tighter together.

"What do we do?" a boar-headed outlaw asked through a tusked mouth. "These automa can't die. We'll never be able to beat them."

Others grumbled in agreement, fear evident in their animal faces.

"We might not," Mezmer said. Her black-tipped ears twitched as she looked at each of them squarely. "But know this, all of you. We fight not for the pleasure of Venetian vermin. We fight for something greater. We fight against the imperial doge and his corrupt empire. And when we die on their puppets' swords, we die knowing we struck fear in the doge's heart. We die with bravery, like the glorious knights of old Abaton.

"The doge tore our families apart and stole our freedom. But we hold no fealty papers. We have broken our bonds of slavery. We chimera are not puppets of the empire! We might never see Abaton's glorious shores, but our deaths will rally our kin to rise up against the doge."

The half-beasts growled and cheered and clanked their weapons.

Pinocchio could not believe what he was hearing. He had thought these half-beasts were little more than runaway slaves who'd become common thieves. But Mezmer and her chimera seemed better than that. They were fighting for something greater: their freedom. Wiq and all the enslaved Abatonians deserved to be free—free from the hated doge and his empire.

Something stirred deep inside Pinocchio at Mezmer's words. This was all the doge's fault. He had enslaved these chimera. He had torn Wiq from his family. And it was this same doge who had ordered Geppetto's family murdered. Hatred boiled in Pinocchio.

The automa charged. Battle erupted. Pinocchio hesitated before running at Scaramouch to begin sparring.

The half-beasts turned out to be very different fighters from the automa. While Harlequin did his usual acrobatics and the other automa fought with showy flourishes, the half-beasts fought defensively, pairing off back-to-back or working together in small formations.

A few automa lost arms. One got his head bashed around backward by a spiked mace. But they kept fighting, unlike in the earlier performances. They weren't pretending to die when they got injured.

Punch signaled to Pinocchio. It was his time to turn against the half-beasts and help Harlequin. But how could he do that now?

The fox Mezmer's speech might have rallied her companions for glorious deaths, but Mezmer wanted to prove something to the doge first. She needed her chimera to fight well. Pinocchio knew he had to help them.

On his seven-league boots, he sprang over clusters of fighters until he found Mezmer. The fox growled when she saw him and nearly skewered him with her spear. But Pinocchio blocked and quickly grabbed Mezmer's spear, pulling her forward.

"Listen to me," Pinocchio whispered urgently. "Your chimera have to stop Harlequin."

"What?" Mezmer gasped, her orange eyes wide.

"He's the best fighter. He's the most dangerous. Take him out and you'll have a better chance at beating the rest!"

Harlequin was already somersaulting their way.

"Here he comes!" Pinocchio said. "Chop off his head. If his head comes loose, his body will stop working."

He shoved Mezmer back before moving away to clash swords with Columbine.

"The heads, darlings!" he heard Mezmer shout to her chimera. "Take off their heads!"

Harlequin landed, striking out wide with both his swords. Sop ducked under one of the swings, but a weasel-headed chimera lost part of an ear to the other.

Mezmer launched herself at Harlequin. She was amazingly fast with her spear, spinning it to block every one of Harlequin's blows. But she wasn't fast enough to take off his head.

Scaramouch was surrounded by a group of chimera. The boar-headed half-beast spiked his mace into Scaramouch's leg, knocking the automa down. When Scaramouch fell, the bear chimera brought his ax down, popping Scaramouch's head off.

"Not bad," the boar said, whistling from between his tusks.

"That's the way!" Mezmer said, struggling to hold back Harlequin. "Sop! A little help, darling. We've got to get this one pinned."

The cat spun around from where he'd just sent an automa's head flying, but before he could run to Mezmer, a group of automa blocked his path.

The badger and the crocodile tried to help Mezmer but kept getting driven back. Mezmer was struggling. She equaled Harlequin in speed, but Pinocchio could see she was tiring fast under his unrelenting assault.

With a grimace, Pinocchio bounded on his seven-league boots, knocking Harlequin down. Al Mi'raj wouldn't like that! He dreaded facing the furious djinni, but what else could he do?

Before Harlequin could shove Pinocchio away, the chimera attacked. The badger's war hammer pinned one arm. The crocodile clamped his jagged teeth onto Harlequin's other arm.

"Now!" Mezmer barked. She spun her spear like a twirling scythe, and Pinocchio scrambled to get out of the way as she swiped the broad-bladed tip.

Pinocchio felt something brush past his feet. As he sat up, he saw Harlequin's head rolling away. Harlequin's eyes blinked wildly, malfunctioning. "Harlequin is not supposed to lose," he complained.

The plan had worked!

Mezmer stood over Pinocchio, smiling down at him. "Thanks, darling."

Pinocchio nodded, excitedly. The chimera had a chance now. They might actually beat the automa! Although the reality nagged at him: What good would it do? This wasn't going to win them their free—

Columbine rushed up behind Mezmer.

"Watch out!" Pinocchio shouted.

Mezmer spun, but before she could block, Columbine's sword drove into the fox's chest. Pinocchio gasped as the tip of the blade came out the back of Mezmer's shirt.

Mezmer choked and fell.

14.

The Doge of Venice

The audience screamed with delight as the battle raged on, but Pinocchio was frozen. He stared at Mezmer.

Sop appeared, hissing and spitting. He flipped Mezmer over and recoiled at what he saw. "No, Mez!" he cried. "NO!"

Mezmer gasped, clutching her blood-soaked chest. "There's ... no saving me, dear," she sputtered. "Keep ... fighting."

Sop beat his fist against the cobblestones. Then he screamed a wildcat howl before charging Columbine.

Pinocchio didn't watch their fight. His eyes were fixed on Mezmer. An awful feeling stirred his insides. The brave chimera was dying.

Pressure and horror and steam seemed to fill Pinocchio's head. But through all that, he was remembering something. From the river. He had seen someone die before....

Captain Toro.

The airman had drowned. And yet, somehow, he'd come back to life. Pinocchio had brought him back to life.

Pinocchio pressed his hands against the fox's wound. "Stay calm," he said. "I can help you."

"Stupid puppet," she whispered. "I . . . can't . . . be . . . h . . ." Her words dissolved into a hiss. She stared up, but no longer saw him. Mezmer's life had spilled out of her too fast.

The clank of steel and the roars of the chimera echoed along with the crowd's exhilaration.

Pinocchio felt something burning in his gearworks. It ran from his chest down into his arms, like a valve being released of its pressure. In the gap between his shirt cuff and his gloves, Pinocchio saw the flesh of his arms transforming. This time it was reversing. Grains of wood rose on the surface. His fingers grew stronger again, turning back into wood.

He yanked off the gloves. His pink fingernails were gone.

Mezmer's eyes shot open, and she gasped an enormous breath, sitting up abruptly. She looked around in alarm and then stared, wide-eyed, at Pinocchio.

"What . . . ?" Mezmer murmured. She looked down at the front of her jerkin. The white patch of fur that poked out was matted crimson with her heart's blood. But as Mezmer felt along the sticky fur, she couldn't find the wound.

As Pinocchio watched this, a strange sensation came over him. Just as it had after saving Captain Toro, Pinocchio's head seemed to fill with a thick mist. The desperation and fear and wonder that were brimming moments before began to vanish. He had only a moment to consider how odd this was. What had he just done? His nose twitched, telling Pinocchio he had done something bad. No, it had not been bad, he reminded himself. He had been trying to help. . . .

The fealty lock in the back of his neck suddenly sparked with energy. He was to obey, not question. Pinocchio rose with a jerk, his thoughts evaporating.

Silence blanketed the crowd. Mezmer climbed to her feet, peering around with disbelief. One by one, the chimera and automa lowered their weapons and stared at Mezmer . . . and then at Pinocchio.

Sop came forward. "How can this be?"

Suddenly a pair of airmen landed. Mezmer reached for her spear.

"Don't move!" one ordered.

Other airmen landed, training their muskets on the rest of the chimera. "Back!" they shouted. "Drop your weapons and get back to the pen!"

Al Mi'raj was storming across the piazza, looking anxiously up at the doge.

An airman shackled Mezmer and called to the djinni, "We're taking them inside. Find a place to hold them."

Al Mi'raj stood gaping at the fox and then over at Pinocchio. "What have you done?"

Before Pinocchio could answer his master, an airman grabbed him by the back of his neck and pushed him forward. "I've been hunting for this one."

The airman from the river. Captain Toro.

Pinocchio glanced back at the chimera. The metal poles of the pen were lowering around them. The crowd was murmuring, and airmen were ordering the piazza cleared. Pinocchio was not concerned with how his thoughts were dimming. There was such panic and fear in everyone around him. But not in Pinocchio. He had nothing to fear. This was what it had been like before . . . before Prester John.

With a last glance, Pinocchio spied the doge staring down at him. The lord mayor was talking rapidly. The doge, however, was ignoring the mayor. His eyes were locked on Pinocchio.

Pinocchio felt no concern. Why should he? That part of his thoughts had vanished. He was back to being a good, obedient automa.

Once inside, Captain Toro hauled Pinocchio into the workshop. The airman remained at the doorway, guarding the entrance.

"Over here," Bulbin said to Pinocchio, leading him as far from the door as possible and pointing to a chair. "Sit down."

Al Mi'raj looked back over his shoulder at Captain Toro before whispering to Pinocchio. "Did you do that to the fox?"

"Do what, Master?"

Al Mi'raj was breathless with disbelief. "I saw her run through with a sword. A chimera can't survive that. No one can." He stared at Pinocchio. "Did you?"

Pinocchio sat rigid in the chair, unable to sort out the question. "Did I what, Master?"

"I'm asking you if you . . ." Al Mi'raj looked over at Bulbin, who was frowning, before taking a deep breath and whispering, "Did you bring the chimera back to life?"

Pinocchio didn't know. He couldn't remember what he had done.

Bulbin didn't wait for his reply. "We all seen it! All Siena seen it!"

"But how?" Al Mi'raj said. "How? I wasn't born in Abaton, but I know about the magic of our homeland. You do too, old friend. Have you ever heard of raising the dead? I haven't. How could an automa possess this power?"

"Resurrections en't impossible," Bulbin said.

"No, but that is the work of Prester John! Only he gives that gift." Al Mi'raj looked back at the airman standing in the doorway. Then he leaned close to Pinocchio to whisper, "I'm ordering you to tell me. Explain how you brought that chimera back to life!"

"I do not know, Master."

Bulbin crossed his arms. "There's been something higgledy about this one. I thunk it was just his model. These Vitruvian Manikins can be a wee queer. But now I seen, there's something more to this one. Someone tinkered with him, eh? I don't know what's been done, but I'll just open him up and see what's going on."

Bulbin split into two identical, if slightly smaller, versions of himself. The other Bulbin ran over to get his tools.

The gnome's words awakened something deep in Pinocchio's mind. Fighting against the fogginess, Pinocchio glanced down at his hands. They'd been different before. Weak and squishy. But now they were strong again. And Bulbin was so small. . . .

"No," Pinocchio managed. "Do not do that. If you touch my panel, I have a charm that commands me to defend myself. You serve Master Al Mi'raj, and I know I should not hurt you. But I would not be able to stop myself."

Al Mi'raj and the Bulbins exchanged looks. The second gnome dropped the tools.

"Have you ever heard of a charm like that?" Al Mi'raj asked.

"No," Bulbin said. "But it could be done. I could imagine how. But who'd bother putting such a thing on an automa?"

"Who put this charm on you?" Al Mi'raj asked Pinocchio quietly. "Answer me."

Faint memories bubbled from the thick recesses of his thoughts.

"It was a prisoner," Pinocchio replied. "Someone named Prester John."

The Bulbins sprang together into a single astonished gnome.

"His Immortal Lordship?" Al Mi'raj gasped. "Imprisoned?"

Voices carried from down the hallway as a group was approaching the workshop.

"But what's Prester John done to this automa?" Bulbin hissed.

"Whatever it is, we can't let the doge discover it." Al Mi'raj rose to greet his masters.

At the doorway, Captain Toro stepped aside, bowing his head as the crimson imperial guards entered. "The lord doge of Venice," one announced through his helmet.

Al Mi'raj and Bulbin bowed. Pinocchio just sat there, waiting for orders.

The doge marched in, draped in heavy red-velvet cloaks trimmed in thick fur. His face seemed to have far too much flesh, a saggy face with bulging eyes and wads of loose skin flapping from his jowls.

The lord mayor said, "My doge, this is the djinni Al Mi'raj, who runs our theater company."

Al Mi'raj bowed lower. "Your presence is an honor, my doge."

The doge pursed his droopy lips distastefully at Al Mi'raj. "What have you discovered about what that automa did out there?"

"Nothing, my doge. We cannot figure out how he did it."

The doge glared at Pinocchio. "Where did you get this automa?"

"We've had him sitting around for ages, my doge," Al Mi'raj said. "Only recently has Bulbin had time to get him operational. Clearly something is still not working right."

The doge turned to the lord mayor. "Do you trust this monster?"

"Y-yes, my doge," the lord mayor said, nodding vigorously.

"Al Mi'raj runs a reputable business and theater. I can assure you. He and his gnome have fealty papers and have been nothing but loyal servants to me and their empire."

"Liar!" a voice cracked.

Everyone froze, their attention turning to the airman standing in the doorway.

"What are you saying, Captain?" the Mayor said, affronted.

Captain Toro's face was a bright shade of purple, his dark eyes locked on Al Mi'raj. The captain's voice shook as he spoke. "That fire eater is lying!"

"*Signore*, I am an ever-loyal servant to Venice," Al Mi'raj said, smiling through his fangs.

"You are a liar and a traitor," Captain Toro spat. "That automa does not belong to you. I know this automa. It is the one that was sent to Geppetto Gazza."

The doge's bulging eyes grew wider. "Ever-loyal servant, Al Mi'raj, tell me again where this automa came from."

Al Mi'raj exchanged a glance with Bulbin before saying, "I don't remember. We must have bought him years ago from a trader—"

"He's lying!" Captain Toro shouted. The imperial guards pushed him back with their spears.

Al Mi'raj stammered, "M-my doge, we purchase disassembled automa all the time, and fix them up for our theater. I swear to you that this automa—"

The doge snatched Bulbin by the throat, lifting the tiny gnome off the floor.

The hand that gripped Bulbin was no ordinary hand. The doge had lost his hand when Geppetto cut it off. In its place was a hand cast of pure lead.

The metal went to work at once on Bulbin. The brown gnome

began to turn a dusty gray, like moist earth growing parched. The gnome gasped, his black eyes rolling back.

"Swear to me, do you?" the doge asked, spittle frothing on his lips. "Do you *swear* upon this disgusting little clod of filth that you've had this automa for years?"

"No!" Al Mi'raj cried. "I remembered wrong. I was confused! Please let him go."

Bulbin went limp in the doge's grip and began to split apart. Little versions of the gnome peeled off like flakes of ash, crumbling to the floor.

"When did you get the automa?" the doge asked calmly.

"Not a week ago, my doge! I don't know where the trader got the automa from."

Pinocchio wondered if he should defend his master and Bulbin, but until Al Mi'raj ordered him to do so, he would wait.

"Could the automa have belonged to the traitor Geppetto?" the doge asked.

"I know nothing about this Geppetto," Al Mi'raj said. "I swear . . . I mean I promise you, my doge, I had no idea it belonged to any Geppetto!"

The doge glared at him. Then he released Bulbin. The gnome thudded to the floor. He gasped a deep breath as warm brown color returned to his face. Bulbin got on all fours, panting and wide-eyed with fear as he gathered the crumbled other gnomes and pushed them back into his body.

The doge removed a handkerchief and began cleaning his leaden hand. He pursed his fleshy lips at Captain Toro. "What is your name, airman?"

"Captain Toro, airman of the Ninth Carabinieri, my doge."

The doge addressed a massive soldier, older than the others, with cropped silver hair and scars crisscrossing his haggard face.

"General Maximian, didn't you tell me that Captain Toro was the first to report that the traitor Geppetto was here in Tuscany?"

The general stepped forward. "Yes, my doge. Apparently Geppetto had been hiding in the village of San Baldovino for months under the name Polendina, pretending to be a shopkeeper."

"And why wasn't he captured when your soldiers arrived?"

The general gave an uncomfortable grunt. "He slipped past us somehow. Although I believe Captain Toro questioned him in his shop before he managed to escape."

"I . . . but . . . there was no automa in his shop!" Captain Toro spluttered. "There was no way to know at the time he was Geppetto. My orders were to search for a man in possession of the automa who escaped from Don—"

"Captain Toro joined our search," the general went on. "Breaking off from his patrol—without orders, mind you—he cornered Geppetto on an aqueduct. However, he lost Geppetto when he was attacked by the automa. Captain Toro then claimed the automa brought him back to life after he drowned."

"The automa did—" Captain Toro began, but the doge silenced him with a glance.

"After what we've all seen today, it would appear Captain Toro could have been telling the truth about this automa. Don't you think, General Maximian?"

The general gave a stiff nod. A smile of vindication crept onto Captain Toro's face.

"An automa who can bring back the dying . . ." The doge waddled around to face Pinocchio. "How is it able to do this?"

Al Mi'raj crouched submissively. "I swear to you, I have no idea, my doge. This is beyond anything Bulbin and I are able to do to an automa."

"I'm certain of that," the doge sneered. "General Maximian, this is the answer to our problem. This automa is just what we need to keep our prisoner alive."

"Yes, my doge," the general replied.

"Is it true then, my doge," the lord mayor whispered, "that you have captured Prester John?"

The doge cut his eyes warily over to Al Mi'raj. Al Mi'raj looked like he would spontaneously combust before he repeated anything he'd heard.

"Yes, we captured the immortal king of Abaton," the doge said, his hands behind his robes as he paced. "But I made the mistake of assuming he would bring the Ancientmost Pearl with him. Sadly, he left it in Abaton for safekeeping. And now, without his precious Pearl, he is dying, at long last, aging into a decrepit old man in my prison at this very moment. But this automa . . ."

The doge rounded on Pinocchio. "This one, whatever Geppetto has done to it, this one might keep Prester John alive long enough."

"Long enough for what?" the lord mayor asked. "What good is keeping him, if he's dying?"

"Oh, I have my reasons, Lord Mayor," the doge said. "Prester John has many uses to me, but only if he is alive. And I will need my former high alchemist. I need Geppetto. General, what is the latest news on the search for him?"

General Maximian began, "Our last report was that Geppetto was spotted fleeing from the river after Captain Toro supposedly drown—"

"I did drown!" Captain Toro squawked.

The doge waved a hand, and General Maximian continued.

"Our men say Geppetto escaped with the assistance of a

blue fairy. He hasn't been seen since, but we have redoubled our efforts and are scouring the countryside, my doge. I can assure you, we will find him."

Captain Toro's face went pale, and when the doge saw it, he said, "What's the matter, Captain?"

Captain Toro mumbled, almost incomprehensibly, "I . . . I saw two travelers just yesterday. One was a fairy. The other . . ."

"You let Geppetto slip past you yet a third time!" General Maximian barked.

The doge fixed his gaze on the trembling captain. "Is this true, Captain Toro? Are you such an imbecile that you spotted a fairy with a man and you didn't suspect it was Geppetto?"

"I . . . she said he was her uncle. She said he was a fairy too."

The doge's voice dripped poisonously. "Can you not tell the difference between a man and a fairy?"

"My doge," Captain Toro pleaded, "he was cloaked. I saw them just as I was learning about the automa in Al Mi'raj's show. It was a crucial discovery! One that led me immediately to Siena. I was going to report it to General Maximian when—"

"Don't give me excuses, Captain!" the doge said, his jowls flapping in rage. "I want Geppetto. I want to know how Geppetto has done this to the automa!"

The room grew quiet.

A moment later, Toro began to mumble, "My doge, I just had a thought. . . . If Geppetto was there yesterday when I heard about this automa, he must have heard it too. He would come here to Siena. He might be here now!"

As the doge considered this, his anger began to wane.

"I can have the city guards begin a sweep at once," the lord mayor said. "We can close the gates and—"

"No," Captain Toro interrupted.

The lord mayor grimaced, but the doge said, "What is it, Captain?"

"We shouldn't scare him into hiding," Captain Toro said. "If Geppetto feels he has a chance to rescue this automa, he might come here. Tonight, even."

"Yes," the doge agreed. "Yes. We must show him that we have not departed with his masterwork of an automa. Show him that he has an opening if he wants to rescue it."

The doge pointed at Al Mi'raj. "Lock the automa in with the half-beasts."

"Yes, my doge," Al Mi'raj said, looking as if he had narrowly escaped a death sentence.

"General," the doge said, "we will set a small guard to show that the automa is here. The rest of my guards and airmen I want back at the mayor's Palazzo Pubblico at once."

"I can stand post here—" Captain Toro began.

"I don't want you botching this again, Captain," the doge snarled.

Captain Toro's face twisted unpleasantly. He stayed silent, bowing his head in submission before following the doge, the mayor, and the soldiers from the room.

Once they were gone, Al Mi'raj snapped his fangs, the black spots on his yellow face growing larger with rage. He knelt. "Are you all right, Bulbin?"

The gnome nodded, still looking shaky.

Pinocchio felt he should be afraid of the doge. He had a vague memory that the doge had done something bad to his former master Geppetto. But the fogginess in his head was too thick. He couldn't muster a worry.

"What you want me to do?" Bulbin asked. "Do we help the doge?"

"We have to," Al Mi'raj said. "We have our own necks to worry about."

"But you seen what this automa can do! If the doge has the power to raise the dead—"

"He also has Prester John dying in a Venetian prison. It might be the only way to save His Immortal Lordship."

"Believe me," Bulbin said. "The doge en't doing this to help Prester John. There's some dark scheme at play here. Something awful."

"There's nothing else we can do, Bulbin. It is not our problem anymore. We'll lock him up with the chimera as ordered. Go with Bulbin," Al Mi'raj said to Pinocchio, "and stay in your cell until the doge's soldiers collect you."

Bulbin sighed. "Get up, manikin."

Pinocchio stood, realizing he might be leaving Al Mi'raj's theater soon. Al Mi'raj was his master, so if Al Mi'raj wanted him to go with the doge, he would obey.

Pinocchio was taken to the dungeon deep beneath the theater and locked in a separate cell from Mezmer and her chimera. After Bulbin left, Mezmer came to the bars separating her from Pinocchio. "Why are you here, automa?"

"The doge is taking me away in the morning," Pinocchio replied.

Sop sneered at him through the bars. "Most likely going to take you apart and figure out how you performed your trick."

"Quiet, Sop," Mezmer said. She nodded to Pinocchio. "Wish I could repay you for what you did, lad. But it's not looking too likely I'll have the chance."

"Repay me?" Pinocchio asked. "An automa has no need for money."

Mezmer laughed. "I mean I'm in your debt. You saved my

life. A knight always honors her debts. I don't know how you did it, but I live another day because of you. All of my darling mongrels, too." She cocked a furred thumb back at the chimera.

A few nodded in agreement, like the boar. Sop and some of the others glanced uneasily at Pinocchio.

"What good is another night waiting to die?" Sop mumbled, licking the back of his hand to smooth the fur around his eye patch.

Mezmer leaned closer to Pinocchio to whisper, "How did you do it, by the way?"

Pinocchio said, "I do not know."

Mezmer watched him with bright orange eyes. Finally she walked away.

One by one, the chimera fell asleep. Pinocchio stood alone against the stone wall at the back of his cell. There was nothing to figure out, nothing to worry about. There was only waiting until his master told him what to do next.

The door to the dungeon opened, and Wiq came in. He whispered, "We have to be quiet."

"All right," Pinocchio said.

"The doge is going to take you away in the morning."

"Yes, I know."

Wiq looked surprised. "But if you do, you'll be in trouble, Pinocchio. You know how dangerous the doge is."

"I do?" Pinocchio asked flatly.

Wiq stared at Pinocchio. "What's wrong with you? Are you just going to let Al Mi'raj give you to the doge?"

"I do what Master Al Mi'raj orders."

Wiq shook his head. "No, you can't. Why are you acting this way? Don't you remember our promise? I thought we were friends."

Wiq pushed up his sleeve, showing Pinocchio the loop of jasmine around his wrist.

Pinocchio blinked at the sight of the bracelet. He looked at Wiq as if seeing him for the first time. He slid up his own sleeve and discovered an identical jasmine bracelet. A memory wanted to break through the fog that was clouding his thoughts. "Friends? We are . . . friends?"

"Did Bulbin do something to you?" Wiq said, his voice shaking. "What's happened?"

"I think . . ." Pinocchio fought against the fog. "I think when I saved the half-beast . . ."

"The fox chimera?"

"Yes, Mezmer," Pinocchio continued. "I lost something. I cannot think right."

"You're acting like . . . an automa," Wiq said.

"I am an automa," Pinocchio replied.

"Not an ordinary one. You can think for yourself! You're different, Pinocchio. Don't you remember? Please remember!"

He was trying to. He wanted to. What had happened to him?

Wiq said urgently, "You're becoming . . . alive, Pinocchio! You're searching for your father. He wants to find you."

Yes, his father. Geppetto! He didn't belong to Al Mi'raj. He belonged with Geppetto. Geppetto wanted him to be his son!

The thought was like a breeze blowing the fog clear from his mind. Pinocchio gave a gasp as his memories began to flood back. With them came a welling of panic. "Wiq! I'm in trouble."

"I know!" Wiq said. "That's what I've been saying."

"And the doge . . . he's planning a trap. He wants to capture my father! I have to get out of here."

Wiq looked beside himself with relief. "You will."

"I will? How?"

Wiq held up a ring of keys.

15.

Escape and Capture

Wiq unlocked the cell. Pinocchio hesitated as he opened the door. The fealty lock in the back of his neck tingled and his nose itched.

"Wiq, I can't. Al Mi'raj ordered me to stay here. If I disobey him, my nose . . ."

Wiq flipped through the jumbled mass of smaller keys. "I stole these from Bulbin's workshop. We just have to figure out which one fits."

As Wiq began trying one fealty key after the other, the chimera woke. Sop came to the bars, his tail slashing back and forth. "Mezmer, get up!"

The fox was awake in an instant. "What are you doing, lad?"

Wiq kept working. Pinocchio felt keys jostled around hurriedly in the back of his neck. "Don't say anything to her," Wiq murmured.

His words weren't quiet enough, and Mezmer narrowed her eyes at Wiq. "Maybe I should shout for the guard."

"No, don't!" Pinocchio said. Then he whispered back at Wiq. "We have to set them free too. They'll be killed otherwise."

"It's too dangerous, Pinocchio. I've got to get you away. I can't release all of them as well."

A key slid neatly into the slot in Pinocchio's neck, clicking the tumblers into place.

"I've got it," Wiq said.

Pinocchio reached back to stop Wiq's hand. "When you turn it, who will be my master?"

"I'm not sure," Wiq said. "I have to say a name, or anyone—the doge, or even one of these chimera—could declare themselves your master. Who should I say?"

"He wants to be your master, automa," Sop said. "Your chum wants to make you his servant so he can escape."

"That's not true!" Wiq said. "I'm helping him."

The one-eyed cat gave a sinister purr. "Sure you are, puppet master."

"Say that Geppetto is my master," Pinocchio said.

Wiq turned the key, and Pinocchio felt that momentary weightlessness, that feeling of freedom. Then Wiq said, "Geppetto is your master now."

Pinocchio wondered what would have happened if he'd gotten Wiq to say *Pinocchio is your master now*. But it was too late. The heaviness sank over him. It wasn't like when Al Mi'raj had become his master. That had been crushing. This felt like a comforting weight, like a heavy blanket. He was glad he belonged to Geppetto again. If only he could find him.

"Whatever happened to Abatonian loyalty?" Mezmer asked coolly. "Free us."

"Yeah," Sop chimed in. "He's just an automa. We're chimera like you. And do you even have a plan to get out of the city? There are airmen everywhere. You'll need us."

"Do you have a plan?" Pinocchio asked.

Wiq shook his head.

"Sop's right, lad," Mezmer said. "If you let us out, we can help you escape. We've snuck out of worse spots."

Wiq looked worried. "I . . . I don't know . . ."

"We can trust them," Pinocchio urged. "I just know it."

"You can," Mezmer said. "I swear to you as a knight of the Celestial Brigade."

"A what?" Wiq asked.

Sop snorted. "She fancies herself one of the legendary Abatonian order."

"I am a descendant of the founder of the Celestial Brigade, the glorious chimera hero Mezmercurian!" Mezmer said.

"So you've told me a million times or two." Sop gave a sigh. "But it is true that if Mezmer gives her word, it won't be broken."

Wiq approached Mezmer with a frown and spoke quietly. "If I let all these chimera out, the airmen will spot you for sure. There are too many of you."

"Trust me, darling," Mezmer said with a wink. "We'll want them all freed."

Wiq looked hesitant but began unlocking the cell doors. The chimera rushed out, growling ferociously. Although their savage displays were disconcerting, Pinocchio realized they were just showing their excitement in their own monstrously peculiar ways.

Mezmer gathered her brethren at the door. She held a hand to silence them and said, "Which way, lad?"

"Airmen are guarding most of the entranceways," Wiq said.

"But there's a door to the back alley. A hidden door. Where Al Mi'raj has his stolen automa snuck in. Al Mi'raj wasn't giving up that secret. There's no guard posted there."

"Splendid," Mezmer said.

Wiq led them up the stairs from the dungeon and through the hallways until they reached the door to the alleyway where Pinocchio had first come in. They rolled aside the barrel at the top of the stairs, and one by one the chimera slipped into the dark. Pinocchio followed Mezmer and Sop. As he did, the door shut behind them.

Pinocchio spun around and saw Wiq peering at him through a small panel in the door. "What are you doing? Aren't you coming?"

Wiq shook his head slowly. "I can't, Pinocchio. You know I can't." He touched a finger to the collar.

"But . . . but we promised to get away together!" This wasn't their plan. What was Wiq doing? Pinocchio shoved his arm through the hole to grab Wiq, but Wiq stepped out of reach.

"I'm not leaving you!" Pinocchio said. "My guts feel like they're boiling. It's my instincts . . . they're telling me this is wrong, Wiq. Don't do this!"

"I have to," Wiq said, his voice strangely raspy. "And you have to. Can't you see, you goof?"

Pinocchio felt something sharp and awful piercing in his chest. "But . . . but . . ." Pinocchio said. "Please! You're my friend."

Wiq brushed angrily at his face. "I know. And you're my friend too. That's why I have to break our promise. I wanted to go, but I can't. You've got to understand. This is the only way for you to get away."

"Come on, dear," Mezmer said pulling on Pinocchio's arm. "Don't make it harder."

Pinocchio shoved her away. He reached through the panel and clasped Wiq's hands.

"Please, Wiq," he cried.

"I'm sorry," Wiq whispered. Then he called to the fox. "You have to keep Pinocchio safe. You can't let the doge's soldiers capture him. He's . . . he's too important. Do you understand?"

Mezmer nodded.

Wiq squeezed Pinocchio's hand. Tears beaded on the fur on his cheeks. "Good-bye, Pinocchio," he said. "If you find your father . . . if he rescues Prester John . . . maybe His Immortal Lordship can find a way to save us."

He shut the panel and was gone.

"Wiq, don't!" Pinocchio cried.

It took Mezmer and Sop both pulling Pinocchio to get him up the stairs and into the alley. "Hush, lad! We have to go."

Pinocchio felt his eyes burn as if hot steam wanted to erupt from them. He slumped to the ground while Mezmer spoke quietly with a small group of the remaining chimera. She clasped each of them by the forearms and said, "You'd have made magnificent knights, darlings," before the group turned and disappeared down the alley.

Mezmer pulled Pinocchio to his feet. He staggered in a daze as she and Sop led him away. It was only a moment later he realized that they weren't following the group.

"Where are the others?" he asked.

"Wiq was right," she said grimly. "If we all stayed together, we'd be caught. They are providing a necessary distraction, so we can hopefully get away."

"But what will happen to them? Will they be captured again?"

"Some. Most will fall in glorious battle against the imperial guards."

"I don't understand," Pinocchio said.

Mezmer stopped and placed a paw to his shoulder. "It is like with your friend Wiq. When friends are loyal and true, they are willing to help one another no matter the cost. Come. Let us not have their sacrifice be in vain."

Pinocchio felt the smallest bit of understanding penetrate the fog of grief encompassing him. Mezmer was right. He couldn't let Wiq down. So he followed her and Sop as they made their way through the darkened streets of Siena.

As they rounded a corner, the muffled sound of musket fire echoed off the buildings, illuminating the night in brief bursts. Distant voices shouted. Then the sky filled with airmen streaking toward the commotion.

Mezmer pulled Pinocchio and Sop into an alley to take cover.

"They found our brethren," she said, looking up worriedly at all the airmen. "Now we have to hope they won't find us."

Pinocchio's thoughts had been consumed by leaving Wiq, but now the sight of the airmen and the sound of the gunfire finally woke him to their present danger.

"So how are we going to escape?" he asked, sticking close to Mezmer's side as the three slid from alleyway to alleyway.

"When we get to the wall," Mezmer explained, "Sop will first make sure there are no guards. He sees better with his one eye than most do with two. Then you'll start to scale the wall, strong automa that you are. We'll hold on to your legs, and Sop will give a special tap if he spies trouble—"

"What should the tap be?" Sop interrupted. "Maybe . . ." He made a *bop-ba-bop, bop-ba-bop* rhythm with his paws. "Or what about a birdcall? It could be . . ." The noise sounded more like a distressed toad than any bird Pinocchio had ever heard.

"Wait!" Pinocchio sputtered. "Are you saying we're just going to climb over the wall and hope we don't get spotted by airmen?"

"That's the general plan," Mezmer replied, her attention focused on the skies and the streets ahead.

"That's a terrible plan!" Pinocchio said.

"Well, it's the only one we have at the moment," Sop said, pushing Mezmer and Pinocchio into a doorway as a trio of airmen streaked overhead.

Pinocchio wondered if going with Mezmer and Sop was a huge mistake.

"I'd give my good eye for a sword right about now," Sop mumbled. "Or better still, a chameleon cloak."

"A what?" Pinocchio asked, Sop's words reminding him of something.

Mezmer pulled him after her. "Doesn't much matter, does it, darling? As we don't have—"

"Do chameleon cloaks disguise you as your surroundings?" he asked. "I know where we might get some."

"What?" Mezmer stopped running and fixed Pinocchio with a surprised look.

"The men who brought me to Siena wore them," Pinocchio said. "But I don't know if they're still here."

"Do you know where they stay in town?" Mezmer asked.

"Not really," Pinocchio said.

Sop hissed. "Then we're wasting time! Let's just go."

In the street ahead, Pinocchio spied a banner with an eagle emblazoned on it. He'd seen banners like that when Rampino brought him to Al Mi'raj's. Each of the neighborhoods of Siena seemed to display a different banner. And Rampino had been staying in the neighborhood where the banners were . . .

"Snails," he murmured. "We have to find the snails."

"The snails?" Sop looked at Pinocchio like he was completely insane.

Pinocchio hurried down the alley. "Just follow me."

Mezmer shoved Sop forward. "Let's see what the lad is onto."

Pinocchio led them down several streets until they reached a neighborhood with rhinoceros banners. "This isn't right."

Sop groaned, but Pinocchio set off in the other direction, and soon they spied panther banners. Yes, he remembered those. Weaving down the narrowest streets and sticking to the shadows so as not to be spotted from above, Pinocchio eventually reached a square with the snail banners.

"Snails," Sop said, giving a nod of understanding. "So where are they?"

"Hopefully in those stables over there," Pinocchio said.

The square was a large one, and crossing it would make them more exposed than they had been in the narrow streets.

"I can handle this," Sop said, adjusting his eye patch. "Wait here."

Sop crossed the square, moving from one shadowy spot to another with surprising stealth, especially for a cat as pudgy as he was. He disappeared into the stables.

Pinocchio held his breath. If Sop woke Rampino's men and a fight broke out, the airmen would notice for certain. But a moment later, Sop slipped back across the square, his arms bundled around not only three chameleon cloaks, but also a pair of swords and a spear.

"Excellent, darling!" Mezmer said, giving the spear an experimental twirl.

Pinocchio threw on the cloak and tested the feel of the sword. Not bad.

"Sleeping off too many bottles of wine, that group was," Sop chuckled, buckling the sword belt and pulling the cloak around his shoulders. He blended in perfectly with the shadowy stone wall behind him. "How do I look? Invisible?"

"Not exactly," Mezmer said. "I can see you when you move. But we'll be invisible enough from the sky." Then she added, "Hopefully. Off we go."

"Wait!" Pinocchio said. "We have to find Geppetto. My fa— I mean, my master is somewhere in the city. He's in danger."

"If you haven't noticed, we're in danger too," Sop said.

"Listen, dear," Mezmer said to Pinocchio, leaning on her spear. "I swore to your friend I'd help you get away, and that's what I'll do. If your master was looking for you, he'll have discovered by now that there's been an escape from Al Mi'raj's theater. The best thing for us to do is leave this city and hope your master comes after you."

"But how will he find me?"

"Not our concern at the moment, dear," Mezmer said kindly before pulling up her hood and setting off.

Musket fire had woken most of Siena. Faces peered out of illuminated windows, but none seemed to notice the three as they made their way to the north gate.

A night guard stood before the closed portcullis. He narrowed his eyes as they approached. "Who goes there?" he called.

Pinocchio really hoped this was going to work. "Rampino," he said in the most gravelly voice he could muster.

"Awful early for you," the guard chuckled. "Where are the rest?"

"Sleeping," Pinocchio said. "These idiots . . . uh, dropped a bag of coins at our last camp. We'll be back later."

The guard cocked his head toward the sounds of the airmen. "Seems suspicious you leaving with these imperial airmen in town."

Pinocchio stiffened and slid a hand to his sword.

The guard burst out laughing. "I don't even want to know what kind of pickle you've gotten into with the imperials, naughty Rampino. Just keep finding us more like the Magpie. I'll keep quiet that you came through. Hurry before you get in trouble."

He opened the gate, and the three headed out onto the steep lane that zigzagged down from Siena. When they reached the main road, Pinocchio looked back at the city. Was Geppetto still there? Would he find a way to escape? If his father had tracked him down in Siena, he had to hope he'd be able to find him still. But now, dawn was coming, and the gunfire was getting worse. They had to get away.

He turned and found Mezmer smiling down at him.

"Nice work back there, darling," she said. "My, aren't you full of surprises. I never imagined puppets could be so clever."

"I'm not a puppet," Pinocchio said.

Mezmer rubbed her furry chin. "No, I suppose you're not. But what are you, exactly?"

Before Pinocchio could answer, Sop said, "Quit yapping and move," as he jogged down the road.

"That must be the djinni's theater," Geppetto said.

Lazuli crouched beside him on the dark rooftop. They peered across at the massive building that bordered the city's central square.

"How are we going to get inside?" Maestro chirped.

Lazuli looked around. "The guards are all below. They've left the terrace at the top unprotected. I can get onto it."

"Why aren't there guards on the roof?" Geppetto asked. "It looks too easy."

"You think it's a trap?" Lazuli asked.

"But for whom?" Geppetto murmured.

The doors to the theater opened down on the street. A djinni emerged, and the guards began barking orders and shouting in anger.

"What's happening?" Lazuli asked.

"I don't know," Geppetto said. They hid in the shadows beside a chimney.

Flying Lions and airmen emerged from atop the Palazzo Pubblico, taking flight and spreading out over the city.

Maestro flicked his antennae. "Someone must have escaped from the theater," he said. "Do you think it could be Pinocchio?"

"Maestro," Geppetto said, fixing the cricket with an urgent gaze. "You have to go look for him!"

Poor Maestro trembled nervously, but in the end, Lazuli could see that his devotion to Pinocchio overcame his fear. With a spring, he disappeared into the dark sky.

Lazuli and Geppetto waited as gunfire erupted somewhere across the city. Shouting voices rose and fell. Lazuli gritted her teeth. Whatever was happening, this was about more than just Geppetto's automa.

Finally Maestro returned, landing on Geppetto's shoulder. "I saw him. At least I think it was Pinocchio and maybe two others. It was hard to tell, since they were wearing chameleon cloaks. I only glimpsed them for a moment before the cloaks shifted—"

"Which way did they go?" Geppetto growled.

"Out the north gate," Maestro said.

Lazuli glanced toward the gunfire on the south side of the city. "Someone's creating a helpful distraction."

Geppetto began to rise from the rooftop. "If we hurry, we can—"

A thump sounded behind them, someone landing, cracking terra-cotta tiles.

"We meet again, fairy," the airman said, aiming his musket at them. "Funny. Your uncle doesn't look like any Abatonian I've ever seen."

He stepped forward, and his face emerged from the shadows. Lazuli recognized him right away.

"Master Geppetto," Captain Toro said. "You never said you had blue-haired family."

Lazuli looked side to side for a way to escape off the roof. She might manage it, but Geppetto couldn't. They were trapped.

"You played a fine trick on me back at that tavern," Captain Toro snarled. "Toro the fool. Toro who has spent his years in this frontier wasteland, when he should have been serving in Venice as an imperial officer of the Fortezza Ducale. Well, you've made a fool of me too many times, traitor!"

He surged toward them. Geppetto backed to the edge of the roof. Lazuli stepped in front of him, her hand on her sword.

"Drop the weapon, fairy," Toro ordered, aiming his musket.

She'd been trained well. She was fast. But not against a gun. There was no escaping Captain Toro this time.

Lazuli slowly unsheathed the sword and dropped it to the tiles.

"You must have had a good laugh," Captain Toro said with a crazed smile. "Back in San Baldovino. On the aqueduct. And then the other day. You must have split your sides thinking you'd fooled me for a third time."

"We thought nothing of the sort, Captain," Geppetto said.

Captain Toro didn't look as if he believed him. The rage and satisfaction on the captain's face was terrifying. "Thought I'd quit after embarrassing myself so many times before the doge and my comrades. But I never quit! I won't fail this time. This is my victory. Tonight, when I bring the doge the traitor Geppetto Gazza, I will show them all that Captain Toro is a hero of the empire!"

Lazuli waved a hand and a roof tile flew at Captain Toro. The airman spun sideways, and the clay tile shattered on his armored forearm.

She reached for the sword at her feet. But before she could grab it, Captain Toro brought the stock end of his musket down, cracking it against her temple.

She staggered toward the edge, nearly falling over. Her vision was swimming with flashes of light. She felt heavy and disoriented, as if she might pass out. *Not now,* she tried to tell herself.

Captain Toro had Geppetto by the elbow. "I've got you this time, traitor."

Geppetto met Lazuli's gaze. She tried to get her eyes to focus on him.

"Go," he barked.

Still holding Geppetto, Captain Toro swung the musket around one-handed and aimed it at her.

Lazuli had no time to weigh her options. She had only an instant to decide. And in that instant, she reached out a hand. A whirl of wind shot her sword into her grip, and she lunged at Captain Toro.

The musket thundered. Pain exploded across Lazuli's chest. She flew backward from the force of the impact, tumbling from the rooftop and down to the cobblestone streets below.

16.

Cricket Music

A peal of thunder echoed across the Tuscan countryside, low and ominous.

Pinocchio sat on the roof of a crumbling mill, hoping to spy Geppetto coming over one of the hills. But besides the steely purple wall of storm clouds blotting out the dawn, nothing out there was moving. Even the skies were finally empty of airmen this morning.

Where were his father and Maestro? When would they come? Now that the doge's fleet had flown off for Venice and the patrols of airmen were gone, they might even be able to sneak back into the city and rescue Wiq. If only his father would get here.

Pinocchio twisted the bracelet of jasmine vines around his wrist.

Mezmer and Sop were asleep below inside the mill. They had found the ruined hiding place a few days before. Although Sop and Mezmer had thought they should keep moving, Pinocchio insisted on staying. If his father was looking for him, they should wait somewhat close to Siena.

Mezmer had warned that they'd be captured if they remained in the mill. And she had almost been right. Twice now patrols had searched the mill, but he and Mezmer and Sop had covered themselves with the chameleon cloaks and hidden in the forest until the soldiers moved on.

Watching the black storm as it drew closer, Pinocchio heard Mezmer and Sop beginning to stir below. They were most likely starting to warm a breakfast of the food they'd plundered from gardens on their escape from Siena. He thought about going down to join them, but didn't want to leave his post.

Sop's voice wafted from the window. "The puppet's kept us here long enough."

Pinocchio sat up straighter, listening.

"Don't call him that," Mezmer said. "And I gave my word I'd help the lad."

"You did!" Sop contended. "You helped him escape Siena. It's time we move on, before a patrol catches us by surprise."

"He still thinks his alchemist is coming," Mezmer said. "You've heard him up there, humming that tune every night as he waits for his master."

"It's depressing, if you ask me," Sop said, clanking around as he worked on breakfast.

Pinocchio hadn't realized they'd been able to hear him humming Maestro's "Orpheus." And it wasn't a depressing song! Humming it was the only thing that gave him an inkling of hope.

"Look, Mez, I like the kid. You're right, he's . . . no ordinary automa. But we can't let him go on thinking this alchemist is going to come, when clearly he's not."

"I know," Mezmer said, with a heavy sigh. A moment later, she asked tentatively, "Back when we were leaving, did you hear what Wiq said, about the alchemist being the lad's father?"

"I heard it. Ridiculous, right?"

Mezmer was silent.

"What!" Sop spat. "You're not serious? Do you honestly think an alchemist could love one of these pupp—I mean, an automa?"

"I think Pinocchio loves this alchemist. Why else would he be acting this way?"

"Puppets don't work like that. Puppets don't feel anything."

"Stop calling him that."

"Sorry, Mez. But really, now! No one would want an automa as a son. It's preposterous!"

Pinocchio felt anger burn his face.

Mezmer was quiet before saying, "The boy Wiq ... he seemed genuinely upset when Pinocchio left, like they were true friends."

"True friends," Sop scoffed. "Probably just sad he missed his chance to escape."

Pinocchio gritted his teeth. That wasn't true! Was it?

"Doesn't really change the fact that we can't stay in this mill forever," Sop went on. "The kid comes with us or he stays. But we've got to go."

Pinocchio slid down the broken tiles of the roof and landed on the ground. He'd show stupid Sop and Mezmer that they were wrong. He just had to wait a little longer.

Mezmer opened the door. "Pinocchio, what are you—"

"Leave me if you want!" he shouted. "Go back to being out-laws or whatever you do. But Geppetto wants me to be his son! He's coming for me. You'll see!"

He began running. Mezmer shouted, "Wait!"

But he kept going. It was good to work his legs, after sitting night after night up on that roof. They felt strong in a way that wasn't just his gearworks. He ran until his legs grew tired, and then he leaped on the seven-league boots, rocketing up into a tree, where Mezmer and Sop wouldn't be able to find him. He pulled the chameleon cloak around him, vanishing into leaves and shadow.

He clung to the branch, panting for breath. He could sit up in this tree forever. He didn't need food. He didn't need to sleep. He would wait here as long as it took for his father to find him.

Heavy clouds loomed low overhead. Fat drops of rain began to fall, a few at first and then coming down all at once. Pinocchio closed his eyes and listened to the pounding rain.

How much time had passed? He was dimly aware that the rain had made his fingers and feet, with their squishy flesh, go cold. It was unpleasant being cold. He tried to ignore it. Tipping his head back, he let the rain patter against his wooden face, which felt no cold or wet.

How strange to be stuck between being wood and flesh, trapped between being an automa and becoming a boy. His fingers felt cold only because flesh wanted to be warm. But wood felt nothing, wanted nothing. Was it better to feel the cold as well as the warmth, or was it better to feel nothing?

He fingered the jasmine loop around his wrist. If he felt nothing, he wouldn't miss Wiq so. But if he felt nothing, if he were an ordinary automa, he never would have befriended Wiq at all. He rubbed his hands together, trying to warm them up.

The sound of the rain reminded Pinocchio of the footsteps of the lonely traveler in Maestro's song. Even within the roar of the downpour, it was as if notes were forming that weren't quite matching the drumming of the rain. Was he just imagining this? Pinocchio cocked his head. No, there was a faint sound forming. He was certain. And it was almost a melody.

Pinocchio sat up straighter on the branch. He tried to answer the melody, to hum the tune, but already the song was fading, drifting off through the forest.

"Maestro!" he called. "Is that you?"

He listened. The song had vanished. Pinocchio was left with only the thrumming of rain against the leaves.

Pinocchio rose to his feet, putting a hand to the trunk to stay balanced. "Maestro?" he called again. "Father? Are you out there? I'm here!"

Thunder rumbled through the forest.

He shivered, the wet and cold seeming to creep up his limbs deeper into the core of his body. Had he imagined it? He pulled the chameleon cloak off his head, hoping against hope that he might hear them coming back.

He cupped a hand to his mouth to scream their names, when something flew straight at him and landed on his nose.

"Pinocchio? Is that really you?"

"Maestro!" Pinocchio gasped.

He couldn't see the cricket clearly in the dark rain, even though—or more likely because—he was right before his eyes.

"Oh, Pinocchio! You wonderful, incorrigible scamp!" the cricket rejoiced, dancing on his nose. "I've been searching for you everywhere! I thought I saw you head out the north gate of Siena, and I followed the road, playing that song through every grove and hedgerow. You wouldn't believe how hard I've searched. And my poor wings ..."

Maestro! Good ol' Maestro. Pinocchio was so happy to see the fussy cricket. He couldn't wait to hear him babble on about different wing techniques for altering the pitch and melody, but first—

"Father!"

Pinocchio brushed Maestro from his face and leaped out of the tree. The landing hurt, stinging his fleshy feet, but he didn't care. He spun this way and that, peering through the rain-drenched forest to find him. "Father, I'm here!"

Maestro fluttered down onto his shoulder. "He's not with me, Pinocchio."

"Is he far behind?"

"He's not here," Maestro sighed. "He's in Venice."

"Venice?"

"The old fool got captured by the doge's men."

Pinocchio couldn't believe this. His knees felt suddenly weak. "No! He couldn't have been."

"Well, he was," Maestro said. "Trying to rescue you. He's been desperate to find you again, Pinocchio."

Pinocchio felt a welling of love for his father. He knew Sop was wrong. His father did want him. Why had he ever listened to that cat?

"Will he escape?" Pinocchio asked. "He has to, doesn't he? We're supposed to be together."

Maestro fidgeted uneasily on his shoulder, his wings rattling. "He won't escape this time. I'm sorry, lad, but . . . What's that?" He leaped around. "Someone's coming!"

Footsteps sounded on the wet forest floor. Mezmer came charging out of the gloom with Sop waddling, wet and grumpy-faced, behind her.

"There you are, dear!" the fox said, relaxing her hold on her spear.

"You know these chimera?" Maestro asked Pinocchio.

"We escaped from Siena together."

Sop adjusted his eye patch and cut a surly eye at Maestro. "Who's that bug you're talking to?"

"I am no mere bug, I'll have you know," Maestro chirped indignantly. "I am Maestro of the Moonlit Court, royal musician to His Immortal Lordship, Prester John of Abaton. What do you say to that, you rogues?"

"You look like a bug," Sop said, crossing his arms over his soft belly.

"Maestro is a friend," Pinocchio said, "to me and to my father."

"There, Mez," Sop said, giving Mezmer a tug on her arm. "We're not leaving him alone. He's got his musical bug buddy. Come on."

"No, don't leave!" Pinocchio cried.

Sop flattened his ears. "And why not? You seemed to want us to go before."

Pinocchio had. But now his father wasn't coming.

Ever since he'd lost Geppetto, he'd been expecting to be rescued. The fealty lock at the back of his neck directed him to wait for orders, like a good automa. But if he wanted to see his father again, he'd have to be the one to rescue Geppetto, not the other way around. The thought made him tremble.

Mezmer flicked her tall ears, tilting her head as if she sensed his struggle. "What is it, darling? Has something happened?"

"It's my father," Pinocchio said and everything began to pour out. "He's been captured by the doge and is imprisoned in Venice with Prester John. . . ."

Although Mezmer had to swat Sop several times to keep him quiet, the fox listened intently as Pinocchio explained how he'd come to Geppetto, how he'd begun changing, and the danger he and his father—as well as Prester John—were in. When he finished, Mezmer gave a gasp of understanding.

"So it's His Immortal Lordship who gave you this power of resurrection. He made you this way. It makes sense now! Why you began acting like an ordinary automa after you saved me."

"Acting like an ordinary automa?" Maestro chirped. "What's this about?"

Pinocchio had been so foggy during those times, but Mezmer was able to fill in the pieces of what had happened at Al Mi'raj's theater as best she could. "Pinocchio is clearly changing. Maybe even becoming . . . alive. But if he uses the power to save the life of another, he turns back into a thoughtless automa. It's as if all the life he's gained leaves him."

Pinocchio knew what Mezmer was saying was true. But he also knew that each time he'd changed back, he'd also eventually become himself again—his true and living self.

"Mezmer, I need your help. We have to go to Venice."

"What!" Sop yowled. "You think the four of us can rescue your master from the doge's fortress? And you thought *our* escape plans were terrible. What you're proposing is ludicrous . . . it's impossible!"

"It can't be!" Pinocchio said.

Mezmer shook her snout. "I'm afraid Sop's right."

Even Maestro seemed to agree. "Pinocchio, I know Master Geppetto is in great danger, but rescuing him . . . well, yes, it's impossible. Think of all the airmen and Flying Lions guarding that floating fortress. How would we get past? I'm not sure we could even enter the city of Venice, much less find a way up into the Fortezza."

Pinocchio's insides were burning with desperation. He had to do this! His instincts screamed at him to take action, no matter how impossible, if he was ever to be reunited with his father. He had to convince the others to follow him.

"You say it's impossible," Pinocchio began. "Isn't it also impossible that a wooden servant could come alive? And Sop, you couldn't believe a human would want an automa for a son. But Geppetto does. Tell him, Maestro."

Maestro flittered. "It's true, but—"

"Mezmer, you and Sop can't possibly want to spend the rest of your lives hiding and dodging patrols of airmen."

Sop's fur rose. "Better than delivering ourselves to the Fortezza's prisons!"

Pinocchio was struggling for a better reason, a more convincing argument, something like what Mezmer had said to inspire her chimera before the battle. It would have to be about more than just helping him rescue his father.

"Tell me," Pinocchio tried, "what is the seemingly impossible thing you and every Abatonian enslaved to the empire wants?"

Sop shifted in annoyance, but Mezmer answered, "To be free."

"Right!" Pinocchio said. "If we can rescue my father, we can rescue Prester John, too, and he could bring us to Abaton. Don't you see? But more so, if we can do that, Prester John could help rescue Wiq and all the other slaves. We have to do this, not just for us—we have to do it for them. For all your enslaved Abatonian brethren."

He saw Mezmer give the slightest nod. She saw herself as a knight with a noble purpose. He would have to appeal to that to inspire her.

"Mezmer, remember what you told the others before the battle. You convinced those chimera to bravely face death to show the doge that you weren't puppets of his empire. Dying is easy.

If you and Sop leave, you'll just be caught one of these days and die a glorious death. But wouldn't it be more glorious to risk your lives for a plan that might actually do some good—something worthy of glory like those knights of old—even if that plan right now seems impossible?"

Mezmer and Sop exchanged glances.

"I've never been keen on your whole glorious-death thing," Sop said.

"But you have to admit you like a good fight, don't you, darling?" Mezmer said.

Sop batted his paw coyly. "You know me too well."

Pinocchio bounced on his heels. "So does that mean you'll help?"

"Well . . . I suppose . . . I would like to see Abaton," the cat said.

Mezmer raised her snout ceremoniously and stabbed the blunt end of her spear into the wet earth. "As a knight of the Celestial Brigade—"

"How did I know . . ." Sop mumbled.

"—I owe you my life, Pinocchio. Glorious combat and daring deeds await us! You have my pledge."

Pinocchio smiled.

"This is insanity," Maestro chirped.

"Glorious, noble insanity," Sop agreed. "Can we get out of this rain and back to our breakfast?"

With Maestro on his shoulder, Pinocchio followed Mezmer and Sop back to the ruined mill, feeling as giddy and light as a soaring magpie. He might be going to Venice, straight into the heart of danger, back to the Fortezza where he'd once mindlessly served the doge, but this time he was going there as a warrior, and as a son. He was going to leave with his father or die trying.

Once they were inside and had their wet cloaks steaming by the fire, Sop stirred the pot simmering over the coals while Mezmer patted a spot on the floor.

"Come sit with us while we eat, Pinocchio, darling," she said. "We've got plans to make."

"So do you know how we can get into the Fortezza?" he asked, settling beside her.

"Not exactly," Mezmer said, "but we know someone who does. Don't we, Sop?"

The cat rolled his eye. "He won't be happy to see us again."

"It's been a long time," Mezmer said.

"That's the problem," Sop said. "Zingaro will be mad you haven't come back sooner."

"Who's Zingaro?" Pinocchio asked, his excitement rising at the prospect of a plan coming together.

Mezmer rubbed her furry chin thoughtfully. "An undine we know."

"An undine?" Pinocchio said. He'd seen other elementals, at least djinn and gnomes, and he had the vague memory of a sylph who'd helped the alchemists repair him back in the Fortezza. But never a water elemental.

Maestro chirped from his shoulder, "I didn't know there were any undine slaves in the empire."

"Not many," Mezmer said. "Most escaped. Sadly for Zingaro, they got a fealty collar on his neck before he got to open water. He was too important. Too smart. He helped design the Fortezza, after all, which is why we need his help. He'll know how to sneak in, if anyone does."

Pinocchio could hardly wait to leave. This Zingaro would find a way for them to get into the Fortezza, to rescue his father!

"But will he help us?" Maestro asked.

Mezmer was about to answer when Pinocchio felt a strange sensation come over his insides. He clutched his gut.

Mezmer gave him a curious flip of her fox ears. "You all right?"

"It's nothing," Pinocchio said. "My insides, they . . . hurt."

"Didn't know puppets could feel pain," Sop said, stirring the pot.

Maestro flittered along Pinocchio's shoulder, giving him a worried look.

Pinocchio's gaze fell once more on the bubbling pot of delicious-smelling stew. "It's not exactly pain. Just a strange feeling in my insides. Like I'm hollow."

"Hollow," Sop chuckled. "You are hollow, except for your springwork and gears. Just now noticing it?"

"Leave him be," Mezmer said.

The rich smells of the stew filled the air. Pinocchio's stomach groaned loudly. The pair looked at him, their furry ears sticking straight up.

"Was that you?" Mezmer said.

"Yes," Pinocchio replied, leaning toward the pot. He could hardly control himself. His mouth grew moist and the aroma made his head go dizzy.

"Give me a spoon," he demanded.

Sop laughed and handed Pinocchio the spoon he'd used for stirring. Pinocchio snatched it and ladled a steaming spoonful.

"What are you doing, dear?" Mezmer barked.

Maestro sprang onto the spoon. "Stop, Pinocchio! You'll ruin your gearworks!"

Pinocchio flicked him away. He brought the scalding concoction into his mouth. The flavor of the onions and tomatoes. The sweetness of the ground corn. The rich, delicious broth.

Mezmer and Sop stared at him, half laughing, half gaping in wonder.

Pinocchio swallowed. The warmth spread down inside him. The hollow pain in his stomach vanished. A new feeling came over him—ravenous desire for more. He shoveled spoonfuls of stew into his mouth.

"Quick! Get the bowls before he eats it all!" Sop shouted, wrestling his spoon away from Pinocchio. Mezmer slopped stew into two bowls and handed one to Sop.

As soon as Sop and Mezmer sat back down to eat, Pinocchio grabbed the pot from the fire, lifted it to his mouth, and drank the rest in several gulps.

Every last trace of wood vanished from his skin.

He was an automa no more.

PART THREE

THE

ALCHEMIST'S
SON

17.

Venice

The Catchfools District at the northern edge of Venice housed the city's Abatonian slaves. Each evening after work, the elementals and chimera returned from the various alchemical workshops and war-machine foundries scattered around the city, back to Catchfools, where the gates on the island's bridges were locked until dawn. No one could leave the district at night.

That didn't mean, however, that there was no way *into* Catchfools at night.

Pinocchio, Mezmer, and Sop walked along the bottom of Battello Canal with bags of sand tied around their ankles. Only the tops of copper breathing tubes showed above the water, although, in the dark, not even the gondoliers rowing past noticed those.

Maestro clung precariously to the top of Pinocchio's tube, complaining nonstop in little chirps. "Quit slouching, Pinocchio! Walk upright. I almost got wet. There are fish circling me. Oh, be careful. And hurry it up!"

Being underwater was now such a different experience. Before, when he'd been a wooden automa filled with gears, he'd simply sunk to the bottom. Now, as a boy of flesh and blood, he had to keep from floating up. And he had to make sure to keep breathing through the tube in his mouth. Breathing was important.

Being alive came with a whole new set of rules for survival. He was figuring them out as he went.

But there were simple delights, too, that came with being human. The tickle of canal minnows flittering against his goose-pimpled arms. The way his hair—which before had only been painted carvings atop his wooden head—now drifted from his scalp in soft strands. Making sure he kept breathing through the tube took concentration, but it had a certain thrill, too, to know that he was responsible for keeping himself alive.

Mezmer tapped him on the shoulder. The pixie bulbs above barely penetrated the watery gloom, but he could see the fox pointing to a large pipe set in the masonry at the side of the canal. Sop pulled off his sandbags and swam into the pipe.

Pinocchio was about to follow when Mezmer pointed up.

Of course. How could he forget?

Pinocchio took the tube out of his mouth and held it aloft with one hand. He lifted each leg to remove the sandbags before springing off the canal's muddy bottom with his seven-league boots. He broke the surface of the water just as Maestro fluttered up from the tube.

The cricket screeched, "What are you doing, you incorrig—"

Pinocchio cupped his hands around Maestro and dropped

back into the canal. When he landed, he sprang through the opening after Mezmer. Once inside, he realized the water was only waist deep in the pipe. He released the panicked cricket.

Maestro shot to the ceiling. "You could have crushed me!"

The others all whispered, "Quiet!"

Pinocchio pushed his wet hair out of his eyes and looked around. "Where are we?"

"Well, Zingaro's an undine," Sop said quietly. "Can't leave the water. So this is his way in and out of his house."

"This pipe connects the canal with his room down there behind that naiad curtain." Mezmer pointed to a faint light at the far end.

Pinocchio eyed the light, not sure what a naiad curtain was. "Are we going into his room?"

"Not unless you want to drown," Sop said. He stretched up on tiptoes to push aside a grate in the top of the pipe. "We'll go in the dry way. Cinnabar won't mind. Too much."

Maestro gave an uncertain flutter of his wings against Pinocchio's neck. "Who's Cinnabar?"

"Just a djinni who lives with Zingaro," Mezmer said.

"A fire elemental and a water elemental," Sop chuckled. "Funny roommates. I guess no one else can stand to live with Cinnabar."

Mezmer gave Pinocchio a serious tilt of her snout. "Whatever you do, dear, don't mention to either of them that you were an automa."

"Why?" Pinocchio asked.

"Others . . . well, they might not understand."

Pinocchio wasn't sure what she meant. Would they not believe he was human? He then remembered how Wiq had hated him at first, because of how the empire's might was built on alchemical creations made by Abatonian slaves. He supposed

Mezmer was right to be cautious, but all the same, it made Pinocchio . . . what was the feeling? Ashamed? Should he be ashamed that he was once an automa?

Heart racing, he followed Mezmer and Sop up through the drain and into a narrow hallway of rough stone. He'd been scared before, but he'd never felt it in his body this way. It made his hands quiver, and he wished he knew how to stop his body from acting so nervous.

"Stay close, darling," Mezmer whispered, taking his arm.

Sop stood before a door at the end of the hall, adjusting his eye patch and smoothing back his whiskers. With a wink to the others, he threw the door open. A djinni leaped up in fright from a table, nearly knocking over his flaming dinner.

"Cinnabar!" Sop said. "Been too long."

Cinnabar slumped against the table, dropping his spoon and slapping a hand to his chest. "Great Abaton! Mezmer, Sop . . . ? Where did you idiots come from?"

Sop pulled off his drenched chameleon cloak and gave a shake of his head, throwing water from his long black-and-white fur. "We had to use the back door. Sorry we didn't knock."

The djinni Cinnabar looked so different from Al Mi'raj, Pinocchio almost didn't recognize him as the same race. He was tall and thin, proportioned much more like a young man than the hulking fire eater of Siena. His horns were only slight nubs protruding from the oily hair at his temples, just above his black-and-yellow-speckled pointed ears.

Cinnabar gave Pinocchio a jerky bow. "Welcome, young master." Then in an undertone to Mezmer he said, "What's the human boy doing here?"

Pinocchio felt a small thrill run through him. The djinni saw him as human.

"We'll explain it all when we see Zingaro," Mezmer said, wringing out her cloak. "Is he around?"

"Of course he's around," Cinnabar said. "Not all of us get to move freely about the empire."

"Moving freely and being free are far from the same thing, darling."

"Your uncle, were he still alive, wouldn't agree, Mezmer," the djinni said, wagging an accusing claw. "And after all you've done—or should I say, *not* done—you're sorely mistaken if you think we're going to help you and whatever shady scheme you've concocted."

"When have we ever asked for your help on a shady scheme?" Sop purred.

Cinnabar began to count off on his fingers, but Mezmer interrupted.

"We're not asking you to help *us* this time," she said. "You'd be helping Prester John."

This caught Cinnabar short, and his fanged mouth fell open.

A low voice said, "I fear there is no helping His Immortal Lordship."

It took Pinocchio a moment to figure out where the voice came from. But as Cinnabar turned, Pinocchio noticed a wall of shimmery fabric draped from the floor to the ceiling, almost like a sheet of immense glass. That must be a naiad curtain! The fabric enclosed the back portion of the room, which he now saw was filled with water.

Mezmer walked toward the silvery curtain. "We know His Immortal Lordship is being held prisoner in the doge's Fortezza. We're planning on freeing him."

"Are you now?" the voice behind the curtain said, each word intoned with what sounded like bursts of bubbles.

Pinocchio stepped closer. A dim light behind the curtain revealed a creature floating in the chamber of water. The undine was long and wispy, like strands of seaweed tangled together in the shape of a greenish man.

"Following the path of the Celestial Order, are you, Mezmer?" Zingaro bubbled skeptically, his large unblinking eyes fixed on her. "Your uncle, rest his soul, filled your head with stories of the glorious Abatonian knights of old, hoping that you'd be the one to help free our people. What would he think to know you took up with Sop and his scoundrels instead?"

"*Scoundrels* is too strong a word," Sop said. "We're more your garden-variety thieves. Still, better robbing villages than chained to the empire's work gangs."

Zingaro shook his tendriled head slowly. "Why should I believe you'd really want to help His Immortal Lordship? Mezmer, who forsook her poor uncle. Mezmer, who left her people in Catchfools when they needed her most. You've only ever done what's helped you."

Mezmer cast her eyes down.

"That's not true!" Pinocchio said. "Mezmer's not like that at all. She's a noble knight!"

Zingaro turned his enormous, lamplike eyes to Pinocchio. "And who are you, young master?"

Those eyes sent a little shiver through him, but he forced himself to meet the undine's gaze. "I'm Pinocchio. My father is the former high alchemist Geppetto Gazza. And he's being held prisoner in the doge's Fortezza, along with Prester John. Mezmer has pledged an oath to help me rescue him as well as Prester John."

"Geppetto G-Gazza!" Cinnabar gasped. "The t-traitor? You've brought his son into our house? If the guards find out, we'll be arrested! You idiots!"

"Don't worry," Sop said, with a dismissive wave of his paw. "The guards won't find out. We weren't stupid enough to let ourselves be followed."

A bell attached to the ceiling jingled. Cinnabar looked at the bell and then glowered at Sop.

"What was that?" Sop asked.

"The front door!" Cinnabar snapped. "The door upstairs to the street. Someone just came in."

"Were you expecting company?" Sop asked innocently.

"No, we weren't expecting company! No one from Catchfools would be out at night. It's the guards! They must have seen you in the canal!"

They all stared at the door. Pinocchio held his breath, listening, but the house was silent. He drew his sword. Sop did the same, and Mezmer raised her spear. Cinnabar ran over to a cabinet and began rummaging through it.

"Cinnabar, didn't you lock the door?" Zingaro asked.

"I locked it! Obviously whoever it is broke it open." The djinni turned around, holding a small handheld crossbow.

"Cinnabar!" Zingaro expelled a jet of bubbles. "You can't attack imperial guards!"

"It's not for the guards," the djinni said, fumbling to pull back the string and load a barbed bolt. "I plan to use it on these idiots and tell the guards they broke in to rob us. I won't be implicated with—"

"You wouldn't," Sop said.

"I would! Unless you get out of here."

"Quick!" Mezmer said, flashing Cinnabar a reproachful scowl. "Back into the canal."

Pinocchio followed them out into the hallway when he remembered, "Maestro!"

Mezmer and Sop kept going, but Pinocchio ran back into the room. "Where's Maestro?"

"GO!" Cinnabar spat.

Maestro's muffled voice came from the cabinet. "I'm not going into that canal."

"And I'm not going to leave you behind, you cowardly cricket!" Pinocchio said, opening the cabinet.

"Idiot boy, I'm warning you!" Cinnabar aimed the crossbow pistol at him. "Do as you're told!"

"As I'm *told*?" Pinocchio scowled. Who did Cinnabar think he was? He wasn't some automa who had to follow orders. He was a human boy now. But he pushed aside his anger, digging around the cabinet for Maestro.

The small crossbow trembled in Cinnabar's outstretched hands. "You have to leave before—" The djinni's words broke off. "Oh, no!"

Pinocchio reared around and saw the handle turning. They were here! Pinocchio hesitated half a moment before an idea struck him.

It was a positively insane idea. But it might just be the perfect thing. If he and his friends were planning to sneak into the Fortezza to rescue his father, then what better way than disguised as imperial soldiers? And here was at least one soldier on their very doorstep. He only hoped it wasn't a whole squadron.

Pinocchio flattened himself behind the door as it began to open. Cinnabar was practically frothing from his fanged mouth as he raised the crossbow pistol.

Don't! Pinocchio mouthed at the djinni. *Trust me.*

Pinocchio drew a deep breath. From behind the slowly opening door, the tip of a sword emerged.

Pinocchio grabbed the door handle and pulled it so hard, the person on the other side came tumbling in. The cloaked figure made a deft roll, coming back to his feet and charging Pinocchio. They clashed blades before Pinocchio made a swift circle with his sword, catching the attacker's cross guard and sending the weapon clattering to the floor. Pinocchio leaped at the attacker, knocking him to the floor, his sword aimed at his face.

Not *his* face, Pinocchio realized in surprise. *Her* face. And she definitely wasn't an imperial guard.

The girl had a long curtain of blue hair—the color of a perfect midday sky—but the angry eyes boring into him were a darker blue, a midnight blue, and they glowed like luminous gemstones. Didn't sylphs have blue . . . ?

She kicked him in the stomach so hard he flew against the wall.

Mezmer and Sop raced back into the room ready for battle, but at the sight of the girl, they lowered their weapons.

"Who is she?" Mezmer asked.

"No idea," Cinnabar said, coming forward with his crossbow pistol raised.

The girl stood lightly and straightened her cape. Slumped against the wall, Pinocchio tried to suck in a breath but found that the best he could manage was an embarrassing little gulp. Whoever this girl was, she sure knew how to kick.

Maestro sprang from the cabinet and landed on the girl's forearm. "Your Highness!" he squeaked. "Princess Lazuli. You're alive!"

"Princess?" Mezmer asked. "Princess of what?"

"Of Abaton, of course!" the cricket said. "She's Prester John's daughter."

Mezmer's and Sop's mouths fell open.

Cinnabar dropped to one knee and bowed his head. "Your Highness!"

Lazuli looked around the room, her eyes narrowed. "Where's my father? I thought . . . I was certain he was here."

"He's not, Your Highness," Maestro said. "And I . . . I thought Captain Toro killed you."

"I'm not that easy to kill," she said, still looking around as if she half expected to find Prester John hiding under a table.

"But I saw you get shot," Maestro said. "How did you survive, Your Highness?"

"Fortunately for me, Captain Toro's musket ball hit this." She pulled a necklace up from the collar of her shirt. On the end was a glass orb, about the size of an apple. A chunk was missing, and the rest of the glass was cracked in a spiderweb network.

"Your Hunter's Glass, my princess," Maestro said sympathetically. "It's broken."

"Better it than me," Lazuli said.

She gave Pinocchio a look. It was definitely a scowl. He had disarmed her, after all, and nearly stabbed her in the face. Not his best introduction, especially to a princess. He wondered if all princesses in Abaton were this lovely. He realized he was staring at her rather stupidly and tried to undo the expression by giving her a scowl back. She looked away, unimpressed.

"After I escaped Siena, I thought the powers of the Hunter's Glass were destroyed," Lazuli said to Maestro. "Until I reached Venice. After I lost you and Master Geppetto, I decided to come here, to see if I could find any of my father's undines still in the lagoon. I was hoping if any had survived the attack, they might have discovered where Father was. But I found none of his undines, and when I reached the city, the Hunter's Glass began glowing. It seemed to be working again, and it led me here. I was sure my father was being held in this house!"

"You thought His Immortal Lordship was being held in Catchfools?" Cinnabar said. "Forgive me, Your Highness, but this is the last place the doge would hold Prester John. Your father was held in the Fortezza until just a few days ago—"

"Where is he now?" Lazuli demanded.

"Gone," Cinnabar said, splaying his clawed hands.

"What!" Lazuli and Pinocchio shouted at the same instant. They scowled at each other.

Pinocchio rounded on Zingaro. "You didn't mention they were gone!"

"I was just about to explain before Princess Lazuli arrived," Zingaro said from behind the curtain.

Lazuli blinked at the silvery curtain, as if just noticing the undine.

"Your Highness," Zingaro said, "it is a great honor to meet you. A great honor indeed to have Abatonian royalty in our home. Allow me to introduce myself. I am Zingaro, and this is my partner, Cinnabar."

He gestured with a webbed hand to the djinni, who gave Lazuli another bow. "We serve in the workshops of the alchemists in charge of the imperial armories," Zingaro continued. "In this position, we are privy to occasional news from the Fortezza, news we overhear from our masters."

"We heard when your father was taken captive by the doge," Cinnabar said. "How the lead chains the doge was using to hold His Immortal Lordship were weakening him. He's been dying, Your Highness."

Lazuli gritted her teeth and looked away, but not before Pinocchio saw the tears spring to her eyes. He'd never been around any princesses before, but he could tell from the way everyone was acting that royalty was supposed to be treated differently from others, with a certain dignity, not gaping at them when they were on the verge of tears.

"I'm . . . I'm sorry, Your Highness," Cinnabar said, gaze lowered. "But this has to account for why His Immortal Lordship has done it."

"Done what?" Lazuli asked.

Zingaro gave a burst of bubbles. "Three days ago, the doge departed Venice with his imperial fleet. A dozen onyx-class flying warships."

"But why?" Mezmer asked.

"Can't you see?" Cinnabar said. "His Immortal Lordship was left with no choice. The lead chains. He wouldn't have survived otherwise. He's . . . being forced to bring the doge . . . to Abaton."

Maestro burst into a flurry of bewildered chirps. "Abaton! But . . . but that would mean . . . !"

"Are you saying my father is allowing the doge to invade Abaton?" Lazuli said, anger flashing in her luminous eyes. "This simply cannot be. He would die first! He would never—"

"I'm afraid he is, Your Highness," Zingaro said.

"But what about my father?" Pinocchio interrupted. "Is he still in the Fortezza?"

"Your father is the only Venetian in centuries to have visited Abaton," Zingaro said. "The doge naturally would have brought Master Geppetto with him."

Lazuli spun around to Pinocchio, blinking hard as if coming out of a daze. "You! You're the missing automa."

Cinnabar began a forced laugh as if trying to play along with the princess's joke. "The young master's no automa, Your Highness. He's Geppetto Gazza's son. Look at him. He's plainly human."

"You're Pinocchio, aren't you?" Lazuli asked. "The automa my father sent to Master Geppetto."

Cinnabar gave a few more dry laughs, but then saw Princess Lazuli's serious expression, and his yellow jaw dropped.

Pinocchio felt as if a cold and crushing slab of silence had fallen on the room. No one said a word.

He took a breath. "Yes. I am."

18.

The Flying Carpet

Lazuli instantly regretted that she had revealed the boy's secret. She could see the panic in his eyes as they flickered from Cinnabar to Zingaro. She had just been so shocked that this was who—what—he was. With his mop of sandy hair and his funny pointy nose, he looked nothing like an automa. He looked real.

Sop started cackling, clapping a hand across his belly as his whole body jiggled. "I wish you could see the look on your face, Cinnabar," he said, wiping a finger under his eye patch.

"You knew!" Cinnabar snarled.

"Of course we knew," Mezmer said coolly.

Cinnabar slithered around Pinocchio, staring at him with fiery yellow eyes. "So this . . . this is nothing but an automa contraption?"

Lazuli could see that Cinnabar had an unmistakable hatred for Pinocchio.

Pinocchio reared up, nearly eye to eye with Cinnabar. "I'm no contraption!"

Cinnabar jerked back before circling around Pinocchio, scrutinizing his face. "Where are its seams?" He touched a finger to the back of Pinocchio's neck. "Look! There's a mark here in the shape of a keyhole! Where his fealty lock was."

Pinocchio spun around and batted Cinnabar's hand away before clapping a hand over the back of his neck.

The djinni snarled a mouthful of fangs. "Don't touch me again, puppet."

Pinocchio put a hand to his sword. Lightning fast, Cinnabar raised the crossbow pistol.

"All right! All right!" Mezmer said, stepping between them. "There's no need for all that."

"Agreed," Lazuli snapped. "Put down your weapons."

Cinnabar looked at her contritely and then lowered the crossbow. "Forgive me, Your Highness."

Lazuli ignored him, her gaze fixed on Pinocchio. "What's happened to this automa?"

Pinocchio frowned at her. She could see the hurt and anger in his eyes. He clearly didn't want to be called an automa.

Mezmer put her arm warmly around Pinocchio's shoulder. "Dear Pinocchio is flesh and blood now, Princess. He's not an automa. He's one of us."

Cinnabar gave a skeptical snort.

"It's true," Sop said, nudging Pinocchio in the ribs. "This ol' scratching post of mine sleeps. He breathes. He eats—"

"A lot!" Mezmer added.

Sop gave a disgusted look. "He even—"

Lazuli held up her hands to stop him right there. "Are you telling me . . . he's human? He's now a complete living human boy?"

They looked at each other and then at Pinocchio to let him answer.

He shrugged. "I'm not an automa anymore."

Lazuli couldn't hold her princess poise any longer. She sputtered, "Master Geppetto told me . . . well, that you were changing. I knew Father had put some charm on you. But this . . . this is not what I expected at all! You seem so . . . so . . ."

"Alive?" Pinocchio said. "I *am* alive."

"Ridiculous," Cinnabar sniffed.

Pinocchio was searching Lazuli's face, obviously desperate to see if she also found it ridiculous. Something about his expression stirred a memory.

When she had been younger, she had been allowed to play with the children of the noble families who visited the Moonlit Court, leading them in games of hide-and-seek in the palace gardens or pretending to be the Celestial Knights of old. But then, after her mother died, her father began to expect her to act differently around their guests. No more silliness. No more cavorting about the flower beds with the other children. She was the daughter of His Immortal Lordship, the protector and king of Abaton. She was to act like a proper princess.

She remembered when a distant cousin she hadn't seen in many years had visited from Mist Cities. Her cousin had asked if they could go chase pixies around the trifle-tree orchards, and Lazuli had said she didn't play childish games anymore. Her cousin had given her a look—not unlike the one Pinocchio was fixing her with now—that seemed to want to know if she was a friend or not.

Though it had wounded Lazuli deeply to see her cousin's face change as she realized Lazuli was not her playmate but the princess of Abaton, Lazuli had known she had to obey her father's wishes. He was Prester John, and she would not let him down. Not then, and not now.

She turned from Pinocchio to the undine. "Zingaro, I need to go after my father."

"Your Highness," the undine replied, sinking a little lower in the water. "We are but slaves of the empire. We have no means of leaving Venice. Even if we did, how would you get past the Deep One, who guards the waters off Abaton? The doge has your father to help him pass the sea monster. But you . . ."

Zingaro looked lost as to how to finish this sentence politely, but Lazuli knew what he would have said if she hadn't been Prester John's daughter. She had nothing. She was just a princess, to be protected and treated with royal respect, not someone to be counted on for a daring rescue mission. Her father would have thought the same thing, had he been here.

"I'm sorry, Your Highness," Zingaro added. "But this is impossible."

"It isn't impossible for her," Pinocchio said.

Lazuli turned to the boy, surprised by the determined look on his face.

"Oh, no," Sop murmured. "Don't get him started on his *impossible* speech again."

Lazuli appraised Pinocchio. "You know how I can rescue my father?"

"No," Pinocchio said. "But I'll help you find a way. My father needs me as well. I'll do anything to help him. I have to! And I want to save your father too. I wouldn't be alive if it weren't for Prester John. Geppetto wouldn't want me as his son if your father hadn't changed me."

How curious that the boy felt grateful to her father. That didn't seem like something an automa would think. And his reason for wanting to help Geppetto . . . This wasn't automa loyalty. This was something else entirely. She had seen it in Geppetto's face when he spoke of Pinocchio. She could see it in Pinocchio's expression now. They genuinely loved each other. It was as simple as that.

A spear of hurt ran through Lazuli. All her life, she had obeyed her father, played the part of the good princess, but for what? Did he love her as Geppetto loved Pinocchio? She wanted that more than anything.

"Yes," Lazuli said, giving a brisk nod. "Our fathers need us."

The smallest smile broke on Pinocchio's face.

Lazuli forced her eyes away from his. "There has to be a way. Maybe we could steal a boat."

"Your Highness," Cinnabar said. "No boat would be swift enough to catch up to flying imperial warships."

"We'll steal a warship, then," Pinocchio said.

"Why don't you just tame a Flying Lion and ride on its back?" Cinnabar said.

"Would that work?" Pinocchio asked.

Cinnabar rolled his eyes. "Don't be absurd."

"What about a flying carpet?" Zingaro said.

Excitement rose in Lazuli. Now, *this* seemed a possibility. Sylph travelers used such carpets back in Abaton, although her father had never allowed her to fly on one.

"Zingaro, you know well enough that all the ones in the empire have been destroyed," Cinnabar said. "To keep the sylph slaves from escaping."

"But Princess Lazuli could make one," Zingaro said, waving a webbed hand.

Lazuli had no idea how, but maybe the others could show her.

"No!" Maestro chirped. "No! No! No! She'd have to . . . No, she can't. As her subject and representative of the Moonlit Court, I have to insist. Not the princess!"

"Why couldn't I?" she demanded.

"Well . . . do you know how they're made, Your Highness?" Cinnabar asked, tapping his yellow fingers together uneasily.

"No," Lazuli replied.

"It requires weaving a sylph's hair into the fabric," Cinnabar said. "Sylphs here in the empire are required by law to keep their hair long. If a sylph slave is found to have cut their hair, it's assumed they have done so to try to make a carpet in order to escape. They risk arrest or worse."

"I'm not a sylph slave."

"Of course you aren't, Your Highness," Cinnabar said. "What I mean is . . . you'd have to cut off all your hair. It wouldn't be proper for the daughter of His Immortal Lordship of Abaton to—"

Lazuli drew her sword. She had gone halfway across the Venetian Empire and back trying to rescue her father. She had faced Flying Lions and mad airmen. She wasn't going to let something like an unseemly haircut stand in her way now.

She swiftly cut a handful of the long blue locks from the side of her head. There was a collective gasp. Cinnabar looked like he might start spitting lava.

"Your Highness!" Maestro hopped back and forth from one of Pinocchio's shoulders to the other in a complete panic.

Lazuli dropped the tangle to the floor and collected another handful of hair from the other side of her head, raising her sword. "I'm not as vain as you might think. As Pinocchio said, I'll do whatever is necessary to rescue our fathers."

She sliced through the hair, leaving behind a jagged patch.

The only one not staring at her in horror was Pinocchio. He was grinning—a wide, approving grin.

The next morning, after Cinnabar and Zingaro had departed for their masters' workshops, Pinocchio continued work with the others on the flying carpet. They wove Lazuli's long strands into a tattered rug they'd taken from the upstairs hall. Mezmer told the princess that the three of them were quite capable of finishing the carpet, but Lazuli insisted on helping.

"The sooner we finish," she said, sending the needle and thin strand of her hair back and forth through the carpet, "the sooner we can leave."

"As you wish, Your Highness," Mezmer said.

Pinocchio thought that Mezmer was acting strangely, not her usual relaxed self at all. While Sop wasn't doting on the princess quite as much as Mezmer, he was obviously keeping his sarcasm to a minimum. And Maestro was constantly watching Lazuli, constantly offering to play her another song.

"Which one would you like to hear, Your Highness?"

Lazuli gave a polite smile. "Any of them will be fine, Maestro."

"How about the Mist Cities Sonata?"

"That would be lovely," Lazuli said, trying to concentrate on the weaving.

"Or if you'd prefer, I could play—"

Pinocchio dropped his needle. "Just play any song!"

Maestro gave him a withering look. "No need to be grumpy. I just thought Princess Lazuli would enjoy some music as she worked. I thought you enjoyed my music too." Maestro turned away from him and started his sonata.

"I do," Pinocchio murmured. Glancing up from his work, he thought Lazuli gave him a slight smirk, but an instant later she had her polite princess expression back on, as she continued sewing.

Pinocchio couldn't figure this princess out. It was as if she had two sides. One side was the royal daughter of Prester John, who commanded absolute respect from her subjects with that haughty jut of her chin. But there was another side that Pinocchio glimpsed too. A flicker of annoyance when Cinnabar groveled and bowed. A flash of something fierce when she spoke of her father. And when she ran her fingers through her spiky new haircut—which looked an even brighter blue now that it was short—she seemed concerned.

He wondered if all girls were this complicated.

"Mezmer," Lazuli asked, clearing her throat, "how long have you and Sop been . . . well . . . ?"

"Been bandits?" Sop asked.

Mezmer cut her eyes at him.

"I was going to say, been free of your bondage," Lazuli replied.

"We escaped from our work gang here in Venice many years ago, Your Highness," Mezmer said. "I couldn't stomach serving a corrupt empire. A knight only serves a just ruler and a just society."

Lazuli raised an eyebrow. "A knight, are you?"

Sop chuckled. "Mez fancies herself a true Abatonian defender, a knight of the Celestial Brigade."

Mezmer lowered her snout. Pinocchio had never seen her act so shy.

"I had no idea I was being joined by a noble knight," Lazuli said, without the slightest trace of mockery. "I'm honored to have your service, Lady Mezmer."

Mezmer was practically glowing. She leaped to her feet. "My spear is pledged to you, Your Highness."

"I thank you," Lazuli said.

Sop and Pinocchio exchanged a look. The cat rolled his one eye.

"Princess Lazuli," Mezmer said, fumbling for the words. "When . . . well, *if* we are able to save His Immortal Lordship and reach Abaton, do you think . . . that I might be permitted to join the Celestial Brigade?"

Lazuli frowned. "I'm sorry to inform you, Lady Mezmer, that the Celestial Brigade no longer exists. It was disbanded centuries ago."

"Oh," Mezmer said, sagging noticeably. She slumped back down and picked up her needle. "What happened to it?"

"Abaton has been a peaceful island for ages," Lazuli said. "There's no war, no bandits—"

Sop gave a cough, like he was getting a hair ball.

"No threat that has needed the Celestial Brigade's defend-ing," Lazuli continued. "I suppose my father felt the brigade was no longer necessary."

Mezmer sewed in silence. Lazuli looked sadly from Sop to Pinocchio.

The cat shrugged. "At least you can say I was wrong, Mez. I always thought your uncle made those stories up, but you were right."

When Mezmer didn't reply, Pinocchio felt a pang in his chest. Mezmer was hiding it well enough, but he knew how upset she must be to have her dream dashed.

"I suppose," Lazuli began, "Abaton is indeed in danger again. If ever there were a need for a knight of the Celestial Brigade, I would say it is now. As the princess of Abaton and the daughter of His Immortal Lordship, I declare that you, Lady Mezmer, are the first in the renewed order of the Celestial Brigade. May your spear and your courage bring peace and safety again to Abaton's shores."

Mezmer looked up, a fierce and determined expression on her fox face.

"Thank you, my princess!" She began sewing as fast as her needle could fly.

When Cinnabar and Zingaro returned that evening, they found the flying carpet finished. Cinnabar closely inspected their work, tracing his claws over every inch of the fabric. The carpet was relatively large—at least ten feet by twelve feet—and while it was grungy and so worn that its pattern was long faded, bright blue strands now sparkled throughout its surface.

"Sloppy knot work here," the djinni declared. "I told you that the automa would make a mess of it."

Pinocchio opened his mouth to argue, but Lazuli cut him off. "I believe I worked on that portion," she said calmly. "Despite my palace tutors' best efforts, I'm afraid my sewing skills are hopeless. Will it fly?"

Cinnabar gritted his fangs and refused to look at Pinocchio, much less apologize. "Of course, Your Highness. You'll be able to leave us tonight."

"Won't you come?" Lazuli said. "I've noticed you wear no fealty collar."

"None of the djinn or gnomes of Venice have to wear collars," Cinnabar said. "We're imprisoned on an island, after all, Your Highness. No djinni would be mad enough to risk getting wet!"

Pinocchio wasn't sure why this was, but he supposed it might have something to do with Cinnabar being a fire elemental. Whatever the reason, he wasn't sorry to leave the djinni behind.

"But this is your chance for freedom, old friend," Mezmer said. "This is your chance to help rescue His Immortal Lordship and save Abaton."

Cinnabar shifted uncomfortably.

"Scared of a little water?" Sop teased.

"It might just be a little water to you!" Cinnabar snarled. "But if I fell off that carpet, it would be like you falling in a sea of fire. Princess Lazuli, I beg that you understand."

She nodded, and Cinnabar gave a sigh of relief.

"Besides, the more we have aboard, the slower we'll travel," Lazuli said. "But the real problem is that carpets like these only go as fast as the breeze. How fast do you think the doge's fleet is traveling, Zingaro?"

"Faster than that, I'm afraid." He stroked the seaweedlike tendrils coming off his chin. "A flying carpet alone won't be swift enough to catch up with the doge's fleet. But . . . yes, there might be a way." Zingaro gestured to Cinnabar. "What about one of the projectiles your master designed? The new propulsion device for the Fortezza's missiles?"

"What is this device?" Lazuli asked.

"It looks like a simple stone pot with a narrow mouth," Zingaro explained. "But if a highly combustible substance, such as powdered salamander, is burned inside, it forces a jet of hot air out the mouth. Creates a sort of rocket."

"Call me crazy," Sop said, "but I'm not sure anything combustible is the best thing to have around a carpet. Especially a carpet that's holding us up."

"It would need to be secured to the back," Cinnabar said.

"That way the carpet would be safe from the flames. But that's not the problem. The amount of powdered salamander you'd need for a voyage this long would be too heavy, Your Highness. It won't work."

Zingaro gave Cinnabar an urgent look. "Unless you were willing to go with them, Cinnabar. If you produced the flame, there would be no need for powdered salamander."

Cinnabar began shaking his head violently. "No! I thought . . . but we agreed . . . I know djinn who have died from falling in water!"

"You won't fall," Sop said. He extended his feline claws to snag Cinnabar's shirt. "I'll hold on to you. I promise."

"It's no good discussing this," Cinnabar said firmly. "We don't even have this projectile. It's locked away in my master's workshop. So you see? It's impossible."

Pinocchio opened his mouth, but Cinnabar jabbed a claw at him. "Don't even start on how nothing's impossible, puppet."

"We could break into your master's workshop," Sop suggested.

Cinnabar spluttered, "You mean . . . steal it? Do you know what would happen to me if I were caught?"

Mezmer waved a hand around at the others. "We're all taking risks, Cinnabar. We need your help if we're to rescue His Immortal Lordship."

Pinocchio didn't want the djinni to come. Cinnabar would never see him as more than just a "puppet" to be tormented. But if it meant the difference between reaching his father in time or not, he could put up with the obnoxious djinni.

"Don't be afraid—" he began.

"Don't you call me a coward, you charading contraption!" Cinnabar's yellow eyes blazed. "How dare you taunt me? What would your kind know about courage? I would give up my very life to save His Immortal Lordship and to protect Princess Lazuli!"

Lazuli raised an eyebrow. "Then you'll come?"

Cinnabar's mouth opened and closed before he managed, "Of course, Your Highness."

19.

Into the Jaws of the Lion

Cinnabar tried to use the excuse that there was no way to reach his master's workshop at night, but Mezmer had the solution: her chameleon cloak. There was still the obstacle of the gates on all the Catchfools bridges being locked, but Sop had the answer here. Being a thief had its advantages. He volunteered to go along, picking the necessary locks and keeping an extra eye out for trouble.

Pinocchio almost wished he could have joined them. To see the majestic city of Venice by night, especially sneaking along its canals and bridges under the cover of chameleon cloaks, sounded thrilling. But that would have meant accompanying Cinnabar. And that sounded about as thrilling as picking out those little crusty brown things that kept mysteriously showing up in his nose—another of the strange aspects of being human.

So Pinocchio had to wait while Cinnabar and Sop set off on their mission to steal the propulsion canister. At first, he and the others were all so preoccupied with final preparations—packing food, attaching the frame that Zingaro had built from stiff strips of naiad scales onto the carpet to support the canister, getting everything up to the rooftop for departure—that worrying about whether Cinnabar and Sop would get caught was pushed aside.

But once everything was completed and they gathered to wait on the rooftop terrace, with the night getting later and later, apprehension began to creep over the group. Mezmer sharpened her spear, casting glances to the street below every few moments. Maestro flittered anxiously from one side of the terrace to the other.

Pinocchio peered down at Zingaro, who was swimming in the canal. When the undine gave a quizzical look up from the surface, eager for news of Cinnabar's return, Pinocchio just shook his head.

Lazuli was lost in thought, pacing circles around the hovering carpet.

"You think they ran into trouble?" Pinocchio asked.

"What?" Lazuli looked up abruptly. "Oh, Sop and Cinnabar? No, I'm sure they're fine. At least I hope so."

"What were you thinking about, then?" he asked. He glanced at the carpet. "Worried if this flaming, rocket-propelled carpet will work?" He had his doubts.

"I'm sure the canister and Zingaro's naiad-scale frame will be perfect. It's just . . ."

"What?"

"It's the Deep One."

Pinocchio frowned. "The sea monster that guards Abaton? What about it?"

"If we don't reach the doge's fleet before they get past it, our voyage will be blocked . . . or worse."

"It wouldn't eat us!" Pinocchio said. "I mean, you're Prester John's daughter; you're the princess of Abaton. Surely it would let you—"

Lazuli shook her head darkly. "Only my father commands the Deep One."

"Then," Pinocchio said, struggling to stay hopeful, "we'll just have to catch up to the doge's fleet before they reach the Deep One."

"Exactly," Lazuli said. "Which is why we need to leave as soon as possible."

Pinocchio began pacing now around the carpet. "What's keeping Sop and Cinnabar?"

Mezmer bolted upright. "I see them!"

Pinocchio exhaled. "Finally." He looked over the edge to report their return to Zingaro.

As soon as the djinni and the cat reached the terrace, Lazuli asked, "Were you successful?"

"If you call nearly getting caught half a dozen times successful, Your Highness," Cinnabar said, holding up the stone canister and casting an exasperated scowl at Sop.

"Get the canister mounted," Mezmer said, taking charge. "I haven't seen any airmen patrolling for hours, so let's leave while we have empty skies."

While Cinnabar attached the canister to the back of the frame, Lazuli stepped lightly onto the hovering carpet and took her place at the front. When Pinocchio, Mezmer, and Sop followed her, the fabric rippled, and they fumbled awkwardly— like crossing a too-soft bed—until they found seats between the food and supplies secured to the frame. Cinnabar climbed aboard last, looking anxious and throwing his arms tightly around the stone canister as if his life depended on it. Possibly it did.

Lazuli waved a hand and summoned a breeze. The carpet lifted. Taking hold of the tassels at the front corners, Lazuli steered them off the roof and down toward the canal, where Zingaro was watching from the watery gloom.

"Princess Lazuli," Zingaro called. "The blessings of your people, both here and in Abaton, go with you. Might I ask, Your Highness, if you are successful . . . if you rescue His Immortal Lordship . . . ?"

Lazuli nodded. "Yes, I know. We'll find a way to bring you all to Abaton. It's time our people are freed. I promise you this, Zingaro."

A fountain of bubbles surfaced. "Thank you, Your Highness. Good luck, Cinnabar. I'm sorry not to join you in freedom."

"I'm not free yet," Cinnabar said, clinging to the canister.

"And Cinnabar, wait until you're away from the city before lighting the projectile," Zingaro said. "We don't want to risk any airmen seeing the flame until you're well away."

Cinnabar nodded.

With a final wave of good-bye, Lazuli pulled the tassels again, steering the carpet up from the canal, above the buildings of Catchfools, and higher up past the palazzos and glowing lights of Venice. Pinocchio cast one last look back at the city as they headed out over the foggy lagoon.

"Keep us above the mist," Mezmer suggested to Lazuli. "There are islands ahead, and we don't want to run into a tree or a ship mast."

Lazuli pulled back on the tassels to gain altitude. The carpet jostled and dipped sporadically as they rose above the layer of thick mist hugging the surface of the water. Cinnabar gave a queasy groan.

"You all right back there?" Sop called over his shoulder.

The djinni didn't answer. His eyes were squeezed shut.

Pinocchio spied the Fortezza Ducale hovering high above, dark and quiet against the night sky. No patrols. Just a little farther and they'd be away from the menacing fortress. Ahead in the mist, the tops of trees poked up, revealing scattered islands separating the Venetian lagoon from the open sea.

Pinocchio gave a sigh of relief. "We've made it."

From the top of a tree ahead, a pair of wings opened, silhouetted in the dark. For a second Pinocchio thought it might be a bird, but then Mezmer cried, "Airman!"

Lazuli banked the carpet as a musket boomed. From the treetops, more wings opened.

"Correction," Mezmer said. "Air*men*."

As their carpet shot over the treetops, Sop said, "Actually, it's worse. Those others aren't airmen."

Pinocchio spied four dark forms taking flight. The first was an airman. But the other three were . . .

"Flying Lions!" he shouted. "And coming in fast."

He drew his sword. Mezmer and Sop wheeled around, then crouched on the bobbing carpet with their weapons ready.

"How fast?" Lazuli asked.

The mechanical lions roared, beating their powerful wings as they closed the gap at a dizzying speed. Mezmer had that manic glint in her orange eyes at the prospect of battle. But Pinocchio couldn't see how they could take on three Flying Lions and an airman.

"Steady, darlings," Mezmer said. "Let them get closer."

"Closer! Uh, why?" Sop asked, adjusting his grip on his sword.

As the lions swooped in, Mezmer shouted, "Down into the mist, Your Highness!"

"But we'll be blind!" Lazuli said.

The blur of steely jaws and massive claws was nearly upon them. Mezmer, Sop, and Pinocchio lunged all at once, their weapons clinking against the armored monsters.

"Down!" Mezmer cried.

Lazuli dropped into the mist, coming so close to the water that a fine spray rose up beneath the carpet. Cinnabar moaned. Pinocchio glimpsed one Lion that dove too fast and splashed into the water. Through the mist, trees came suddenly into view. Lazuli tilted the carpet sideways to squeeze between the trunks. Pinocchio and the others had to cling to the edge to keep from spilling out.

"We're going to crash if we stay down here," Lazuli said. "I'm taking us back up."

"Wait!" Mezmer ordered. "Cinnabar, get ready to ignite that canister."

Pinocchio wasn't sure the djinni heard. He wasn't even sure he was still conscious. Pinocchio grabbed Cinnabar by the shoulder. "Can you light it?"

The djinni managed to open his eyes, but he didn't reply, his face fixed with fear.

More trees appeared from the gloom, and Lazuli inclined the carpet sharply. They rose out of the blanket of fog and right into the surprised airmen. Flopping on the carpet, one airman fumbled to bring his musket around. With only a split second to react, Pinocchio slashed at the fabric of his wings, and Mezmer and Sop heaved him over the side, where he disappeared with a splash.

"Where are those last two Lions?" Mezmer called.

Sop pointed. "Closing in behind us."

"Cinnabar, light that rocket!" Mezmer ordered.

The djinni didn't move. He had his arms wrapped around the canister and was staring at the dark streaks diving toward them.

Lazuli brought a swifter wind up beneath the carpet, but Pinocchio could see they weren't going nearly fast enough. The lions would reach them any second.

"Cinnabar!" he shouted. "What are you doing?"

"Just a moment," Cinnabar muttered.

Pinocchio felt his heart thundering.

The pair of Flying Lions was almost on them when Cinnabar cried, "Hold on!"

A blast of white-hot flame erupted from the mouth of the canister, engulfing the roaring Lions. The carpet shot forward so fast, Pinocchio smacked against Cinnabar. The Lions' wings burned away in cinders, and the mechanical beasts crashed into the lagoon.

"You did it!" Pinocchio shouted at the djinni.

"Get off me," Cinnabar growled, giving him a shove.

In that moment, Pinocchio didn't care about obnoxious old Cinnabar. He threw his arms around Mezmer's and Sop's shoulders and gave a wild whoop to the wind.

They laughed along with him, while Lazuli cast back a smile. They were finally on their way, rocketing over the top of the misty island and out into the clear moonlight sparkling on the sea.

20.

The Sea Monster

Lazuli was exhausted. The journey to reach the Indian Ocean had taken four days. If it hadn't been for Cinnabar and the canister, she never could have kept the carpet flying that long. But now, with only crystal-blue water in every direction, the ocean wind was doing most of the work, and she was able to let others take turns steering.

Although the long days in scorching tropical sun had done little to her own pale skin—except raise a few blue freckles on her nose—the journey had burnished Pinocchio's skin golden tan. He retreated from the sun as best he could beneath his chameleon cloak, twisting at the band of jasmine vines on his wrist, mostly lost in thought.

The fur on Mezmer's and Sop's faces was plastered back by the ferocious, salty wind. Lazuli was surprised that Cinnabar kept his hood pulled low over his face. Djinn generally didn't mind the baking sun. Maybe it was an excuse to cover his eyes against the boundless watery danger below. Lazuli was certain she'd heard Cinnabar uttering prayers, or possibly curses, from time to time.

The concern over whether they'd catch up with the doge's fleet in time was ever present in Lazuli's mind.

"Abaton is southeast of Arabia," she said to the others. "We've been going in that direction since we left land. But this ocean is vast. We could have flown past the fleet and might not know."

"Should you try the Hunter's Glass?" Pinocchio asked.

She took the cracked orb out, skeptical that it would help. She held it in her hand a moment before a faint light flickered. Then it pulsed bright, the glow filling the entire orb, not pointing in any single direction.

"It's clearly broken," she said, before tucking it away.

"Don't worry, Your Highness," Mezmer said. "The doge's fleet is huge. Sop might only have one eye, but it's keen. Even if we're off course, he'll spot them."

Sop gave her an assuring nod before adjusting his eye patch and scanning the distant horizon.

Maestro began playing a song to try to relax their pent-up nervousness. Pinocchio peeked out from beneath his chameleon cloak after a few moments. "What's that you're playing, Maestro?"

"'The Old Man and the Leviathan,'" the cricket replied, without interrupting the droning melody playing on his wings.

"I like it." Pinocchio rolled over onto his back.

"My father taught it to me, but told me never to play it at the Moonlit Court. I suppose it wasn't one of His Immortal Lordship's favorites."

"What's it about?" Lazuli asked, wondering why her father didn't like the song.

"A young sailor who gets swallowed by the Deep One. In the song, the sailor lives in the belly of the sea monster until he is an old man. One day, the Deep One belches him out. The old man comes ashore only to discover that the world is much changed and unfriendly, and the old man longs to be back in the sea monster."

"You really know how to cheer us up, Master Cricket," Sop said.

Maestro brought his wings to an abrupt stop. "Maybe a different song?"

Pinocchio chuckled. "Maybe so. Play one of my favorites. How about 'Orpheus'?"

As Maestro began, Pinocchio turned to Lazuli. "Did you see the Deep One when you and your father came to Venice?"

Lazuli tried not to frown as she remembered how the seas all around had churned violently, how she had shivered at the unbearably loud groan coming up from the watery depths, and how her father had stood on the bow and called for the Deep One to go back down, to let them pass, before the seas grew calm again. But she had no desire to frighten them all with this memory.

"No," she replied. "Thankfully not."

Pinocchio returned to twisting the jasmine vines around his wrist. Lazuli could tell from the way he always touched it that the bracelet was important to him.

"Did Master Geppetto give that to you?"

Pinocchio raised his eyebrows. "Oh, this? No. My friend Wiq gave it to me." He sighed. "We were imprisoned together in Al Mi'raj's theater. Wiq helped me escape. I had to . . . leave him behind."

She heard how his voice caught on the final words. "You miss him?" she asked.

Pinocchio nodded.

"Do you manage to make friends everywhere you go?" she asked.

Pinocchio saw her smirk and returned it. "Clearly not everywhere I go," he said with a nod back to Cinnabar. "What about you? You must have friends you miss back in Abaton."

Lazuli set her jaw. "It's not that simple. My father . . . he expects me to . . . represent the Moonlit Court properly."

"What's that mean? He doesn't let you have friends?"

Lazuli wasn't sure how to explain this to Pinocchio. How could he understand what it was like to have her responsibilities?

He seemed to sense her hesitation. "Doesn't he want you to be happy?"

"Of course he does," she said. Between the wind and Maestro's song, she thought the others couldn't hear her, but she lowered her voice to be sure. "It's not the same as it is with you and Master Geppetto. My father loves me as he loves all his Abatonian subjects, but . . . I'm not sure he really loves me as his daughter."

She frowned as Pinocchio gave her a sad look. She didn't need his sympathy. A princess didn't need her subjects' pity. But then, Pinocchio wasn't her subject. If he was, she certainly wouldn't be discussing this with him. This was the sort of thing only friends discussed. It had been so long since she'd had anyone like a friend to talk to.

"I remember Geppetto saying," Pinocchio began quietly, "that it must be difficult for your father to see so many of his children die, because your father is immortal and his children aren't. I'm sure that's why he acts that way. But he has to love you. Parents always love their children."

Lazuli wanted to believe that.

"It doesn't seem fair, though!" Pinocchio whispered sharply. "Why should your father let his children grow old and die when he gets to live forever? That doesn't seem like what a parent should do."

"Father protects Abaton," she said. "Being the ruler is a heavy responsibility. I wouldn't want that. What good is living forever if you're stuck in the palace all the time? I'd rather have some adventures. I'd rather live an exciting life and be free. Wouldn't you?"

She had never admitted this to anyone before. It felt good to say it out loud, even if it was a hopeless dream.

"I'm just glad to be alive," Pinocchio said.

She smiled, suddenly aware of what it must be like for him to be so newly human. "I forget," she said. "That you were an automa."

Pinocchio shifted uncomfortably. "I'm glad. I don't like being seen as the boy who was once an automa."

"And I don't like being seen only as the daughter of Prester John, princess of Abaton," she whispered. "You know, you're the only one who doesn't call me Your Highness. You're the only one who treats me . . . normally."

"Is that all right?"

"Of course it is."

Pinocchio seemed pleased. But an instant later a puzzled look came to his face. "But what I don't understand about your father . . . If he really loves Abaton, why would he allow the doge to invade it? It seems like he'd rather sacrifice himself first."

"He would," Lazuli said. "And I've been wondering the same thing. I don't believe my father is going to allow the doge's fleet to reach Abaton."

"Then why has he come all this way?" Pinocchio asked.

"I'm not sure," Lazuli said. "My father is up to something,

but I can't figure out what it is. Whatever he's planning, I can't see how it's going to work. He needs our help. And I plan to show my father I'm capable of doing more than just being a proper princess of the Moonlit Court."

Sop gave a sudden hiss, and Lazuli sat up.

"What is it?" Pinocchio asked.

Sop pointed straight ahead to a range of voluminous clouds. At first that was all Lazuli saw, but then, as she looked closer, she spied a dark haze—like a distant swarm of insects—floating among the white wisps.

Maestro sprang onto Pinocchio's shoulder. "My eyes aren't as good. What do you see?"

"I'm not sure."

"Could it be the doge's fleet?" Lazuli asked.

"No, I don't see any ships," Sop said. "It's something . . . smaller. I'll take us in closer."

As Sop raced the carpet onward, the dark shapes began to take form. None of them were big enough to be a warship, but they weren't small either.

They passed a piece of wood hovering in the air, and then another and another. . . . Lazuli eyed it all with growing bewilderment. Soon the sky around their carpet was filled with broken timbers and splintered wooden beams, all floating in the wind.

"What is it?" Lazuli asked.

"I . . . I think it's wreckage," Mezmer said.

"But from what?" she asked.

Pinocchio gave a gasp. Ahead, clinging to several of the timbers in the middle of the debris field, were about a dozen men. What were they doing up here? But as they grew nearer, Lazuli spotted the red cloaks they wore and the golden lions emblazoned on their chests.

"They're imperial soldiers," Mezmer said, her snout hanging open with disbelief.

"But where's the doge's fleet?" Lazuli asked.

"This *is* the fleet, Your Highness!" Mezmer said. "It's all that's left."

Lazuli's heart was racing.

"But what happened?" Pinocchio said, his voice growing panicked. "Where are the others? Where's my father?"

A musket shot sounded. Sop banked the carpet sharply, and Lazuli spun around. A group of airmen was closing in fast behind them.

"Where did they come from?" Mezmer said, getting protectively behind Lazuli.

"Hiding in the debris," Cinnabar snarled, loading a bolt into his crossbow. "Sop, bring us around!"

"No!" Lazuli barked. Attacking these airmen seemed unnecessarily cruel, especially given that they were stranded up here above all this ocean. They were enemies, but they were still people. "Fly faster, Sop. They won't be able to catch us."

Another shot boomed, whizzing close but missing. Cinnabar growled, but when Lazuli cut her eyes at him, he said nothing.

Pinocchio was on his stomach, watching the pursuing airmen. "Is that Captain Toro?"

Lazuli spun around. One of the airmen was ahead of the others, his wings beating mercilessly. "I think you're right!"

"You know that airman, Your Highness?" Mezmer asked.

"He's the one who shot me."

Cinnabar snarled again, shaking his handheld crossbow pleadingly. "Then we must make him pay, Your Highness!"

"That is not the Abatonian way," Lazuli said, unable to stop herself from giving the djinni a revolted look. "Keep going, Sop."

Captain Toro fought hard to catch up, but matching the speed of the rocketing carpet was hopeless. Soon Sop maneuvered them out of the debris field. Everyone was dazed with shock, but none more so than Lazuli.

"So what—what happened to the fleet?" Maestro stammered, trembling at the edge of Pinocchio's collar.

"What else?" Sop said. "They were devoured." Even the sarcastic cat couldn't hide the tremor in his voice.

"But the Deep One wouldn't have attacked Prester John," Pinocchio said in disbelief.

Unless . . . Lazuli felt her insides sink. "I should have realized."

"Realized what?" Pinocchio asked.

"What my father was doing." Her mind was spinning. "I knew he would never allow the doge to invade Abaton, but . . . I never imagined . . ."

"What do you mean?" Mezmer asked.

"My father tricked the doge into believing he'd lead him to Abaton," Lazuli said. "Made him believe he would exchange Abaton for his life. But really, it was a trap! My father didn't command the Deep One to go back. He allowed himself . . . to be devoured, along with all of the doge's fleet."

"But that would mean . . ." Pinocchio said with breathless terror. "My father!"

Lazuli's heart ached at the despair in Pinocchio's voice. If only her father had known she was coming, if only he could have believed she was capable of saving him!

Pinocchio grabbed her by the arm. "Try the Hunter's Glass!" he shouted. "I have to know."

"You will not speak to Princess Lazuli that way!" Cinnabar snapped.

"It's all right, Cinnabar," Lazuli said. She looked pleadingly at Pinocchio. "It's broken. You know it's broken."

"When you try to search for *your* father," Pinocchio argued. "But what if you used it to search for Geppetto?"

She shook her head. "Broken is broken, no matter who I search for."

"Just try it! Please!"

Lazuli pulled out the cracked glass orb. "Do you remember any object Master Geppetto would have on him?"

Pinocchio squeezed his eyes shut. "He wore a pin on his shirt. A jeweled rose that belonged to his wife."

She remembered seeing it. She handed the Hunter's Glass to him, saying, "Visualize that pin."

Everyone was quiet as Pinocchio pinched the Hunter's Glass between his thumb and index finger. The glass orb began crackling with light. For a moment Lazuli thought it would do as before, and glow all over. But instead, a single point of light appeared on the Hunter's Glass.

"Is it working?" Pinocchio gasped. "It's pointing to Father!"

Lazuli watched, at first with awe that the Hunter's Glass did seem to be working, and then with sad resignation as she saw the point of light stop near the bottom of the orb. It wasn't pointing into the sky, but down toward the ocean ahead. She took the glass back, stowing it once more beneath her shirt, not wanting to see the awful truth.

"Then . . . they were swallowed," Maestro said, in the tiniest chirp.

Pinocchio sank back on the carpet, covering his face. Mezmer put her arm around him and pressed her soft snout soothingly against his cheek. "I'm so sorry, my darling boy. I'm so sorry."

The others were quiet until at last Cinnabar spoke up. "But what are *we* going to do?"

"Go back to Venice?" Sop said.

"Never!" the djinni spat.

"What other choice do we have?" Sop asked. "The closest land is probably Mughal India. If we—"

"We should keep going," Pinocchio murmured.

"To where?" Lazuli asked.

He looked up, his eyes rimmed red but filled with something fiery and determined. "To Abaton."

"More contraption nonsense," Cinnabar scoffed.

Pinocchio ignored the djinni, his eyes fixed on Lazuli. "We might have failed to save our fathers, but I won't fail the ones we left behind." His fingers twisted at the bracelet, Wiq's bracelet.

He turned to Cinnabar. "What about Zingaro? What about all the others who are still enslaved by the empire? Someone has to free them. We need to reach Abaton and return with help. And Abaton needs you, Lazuli! We have to get you home to your people."

Lazuli felt something cold and terrifying run through her.

"Said like a noble knight, darling," Mezmer said, raising her snout with chivalrous approval at Pinocchio.

"But what about the Deep One?" Sop asked. "It's out there somewhere. How can we get past it when the doge's fleet couldn't?"

"Captain Toro and those airmen back there escaped," Pinocchio said. "Our carpet is small compared to the doge's fleet. It's possible we could maneuver around the Deep One. We just might get past."

"Your Highness," Cinnabar said, spreading his hands with exasperation. "This seems highly unlikely."

What Pinocchio was proposing seemed downright suicidal, but as Lazuli gazed at him, she knew it was their only hope.

"Maybe so, Cinnabar," Lazuli said. "But it's not impossible. Let's go."

They continued southeast, toward Abaton. The sun set, and glittering stars spread across the evening sky. Sop scanned the ocean for any signs of the Deep One. He caught Pinocchio's eye at one point and gave him a sympathetic nod. Pinocchio forced a weak smile, but couldn't stop the despair crushing down on him.

His father was gone. He would never come back.

They all fell into an apprehensive silence, unable to talk about what had happened, unwilling to voice their fears of what was to come, until finally Lazuli called to Sop. "You keep looking behind us," she said. "What do you see?"

"I think we have a straggler."

Pinocchio peered hard into the darkening distance. Something was flying behind them. It might have been a bird, except that since leaving the wreckage of the doge's fleet, they hadn't seen any seabirds. Pinocchio knew who it was, who it had to be.

"Captain Toro," he said.

"He really doesn't know when to quit," Sop said.

They flew deeper into the night, passing occasional fields of hovering debris where the remains of the doge's fleet had scattered on the winds. The moon rose, large and luminous, as Pinocchio took his shift steering the carpet. The others lay on the carpet sleeping, except for Cinnabar, who snored with his head resting on the top of the flaming canister.

Pinocchio was nearly nodding off himself when he felt something strange. At first he thought it was a vibration, but then he realized it was a sound. A deep sound. Something so low that it was more felt than heard.

"What is that?" Mezmer mumbled, waking in an instant.

Pinocchio searched the ocean. The surface was a shimmering field of moonlit sparks. But the sound—that unsettling groan—was getting louder and louder, until everyone was awake and frantically peering over the sides of the carpet.

"Look!" Lazuli said.

Ahead, the moonlight reflected on the ocean vanished, as if a dark stain were spreading out. It was hard to see, but Pinocchio watched while doing his best to keep steering the carpet.

The ocean seemed to bulge like a volcanic dome was rising to the surface. And then it was as if a crater formed atop the volcano's peak, opening into a massive watery cavern that could have swallowed an island. Many islands. Many large islands. The groan echoed so deep and primordial and terrifying, it seemed to rumble through Pinocchio's bones. His hands felt weak on the tassels as he watched an incomprehensible amount of water rush down into the gaping hole.

No, not a hole. That was no mere hole. It was a mouth. How could something have a mouth that large?

Pinocchio looked back to see if one of the others wanted to take over steering. Lazuli appeared frozen. Sop's feline pupil had grown into a huge black orb brimming with terror. Mezmer clung to the edge of the carpet, her ears flat against her head. Cinnabar hugged the canister with his face buried in his elbow.

Clearly, none of the others wanted to take over. It was up to him to get them past.

A vast cavern of darkness split the ocean's surface. Crashing water, like a thousand thundering waterfalls, filled the air with mist. The groan became an earsplitting roar.

Pinocchio tried to hum to steady his nerves. He tightened his grip on the tassels, ready to maneuver around the monster as it rose for them. He couldn't help but think of his father and what he must have felt as the Deep One attacked the doge's ship.

That monster had devoured his father.

He realized he was humming the song Maestro had played about the sailor who had been swallowed by the Deep One and lived inside the creature. Was it possible that his father had survived, like the man in the song? Could his father be alive down in the Deep One?

The monster rose.

"Faster, Cinnabar!" Mezmer yowled.

Pinocchio began to bank the carpet as the yawning void of the monster's mouth reached higher. How was he going to get past those mountainous teeth? He forced his concentration from his father to evading that colossal maw. He had to get past. The Deep One had to let them pass.

At that moment, the Deep One seemed to slow, and to Pinocchio's surprise, it started sinking back down.

"What's it doing?" he heard Sop shout over the roar. "Did it miss us?"

"I don't think so," a quivering Maestro said from Pinocchio's collar.

The Deep One's head descended toward the ocean, sending up towering waves in all directions.

"It's not swallowing us!" Maestro squeaked excitedly. "It's letting us go!"

"But why?" Pinocchio shouted.

"Princess Lazuli," Maestro answered. "It must be because Prester John's daughter is here."

"That—that can't be right—" Lazuli stammered. "Only Father commands the Deep One! Maybe he's still alive inside. Maybe he's commanding it to let us pass."

Pinocchio felt a jolt of something desperate and dangerous and utterly foolish rise up in him. If Lazuli believed her father might be alive inside the Deep One, then there might be hope that Geppetto was also. Pinocchio could imagine how the enormous creature had swallowed some of the doge's ships whole. They might have survived.

In that moment, he thought of Wiq and what his friend had said about trusting his instincts, about listening to that voice deep inside that told him the right thing to do. Listening now, Pinocchio knew he had but one final chance to rescue his father. And he'd have to be quick.

Pinocchio dropped the carpet into a dive. He had to get in that mouth before it closed. His father was down there. He needed him.

The others shouted as the carpet rocketed nearly straight down.

"What are you doing?" Lazuli screamed.

"Saving them!" Pinocchio managed through gritted teeth.

The Deep One was submerging. The surface of the water rolled and boiled as the jaws began to close. With only seconds left, Pinocchio pitched forward, nearly flat against the carpet. Lazuli clung to his arm, screaming, but not nearly as loud as the earsplitting yowling of Sop.

The teeth were crashing together. Pinocchio wasn't sure they'd get through. Any moment, he expected to be crushed. He pushed the carpet faster, aiming for the gap between those massive fangs.

The Deep One's mouth began to disappear beneath the swirling froth of the water.

"It's too late!" Lazuli screamed.

"No it's not! Everyone, hold your breath." Pinocchio knew this was their only chance. If he didn't take it, his father would be lost to him forever.

He plunged the flying carpet straight into the sea, hitting the churning water with a dizzying impact that shot them down, arrowlike, through the gap in the teeth and into the black depths.

21.

The Darkness of the Deep One

The water slowed them almost immediately. Pinocchio felt himself thrown sideways, and pulled this way and that by the currents. He clung with one hand to a corner of the carpet. With his other, he held Lazuli. He could only hope that the others had their claws deep in the carpet.

The swirls and surges swept them in a disorienting, chaotic tumble. Pinocchio had no idea how long it lasted, only that his breath was being crushed out of him. If he had still been an automa, he wouldn't have worried about needing air. But now he fought to keep from inhaling water and drowning. For a few moments, he was certain he had blacked out.

Soon he became aware of the current dragging them, a wave thrusting them . . . but where? Out, down, up? He wasn't sure.

But then he broke the surface and was flung onto a slimy shore before the wave retreated.

He was certain that he was dead. There was utter darkness encompassing him. A blackness like Pinocchio had never imagined. A blackness as silent and hollow as Alberto's tomb. When he'd seen Geppetto's dead son, he'd had no idea what it meant to be dead. But now, this seemed to be it.

He lay flat on his back, panting for breath. Was he still breathing? If so, then he had to be alive. Someone started coughing beside him and then retching up a lungful of seawater. Whoever this was clearly wasn't dead either, although almost.

"Lazuli," he gasped. "Is that you?"

"No, it's"—another lungful of water was coughed up—"me," Sop said.

Pinocchio felt a weak grip take his arm. "I'm here," Lazuli whispered. The luminescence from her blue eyes was the only dim light in all this darkness. "But where is here?"

Before he could answer, his heart suddenly exploded in panic. "Maestro! Where's Maestro?"

His strength reignited with guilt and terror that the poor cricket had been drowned. Then something tickled his neck.

"*Now* you think of Maestro," a quiet, exhausted voice chirped. "Not *Maybe I shouldn't fly us headlong into the ocean without first making sure Maestro is safely inside a bottle or something.* No. It's only after you nearly drown me that you concern yourself with my well-being."

Pinocchio could only laugh, half sobbing with relief, as the cricket came down onto his arm. "I'm so sorry, Maestro!"

"You should be," he said. "You're lucky my wings weren't torn off. I'd never be able to play music again. What were you thinking? Why did you do that?"

But Pinocchio had no time to explain yet. "Where are the others?"

Lazuli's eyes cast dim light down the shore as she looked around.

Shore. Pinocchio pressed a hand to the ground. Parts were slippery and oozing. Beneath was a crusty surface. He hoped he was only touching algae-covered crustaceans. He pulled his hand back in disgust.

"And where are we?" Lazuli muttered.

"From an anatomical standpoint, I don't even want to hazard a guess," Maestro said. "But generally speaking, we're somewhere in the belly of the beast. Thanks to Pinocchio."

Their voices had a strange resonance. Not echoing, exactly, but definitely as if the sound was swirling around somewhere large and cavernous. It was oppressively warm. The air was thick with sour fumes. By any standards, being inside a sea monster was revolting.

But there was something fascinating about it as well. Despite his disgust, Pinocchio had to admit it was a bit amazing. They were alive inside the gut of the monster.

Sop gagged. He clearly didn't agree.

"You all right?" Pinocchio asked.

Sop was silent for a few seconds and then said, "Scratching post, ol' pal, if I weren't so exhausted right now, I'd claw your face off."

"Glad to hear it," Pinocchio said.

Down the shore, something urgent was happening. Mezmer's voice seemed pitched with panic.

"What's the matter?" Lazuli called, the glow of her eyes searching for the fox.

"Cinnabar," Mezmer said. "Cinnabar! Can you hear me?"

Sop leaped to his feet and ran. Pinocchio felt frozen to his spot, as a horrible feeling of dread poured over him. Cinnabar! He'd completely forgotten about Cinnabar when he'd flown them into the ocean.

"He's alive," Mezmer said when they reached her. "But he's unconscious. Maybe . . . Cinnabar!" she cried, obviously trying to revive the djinni.

"His elemental heat has been doused," Lazuli said.

"What do we do?" Pinocchio asked, churning with guilt. He didn't much like Cinnabar, but he'd never wanted to harm him.

"Fire," Mezmer said. "We have to get him in a fire."

"How do we make a fire down here?" Lazuli asked.

A voice came from the dark, "You'll need wood."

They all froze. Pinocchio knew that voice. If he never heard it again, it would still be too soon. He drew his sword in a flash and aimed it at the airman.

"Captain Toro," he said. "How did you get here?"

Illuminated by Lazuli's eyes, Captain Toro had his hands raised, showing that he was unarmed. Maybe he had lost his musket. He certainly had lost his helmet. His hair lay in wet ribbons across his shadowy face, although even the dim light didn't mask his permanent scowl.

"Same as you."

"Let's ask that a different way," Sop said, brandishing his sword. "Why did you come down or in or . . . wherever we are here?"

"The same as you," he replied. "To rescue my master."

"You're insane," Sop said. "Of course, since Pinocchio is the one who flew us in here, he's equally insane. Why do I have to be surrounded by crazy humans?"

Captain Toro stared at Pinocchio. "So you are Geppetto

Gazza's automa? When I saw you fly past, I thought for a moment it was you, but then . . . you're not an automa anymore."

"No, I'm not," Pinocchio said, without lowering his sword.

"What do we do with him, Your Highness?" Sop said.

Lazuli came forward, and Captain Toro's surprised eyes grew even wider. "You! You're the blue fairy who . . . I . . ."

"Attempted to kill," Lazuli said. "I'm afraid so. Now you should leave, Captain Toro."

Captain Toro peered out into the darkness, worry wrinkling his face. "Where?"

"Anywhere but with us," Sop said.

"I can help you," Captain Toro said, looking pleadingly to Pinocchio.

"We don't need your help," he said.

"You do," Captain Toro said. "You need wood for the fire eater there. I've lost my musket, but look, I still have dry gunpowder." He touched a canister on his belt. "Do you have another way to start a fire?"

Pinocchio glanced around at the others. He knew they didn't. Coming close to Lazuli, he whispered, "We're not befriending him. We're just calling a temporary truce until we can figure things out. Besides, the most important thing now is to help Cinnabar."

"Pinocchio's right, Your Highness," Mezmer said.

Lazuli gave a reluctant nod.

Pinocchio sheathed his sword. "Come on, Captain. You can help Lazuli and me look for wood."

Mezmer rose. "Your Highness, if you're going, I should stay with you. I pledged my spear to protect you."

"I'll take care of the princess, Mez," Sop said. "I can see better than you in the dark."

"Thank you, Mezmer, but Sop's right," Lazuli said. "Watch over Cinnabar."

The fox nodded and knelt next to the unconscious djinni.

Captain Toro lowered his hands and began to follow. "I don't have a weapon. Do you think there's anything to be concerned about out there?"

"Besides a squadron of airmen and the doge of Venice?" Sop said. "But I guess you don't have to worry about them."

Captain Toro still peered around with concern.

"Afraid of the dark, Captain?" Lazuli said, leading the way.

"Of course not." But the airman stayed at the back.

Walking was not easy over this slimy, uneven terrain. Lazuli's eyes cast only so much light. Pinocchio slipped several times and kept banging his shins against barnacle-covered debris.

"Fairy," Captain Toro said. "Why do the others call you Your Highness?"

Maestro fluttered uneasily on Pinocchio's shoulder.

"I am Princess Lazuli of Abaton, daughter of His Immortal Lordship, Prester John."

"Are you now?" Captain Toro said. "How did you get—"

"Enough questions, airman," Sop said. "Keep looking for wood."

They came across boards, clearly the broken wreckage from ships the Deep One had devoured. But the wood was so waterlogged, it was hopeless for burning.

"We need to locate the fleet," Captain Toro said. "Any ships that survived should be floating, which will keep them dry. We can use wood from the bunks."

Pinocchio looked into the cavernous black above him. "How are we supposed to find floating ships?"

"You could fly up there, Captain Toro," Lazuli suggested.

The airman shook his head. "It's too dark. I wouldn't know what I was about to fly into."

"Like into the Deep One's lower intestines," Pinocchio said.

Sop made a noise like he was about to lose what remained in his own lower intestines. The poor cat really wasn't handling this very well.

"The crew would stabilize the ship to keep it from drifting," Captain Toro said. "We just need to find where they've dropped an anchor."

"Why didn't you say so?" Sop said. "We just passed one."

"Where?"

"Back here," Sop said, leading them back. "At least I thought it was back here. I almost tripped on—" He fell over.

Captain Toro ran toward him. Sop reached for the airman's hand for help up, but Captain Toro grabbed the anchor instead. "Fairy, bring your eyes closer."

The blue light of Lazuli's gaze illuminated a chain rising up in the dark.

"Hello!" Captain Toro called. "Anyone up there?"

Nothing answered, except for a faint scuttling in the dark. Toro grabbed the chain and tugged. The chain gave a few feet. "Help me pull," he said.

They all took hold of the chain and, hand over hand, grunting with the effort, hauled down the doge's ship until the hull reached Lazuli's luminous gaze. Pinocchio's heart raced with the hope that he was going to find Geppetto aboard.

"Hook the chain onto the spire of the anchor," Captain Toro grunted.

They managed to attach the chain so that the ship floated just above their heads. Captain Toro threw out his wings and with a single swoop flew onto the deck. Lazuli scampered up the chain effortlessly. Pinocchio and Sop managed to climb up, but not nearly as easily as the other two.

When Pinocchio was over the rail, Lazuli said, "It's abandoned."

Pinocchio frowned. "Where did they all go?"

Captain Toro emerged from below deck. "It's only been a few days. They had barrels of gunpowder, caskets of water, tons of food stores, but now everything's gone. Even the bunks are missing. Entire bunks. There's no way they could have carried all that. And why would they even leave the ship?"

"To search for a way out of the Deep One?" Pinocchio mused.

Captain Toro shook his head. "The doge might send out a patrol. But he'd never leave his ship."

"Unless they were in some sort of danger," Lazuli said.

"From what?" Maestro peeped.

The faintest scattering of movement sounded from out in the dark. Pinocchio gripped his sword tighter.

"What was that?"

"Someone looted the ship," Captain Toro suggested. "Maybe it's them?"

Lazuli leaned over the railing. The light from her eyes didn't reach far and certainly didn't illuminate anything lurking in the blackness that Pinocchio could see.

"What's down there, Sop?" she asked, a nervous edge to her voice.

"I can't tell," Sop said. "It's all black— No! Eyes. I see eyes!"

Captain Toro barked, "Give me a weapon."

"You should do a better job keeping up with your stuff, Captain," Sop said, giving Toro a shove. "Come on. Let's pry up some boards and get them back to Cinnabar."

"I said you could use the bunks," Toro said. "I won't have you tearing apart the doge's ship!"

"The bunks are gone," Pinocchio said. "We need wood."

Sop gave his sword a playful twirl. "If you want our protection, you'll help us out. You scratch my back or I'll scratch yours."

"Besides," Pinocchio added, "the doge abandoned the ship. It's not doing him a lot of good down here anyway. A few timbers are all we need."

Toro grumbled but helped them pry up a section of the decking.

As they climbed down from the ship and set off back to Cinnabar, Pinocchio thought he saw eyes blinking out at him. They were faint and disappeared quickly, but he grew certain he was not imagining them. "Whatever is out there," he whispered, "seems to be following us."

"I wish they'd quit skulking and show themselves," Sop said.

"Be careful what you wish for," Captain Toro said. "There's no telling what they are. Or what they eat. Anything that lives down here can't be too picky about its meals."

"I bet they'd have no qualms about eating crickets," Maestro whimpered.

"Cricket eaters are the least of my worries," Captain Toro said.

Pinocchio heard whispers of movement, something slipping easily across the soggy patches of algae. He picked up his pace. When they reached Mezmer crouching over Cinnabar, he said, "We're not alone."

"I know," Mezmer said. "Any idea what they are?"

"No," Lazuli answered. "But hopefully a good fire will keep them at bay."

They stacked the wood in a pyre and placed Cinnabar on top.

Captain Toro opened a sachet of gunpowder and poured a line around the boards. From his belt he removed a flint striker; then he looked at the others and said, "Ready?"

Mezmer nodded. "Light it."

Captain Toro snapped the flint striker, scattering sparks across the powder. With a startling brightness, the gunpowder ignited. Pinocchio had to cover his eyes, but by the time they adjusted, the boards had caught fire and Cinnabar was engulfed in smoke and dancing tongues of flame.

Pinocchio sighed. He was going to be one angry djinni when he woke.

A low groan echoed and the ground shuddered.

"What was that?" Maestro chirped.

Sop fanned his hands at the flames. "Hurry and wake up, you stupid djinni, before the Deep One gets indigestion!"

Faint flickers of movement appeared in the dark, accompanied by little shrieks of distress. Whatever was lurking out beyond the perimeter of the fire's light seemed upset.

Captain Toro chuckled. "That'll send them scurrying back to their holes." He cupped a hand to his mouth and shouted, "This is called fire, you beasties! We only mastered it millennia ago."

A dark clod splattered against Captain Toro's face.

Sop laughed. "I guess they've mastered flinging slime."

Captain Toro gave a disgusted groan as he scraped the tangled seaweed and muck from his face. "Give me your sword. I'll find the creepy that threw that!"

Already more clods were raining down on them. Pinocchio turned his back to the incoming missiles. "What are they doing? These don't even hurt."

"Annoying us into surrender?" Sop guessed. Dripping seaweed covered his arms as he tried to shield himself.

"They're putting out the fire!" Mezmer cried.

She was right. Hissing cakes of muck were already half covering Cinnabar. The fire was dying. Plumes of smoke filled the air.

"Protect him!" Lazuli shouted.

The back of Pinocchio's chameleon cloak was already so covered that he felt like a knight half dressed in a slimy suit of muck armor. But try as they might, the five of them couldn't shield Cinnabar from the filthy volley coming from all sides.

"How many of them are there?" Pinocchio said.

"I think we're about to find out," Captain Toro growled.

The fire sputtered out. In the light of the dying embers, shadowy figures closed in on all sides.

22.

Barnacle and Flame

Through the smoke, Pinocchio couldn't yet make out what the creatures looked like, but some carried crude spears. Mezmer directed her troop into positions surrounding Cinnabar, their scanty weapons outstretched. But they were completely surrounded and hopelessly outnumbered.

"Hold steady, darlings," Mezmer growled, her spear raised.

As the mob of creatures crept closer, one by one, dim green lights began to glow from their heads. What at first sounded like monstrous mutterings seemed to form words.

"What are they saying?" Pinocchio asked.

Captain Toro shook his head. "Gibberish. They're just beasts."

"No, I hear them too," Lazuli said. "It's sounds like they're saying, 'Mother.'"

At that moment, the nearest creatures came into view. They

weren't human, but they were humanoid in shape, and covered in barnacles, crustaceans, and seaweed. The green lights were shining from open shells atop their heads.

"Mother," they said. "Mother."

Sop shook his sword at them. "We're not your mommies, barnacle faces!"

"No fire," they murmured. "Mother hates fire. No fire."

Pinocchio noticed that the Deep One had become still again. "Mother must be—" he began, but his wrists were suddenly locked in a strong grasp. It wasn't by one of the creatures. It was Captain Toro.

The airman snatched the sword from Pinocchio's hand and charged toward the nearest of the creatures. Pinocchio could barely tell what happened next. The captain threw out his wings, scattering smoke and bits of muck. And then he had one of the barnacle creatures by the tangle of seaweed attached to the creature's head.

He held out his sword and shouted, "Get back, you savages! Get back or I'll kill him."

The little creature in his grasp squealed, wriggling to get free. The others of its kind broke into terrible cries, scurrying around in such a dark mass that Pinocchio knew there must be many more then he had imagined before.

"Back!" Captain Toro shouted.

They didn't flee. In fact, more of the lights appeared, shining unexpectedly bright in their faces. A mass of spears took aim at Captain Toro. "No! Free her! Let her go!" the creatures squeaked.

"I'll kill your companion if you don't get back," the captain warned.

Pinocchio rushed forward. "What are you doing, Toro?"

"Saving our hides," he snarled.

"You're scaring her."

"Who?" Captain Toro said.

"Her," Pinocchio said, gesturing to the creature in his grasp. "They've done us no harm."

"Are you insane, Pinocchio?" Sop called. "Have you not seen the horde of things surrounding us? Not to mention all the spears pointing at you."

"They attacked first," Captain Toro said.

The little creature in Captain Toro's grasp kicked helplessly. "We didn't harm you. Just protecting Mother. Mother doesn't like fire. Fire hurts Mother."

In the dim light, Pinocchio could see the little creature's blinking black eyes peering out from a gap in the barnacles encasing her face. There was a bright intelligence in her eyes— kindness, even.

"See," Pinocchio said. "They were just trying to put out the fire. If they had wanted to harm us, they would have. They have weapons. And sufficient numbers."

"Let Gragl go!" the creatures squealed at Captain Toro.

The Captain snarled at Pinocchio. "How can you trust these things? Just look at them. As soon as I let her go, they'll kill us."

"No we won't," Gragl said, wriggling in Toro's grasp.

Lazuli drew her sword and aimed it at Captain Toro. "Pinocchio's right. You heard her, Captain Toro. Let her go."

Mezmer came on the other side of Captain Toro and leveled her spear at him.

Captain Toro spat angrily at Mezmer and Lazuli. Then he lowered his sword and released the creature. When she scuttled off, others of her kind rushed forward to surround her.

Gragl flipped open a clamshell attached to her forehead. Inside was a little luminescent mussel. Not much light on its own. But combined with the hundreds of other glowing mussels on the foreheads of the rest of the barnacle people, the light was plenty.

Gragl glared up at Captain Toro. "Your sword could have done nothing to me anyway."

She tapped her knuckles against the side of her face and then against her shoulder. It gave the dry sound of stones crunching against stones, shells rubbing against shells.

Pinocchio grinned as he snatched his sword back from Captain Toro. These barnacle people had natural armor in addition to their built-in lanterns. Fascinating.

"So if your new friends are so harmless, what happened to everyone from the doge's ship?" Captain Toro growled. "The ship was looted. Everyone aboard is gone without a trace. See if your little clam-faced friends can explain what they did to them."

Captain Toro might have been a brute, but he did have a point. Pinocchio turned to the barnacle people. "Where's my father? Where is Prester John?"

The barnacle people broke into whispered mutterings.

Pinocchio exchanged a concerned look with the others before saying again, "We're looking for—"

Gragl looked up at Pinocchio with unmistakable amazement sparkling in her eyes. "Your father is His Immortal Lordship?" The other creatures fell into expectant silence.

Pinocchio realized their mistake, but before he could explain, Gragl added, "Sadly, His Lordship is no longer immortal. Your father is dying." She gulped miserably.

"Quiet, Gragl," another scolded. "You'll upset the boy."

"Actually, my father is—" Pinocchio began, but Lazuli cut him off.

"Your father is in need of our help, Pinocchio." She gave him a meaningful frown. "Right? You need to be with your father."

"Oh, of course I do," Pinocchio said. "Can you take us to him?"

The barnacle people whispered to one another.

"What's the problem?" Mezmer asked.

Gragl looked at Mezmer and Sop in turn before saying to Pinocchio, "My people fear that you will eat them."

Several of the nearest began scuttling back nervously.

"Eat them!" Sop said. "Trust me. That's about the last thing you have to fear from us."

"Why would you think that?" Pinocchio asked.

Gragl pointed to Cinnabar. "Were you not trying to cook your companion?"

"Oh, ha!" Pinocchio said, chuckling with the others as the barnacle people stared with dark, worried eyes. "No, we weren't cooking him."

"He's a djinni," Lazuli explained. "An elemental being of fire."

"Then what's he doing here?" Gragl asked.

"I'm sure he's going to be wondering the same thing when he wakes," Pinocchio said, not looking forward to explaining this to Cinnabar. "He needs help."

"He needs fire," Mezmer added from where she was removing the soggy mound off Cinnabar. "And soon, or he might die."

Gragl gave an anxious twitch. "Mother does not like fire."

"Who is this Mother anyway?" Sop said.

Some of the barnacle people looked up. Some looked down. Others simply peered around at the darkness. "We are inside her," Gragl said.

"What? Oh!" Sop said, his feline eye widening. "The sea monster is Mother."

A low growl ran through the barnacle people. Gragl snapped, "Mother is no monster. She takes care of us."

"She provides for us!" another chimed in, holding up a spear. Pinocchio now saw that there were several large fish stuck midway down the spear.

Pinocchio held up his hands. "Our mistake. But you must have fire. Don't you cook your fish before you eat it?"

A tongue emerged from Gragl's encrusted face. "Yuck! Burn a perfectly good fish before eating it? How disgusting!"

One of the barnacle people whispered to Gragl. She nodded her head. "Yes. You should come with us. Bring your friend. We might be able to help him."

Gragl and her people led them across the cavernous stomach-scape. Pinocchio couldn't believe how many of Gragl's kind there were. It was like being accompanied by an entire city of inhabitants. Little bobbing lights spread out around them by the thousands.

"Where are they taking us?" Captain Toro asked.

"To those cliffs, I suppose," Pinocchio said, pointing to the massive sheer wall coming into view.

"Those aren't cliffs, technically," Maestro said.

Sop made a distressed noise. "Stop. Just stop talking about it."

At the base of the cliff, Gragl led them single file up a series of stairs that were thankfully less slippery and algae-covered than the shore. Not all the barnacle people followed them. Some were ascending different paths. But most of Gragl's kind remained below. Pinocchio couldn't tell what they were doing. All he could see were little bobbing lights wandering this way and that. Maybe they were still scavenging or hunting for fish that had washed into the great stomach of the Deep One.

After an exhausting climb, they reached a cave set into the side of the cliff. Inside were the rough materials of a home. Beds made from bundles of dried sea grass and tattered sailcloth. Tables and benches fashioned from broken timbers.

"You live here?" Pinocchio asked.

Gragl nodded. "Along with my family." There were a few dozen others busily skinning fish, cracking shellfish, and chopping seaweed. Pinocchio was hungry, but he wasn't sure he was *that* hungry.

Mezmer came in last, Cinnabar hanging limply over her shoulder. She was panting, her tongue drooping from between her teeth. "You said you could help our friend, dears?" she grunted. "He needs fire."

"Bring him back this way." Gragl motioned to a tunnel at the back of the cave.

They reached another cave that was hot and thick with smoke. In the middle was a massive bowl, as big as a fountain, dancing with low blue flames and tended by a group of the barnacle people. Placed inside the bowl of fire were several large, closed clamshells. Bubbles hissed from the edges.

"What is this?" Lazuli asked. "I thought you didn't cook your food."

"This isn't for cooking," Gragl said. "For drinking."

Before Pinocchio could get an explanation about this, Mezmer said, "That fire! We can use it?"

"It truly won't harm your friend?" Gragl asked, stepping to one side so Mezmer could approach the bowl.

"Just the medicine he needs," Mezmer said. "Sop, darling, give me a hand."

The two took Cinnabar by the wrists and ankles, keeping clear of the flames, and laid the djinni in the fire.

"I see no wood in there," Mezmer said. "What are you burning?"

"Oil," Gragl replied.

"Mother provides," another of the barnacle people said.

Others muttered reverently, "Mother provides."

"How long will it take?" Gragl asked.

"Not sure," Mezmer replied, watching Cinnabar anxiously as the flames danced across him.

"Are you thirsty?" Gragl asked.

Several barnacle people were hooking a stick through a notch at the top of one of the shells and working together to pull it onto the floor. One of them prodded it open. Steam plumed out. Inside was a bucket half filled with water.

"This one is still hot, but we have others that are cooled." She shuffled over to a collection of containers and brought back a bucket.

"What is it?" Sop asked.

"Water," Gragl said. "Freshwater. It is bad to drink seawater, you know."

"Yes, but—" Lazuli began.

"Oh, I see!" Maestro chirped from Pinocchio's shoulder. "They distill the seawater into these buckets. The boiling removes the salt. Right?"

Gragl nodded, a small smile on her crusted face. "Yes. Freshwater." She offered Pinocchio the bucket. "Drink."

Pinocchio glanced at his companions. Their looks weren't exactly encouraging. He hesitantly lifted the bucket to his mouth. It was fishy, but the slight salty taste wasn't quite as concentrated as seawater. He forced a smile. "Uh, yes. Not . . . bad?"

Gragl gave an encouraging nod and passed the bucket to Lazuli. They all took turns drinking the rank water.

From the fire, Cinnabar gave a groan. Mezmer rushed over to

the bowl. Pinocchio could now tell that the bowl was also a massive shell. The Deep One sure swallowed some surprising things.

"Cinnabar, old friend, can you hear me?" Mezmer asked. "Are you all right, dear?"

The djinni slowly sat up on his elbows. He looked around with dim-eyed confusion, like a person waking from the heaviest sleep. "Where am I?" he mumbled.

"We'd better hold off on that for now," Sop said. "Your elemental fire went out. How do you feel?"

"Better," he whispered, lying back in the bed of flames and giving a little moan of contentment. Then he shot back up, his eyes wide. "Wait! Why did my fire go out? We're inside the Deep One, aren't we? We've been swallowed!"

Cinnabar jabbed his finger at Pinocchio in a way that made it obvious that if his finger had been something more pointy and lethal, he would be stabbing it into Pinocchio. "This is all your fault, you idiotic puppet! You flew us in here on purpose. You've trapped us in this . . . forsaken hell-world!"

"I don't think it's as bad as that," Pinocchio said. "It's quite fascinating down here, really."

Gragl blinked up at him adoringly.

"Fascinating? Fascinating?" the djinni sputtered with rage. Lying in a bed of flames only made him look more terrifying. "This is a place of no escape. This is a place of death!"

"It isn't a place of no escape," Gragl uttered in the tiniest whisper.

Cinnabar's eyebrows wrestled between fury and disbelief as her words sank in. "What is that nasty little creature, and what is it babbling about?"

Pinocchio scowled. Despite his guilt about nearly killing the djinni, he definitely wasn't glad to have his loathsome mouth back.

Lazuli knelt before Gragl. "Is there a way to leave?"

"There must be," she replied. "Prester John escaped."

"What?" Mezmer snapped. "His Immortal Lordship has already left?"

Pinocchio felt his stomach sink.

"No, he's here now," Gragl explained. "He's returned to Mother at last. What I meant was that he escaped before, long ago. Before he was king of Abaton." She paused and cowered at the confused faces surrounding her. "Did you not know? Had you not heard that this was Prester John's original home?"

"No," Mezmer said.

Even Lazuli looked surprised by this news.

Gragl gave a proud smile. "See? This is not a place of death. This is where Prester John won his immortal life."

"None of you die here?" Lazuli asked.

"We die," Gragl said, "like you die. Only Prester John has the gift of immortality. Mother gave him the Ancientmost Pearl." She sighed heavily and fixed Pinocchio with a teary-eyed gaze. "But now it is gone and your father is dying."

"Not if we can help it," Cinnabar growled. "Can you take us to His Immortal Lordship?"

Gragl gave an enthusiastic nod, which, given that her neck was covered in shells, looked more like she was wobbling forward and back.

"Is he nearby?" Pinocchio asked.

"Your father has gone with his attendant to his ancestral home," Gragl said.

Her words filled Pinocchio with such giddiness he almost

leaped in the air. "The attendant!" he said. "Did you say he's with someone? Was his name Geppetto?"

"Yes, I think that is right."

Maestro hopped from Pinocchio's head to his shoulder, and Lazuli flashed Pinocchio a smile. Geppetto was alive!

"How far away are they?" Pinocchio asked Gragl.

"Not far."

"A few hours? A few days?"

Gragl blinked, confused. "What are hours and days?"

Maestro said, "There's no sun down here. No way to measure time like we do."

"Oh," Pinocchio said. "Well, I guess we'll find out how far it is when we go."

While Cinnabar recovered, Pinocchio and Lazuli talked Gragl into letting them cook fish in a different fire, away from the fuming djinni, and the others gathered supplies for the journey.

Pinocchio was anxiously aware of Captain Toro squatting in the shadows at the mouth of the cave. Gragl's people eyed him nervously and avoided him as best they could. When the airman finally rose to his feet and approached Pinocchio, the barnacle people scattered back.

"Where are my men?" he asked.

"How should I know?" Pinocchio replied.

"Ask her," Captain Toro demanded, pointing at Gragl.

Why Captain Toro couldn't ask her himself irritated Pinocchio, but he had noticed that Gragl only seemed comfortable talking with him.

"Gragl," he said gently. "Prester John arrived here aboard a ship with others. Where are the others?"

"The ones who held him prisoner?" she said.

"Yes," Pinocchio replied.

"They were bad men. We helped free His Immortal Lordship from these bad men."

"What did you do to the doge?" Captain Toro roared. "What's happened to him?"

Gragl trembled behind Pinocchio. He gave Gragl an assuring pat, which wasn't particularly pleasant since he was patting the muck-covered seashells encrusting her shoulder.

Gragl said, "His soldiers have gone in search of the other dirt-born."

Pinocchio exchanged a perplexed look with Lazuli before asking Gragl, "Dirt-born?"

Gragl pointed a gnarled finger at Captain Toro. "Like him. And like you, son of his Immortal Lordship."

"You mean humans?" Captain Toro said. "There are humans down here?"

"The ones who have been swallowed by Mother. There have been others before your ship. Many others. They dwell in settlements. We trade with them. They leave my people alone if we share what Mother delivers to us."

Lazuli asked, "Are there Abatonians like us down here as well?"

"There have been some," Gragl said. "The dirt-born take them. We never see them again."

Lazuli scowled. "What happens to them?"

Gragl looked at Captain Toro. "Unlike His Immortal Lordship's son and his attendant, most dirt-born are savages. There is no telling what they do to them. They might keep them as slaves. Or do worse things."

Captain Toro turned angrily and began to head out from the cave.

"Where are you going?" Pinocchio called.

The captain growled back at him. "I have to find my lord the doge."

"You'll never find him in that darkness," Pinocchio said.

Captain Toro ground his teeth, looking like he might explode with anger. "If I only had some light . . ."

"Gragl," Lazuli said. "The lights in the shells on your head? Do you have one that you can give to Captain Toro?"

Pinocchio began to argue, but Lazuli held up a hand to silence him.

Gragl looked hesitantly from Captain Toro to Lazuli. "You want him to have one?"

"If you can spare it," Lazuli said.

Gragl opened the shell on her forehead and scooped out the little slimy glowing mussel. "We have many more. He can have this one." She held it out to the captain.

"It barely puts out any light," Captain Toro complained.

"Do you want it or not?" Lazuli asked.

Reluctantly Captain Toro took the mussel.

"You must keep it moist," Gragl said, "or the light will die."

Captain Toro rose and without a backward glance—much less a thank-you—headed out from the cave. He flung open his wings once he was outside and disappeared into the darkness.

Pinocchio gave Lazuli a bewildered look. "Why'd you help him? I thought you didn't like him."

"I don't," Lazuli said. "But it seemed the best way to get rid of him."

Gragl smiled and went off to retrieve another light.

23.

The Secret of the Ancientmost Pearl

ven when Cinnabar's elemental flame was restored, he seemed no happier about their situation. He raged about how this was all Pinocchio's fault, snarling and snapping all the way down the steep, crude stairs until they reached the soggy floor below. That shut him up. The djinni had to focus his attention on not falling into any of the black ponds or slipping on the precarious paths of seaweed and slime.

Marching off into the cavernous dark set their group on edge. While Pinocchio was fascinated by the enormity of this underworld, he couldn't help but feel a creepy tingling along his spine at the thought that a band of castaway dirt-born savages might be waiting to capture them. He held his sword at the ready.

A dozen or so of Gragl's barnacle people led the way. Pinocchio was glad for the light shining from the shells fixed to their heads, but it only made him more aware of the vast darkness surrounding them.

"What do you see ahead?" Maestro whispered from his shoulder.

"Nothing," Pinocchio said. "Absolutely nothing."

He soon gave up trying to spy any features or to figure out how long had they traveled. There was no way to measure time except by their footsteps, too innumerable to track. The journey felt like days. They paused on occasion to eat and drink and pushed on until they staggered with weariness.

Gragl assured Pinocchio and the others that her people would keep watch while they slept. If sleep was anything for the others like it was for Pinocchio, then it was a miserable sleep filled with dreams of black floods and mountainous, devouring teeth. Waking with no dawn was disconcerting, and they resumed their journey grumbling and sullen.

Later Gragl said, "We are nearing the dirt-born settlements. We must travel quietly and with no light so that we won't be found. We trade with them, so they will not harm my people. But if they found you . . ."

When the lights of the scattered settlements came into view, Pinocchio saw that they were built from pieces of wrecked ships and scavenged items. Each was like a small fortress, towering and walled and glowing from within with orange, oily light.

The landscape was irregular, rising and falling with strange mounds. Gragl navigated them along a twisty path through the shadowy features, past the settlements, until at last Pinocchio saw empty darkness ahead. He thought it odd that he was actually glad for the dark again.

Pinocchio whispered to Gragl, "Are these the only settlements?"

"No," Gragl replied. "Just the nearest to the mouth, and the only ones I have visited. I hear there are more, deeper in Mother. They say there are even dirt-born cities."

Pinocchio was trying to wrap his head around this when Sop hissed, "Someone is coming!"

Over to one side, from the last of the settlements they had yet to pass, bobbing lights approached. They weren't the dim green of the barnacle people's luminescent mussels, but yellow, flickering lights that looked like oil lanterns.

Gragl pulled Pinocchio's hand. "It is a band of dirt-born. There is no telling whether they are attacking another settlement or trading. These savages are friends one day and enemies the next."

Mezmer stepped closer to Lazuli, spear raised, ready to defend the princess as a good knight should. Lazuli, with her sword out, didn't seem to need much defending, but she clearly didn't have the heart to tell the chivalrous fox otherwise.

"What should we do?" Pinocchio asked.

Gragl pointed to the darkness ahead. "Hurry that way! Stay hidden. We will distract them."

Voices were growing nearer. Gragl rushed off with her people to intercept the dirt-born before they discovered Pinocchio and the others.

"Come on," Sop said. "I can see well enough."

Once they were on the far side of one of the mounds, they crouched together and waited. Pinocchio hated not being able to know what was happening to Gragl. He tried to listen, but the sounds were too faint.

"I'm going up on this mound to see what's going on," Pinocchio said.

"Gragl told us to stay hidden," Lazuli said.

"I will be," Pinocchio said, pulling the chameleon cloak around him.

He leaped to the top of the slimy mound on the seven-league boots and knelt down. He could see the cluster of green lights from the barnacle people as they spoke with the dirt-born. The dirt-born looked like warriors. They wore a strange assortment of armor cobbled from pieces of timber and bones and carried an array of crude weapons.

Maestro chirped quietly from his shoulder, "Gragl and her people don't look in danger. I think—"

A horn sounded, echoing across the stomachscape, followed by raucous cries and war whoops. Pinocchio turned toward the sound and saw another group of dirt-born sweeping out from behind mounds and charging the party talking to the barnacle people.

"What's going on?" Sop hissed up to Pinocchio.

Pinocchio went cold. The two groups were about to battle. He and his friends were trapped in between them. He jumped from the mound, nearly colliding with Mezmer. "Quick! They're coming our way."

Mezmer spun her spear. "Glorious battle!"

"No!" Pinocchio said, giving her a shove. "There are too many."

They ran, winding through the maze of mounds in a frantic race to escape the charging hordes. But in the dark, Pinocchio soon found he was separated from the others. Where were they?

He rounded a mound and spied Lazuli ahead. She had obviously also lost the others. The bloodthirsty shouts of dirt-born were coming from behind the next mound. They were about to get caught.

Just as a trio of warriors came around, Pinocchio leaped at Lazuli, knocking her to the ground. He threw his chameleon cloak over them.

"Be quiet!" he whispered.

The sound of heavy feet passed inches from them. Once they were gone, he pulled the cloak off and tugged Lazuli to her feet.

"Thanks," she said. "Where are the others?"

"Don't know," he said. "Keep going. And stay close!"

The screams and clamor of battle grew behind them. He and Lazuli ran until they found themselves away from the mounds, away from the lights of the settlements, and in a flatter portion of the stomachscape that sloped down into empty darkness.

Pinocchio looked back toward the now-distant sound of battle. He hoped the others hadn't gotten caught. A flickering yellow light came toward them. Pinocchio and Lazuli drew their swords in unison.

But it wasn't a dirt-born's lantern. It was Cinnabar's hand, encased in a thin flame. Mezmer and Sop stumbled after him, panting for breath.

"Princess Lazuli, forgive me!" Mezmer said. "I swore to protect you and—"

"It's all right," Lazuli said, brushing away her apologies. "What happened to Gragl?"

"No idea."

"We have to go back for her," Pinocchio said.

Cinnabar stood in his path. "Are you mad? We'll get chopped to pieces by those savages. She'll catch up to us."

But as they waited and the distant sound of battle finally went quiet, Gragl and her people never came.

"What are we going to do?" Maestro chirped.

"We have to wait for her," Pinocchio said.

"What if she doesn't come?" the cricket asked. "What if she's . . . well, you know."

Sop flicked his feline ears. "Dead? I doubt it. Those crusties are tough. But they do seem a bit jittery. Might have scattered in panic at the battle."

"Or headed back to the safety of their caves," Cinnabar said.

"She wouldn't leave us," Pinocchio said.

"Then where is she?"

Pinocchio looked into the darkness ahead. He had no answer. He was worried for Gragl, but he was also worried that they were now lost in the vast emptiness of the Deep One.

"We can't just stay here," Lazuli said. "We have to reach Father."

"How will we find him? We don't know where to go."

Lazuli pulled out the Hunter's Glass. "It showed us Master Geppetto before. Let's see if it works again."

They all huddled around Lazuli, peering at the glass ball illuminated by Cinnabar's hand. Lazuli closed her eyes. A moment later a single point of light formed, then wound its way around the surface of the glass until it stopped on one side.

Lazuli opened her eyes, and they all stared out into the darkness ahead.

"That way," Cinnabar said with a satisfied smile.

As they headed off, Lazuli didn't put away the Hunter's Glass, and a puzzled look formed on her face.

"What's the matter?" Pinocchio asked, walking beside her.

"Well, the glass seemed broken when I was trying to find my father. But it works when I search for Master Geppetto."

"Then try it for your father again," Pinocchio said.

The others stopped while Lazuli held the orb and closed her

eyes. The Hunter's Glass began flickering, before the entire globe swelled with light.

"It's not pointing anywhere," Sop said. "Broken?"

"But it can't be," Lazuli replied. "It just worked when I thought of Master Geppetto's jeweled rose pin."

"So you focus on an object and not the person, Your Highness?" Mezmer asked.

"That's how it works," Lazuli replied. "The Hunter's Glass locates objects, not people. Before Pinocchio changed, Master Geppetto was able to use it to locate him, because Pinocchio was an automa."

Pinocchio felt his face go hot. He didn't like thinking that he hadn't always been a person.

"But if I try to use it for Pinocchio now . . ." She closed her eyes. The Hunter's Glass remained dark. "See," she said, opening her eyes. "But if I visualize his boots . . ." She closed her eyes again.

Lights speckled across the surface of the Hunter's Glass before filling it completely with bright light.

"Oh!" she said. "I thought it would just point to him. But that was the same as . . ."

Something cold crept over Pinocchio. He didn't yet understand why, but he knew there was something strange at work here.

"Princess Lazuli," Maestro began tentatively. "Why did it get so bright when you thought of Pinocchio's boots?"

Lazuli's brow furrowed as she thought. "Maybe . . . because they're so close, because Pinocchio is right here."

"But it did the same thing when you visualized His Immortal Lordship, didn't it?" Cinnabar said edgily.

An electric tension seemed to pass through them all. Pinocchio felt dizzy with panic, although he couldn't say why.

"But I wasn't visualizing my father," Lazuli whispered.

Her eyes grew wide and glowed as bright as Pinocchio had ever seen them. She stared at him in disbelief.

"What were you visualizing when you were looking for your father?" Pinocchio asked.

Lazuli seemed to have to force herself to speak. "No . . . it can't be."

"What?" Pinocchio asked.

Lazuli hurriedly closed her eyes and murmured, "If I visualize Father's crown . . ." A single point of light traced its way from the top to the same side of the Hunter's Glass that had pointed to Geppetto.

Lazuli stared at it and then closed her eyes once more. This time the globe sparked all over before growing bright.

"What of your father's did you just visualize?" Mezmer asked.

Lazuli was trembling. "The Ancientmost Pearl," she whispered. "I have been searching for my father all along by visualizing the Ancientmost Pearl."

Cinnabar pointed at the glowing orb in Lazuli's hand. "But that would mean, Your Highness, that the Ancientmost Pearl is right here."

"And not with His Immortal Lordship," Maestro added.

"I know," Lazuli said.

"But where is it?" Pinocchio asked. Even as the words came out of his mouth, the realization dawned on him.

"It's inside me," he said.

Lazuli gave the slightest nod, as if she wished more than anything it weren't true.

"How can that be?" Mezmer gasped.

"When Father was captured by the doge," Lazuli said, "he hid the Ancientmost Pearl inside Pinocchio. To keep it safe. It's the Ancientmost Pearl that's brought Pinocchio to life."

Maestro rattled his wings wildly. "But I saw what was inside Pinocchio. It was only a pinecone!"

"Father must have transformed it with a glamour to look that way," Lazuli answered, "in case someone managed to open Pinocchio up."

"But he also put a charm on me so I would protect the Pearl," Pinocchio said. "Lazuli, does that mean your father didn't send me to Geppetto so I could be his son?"

Lazuli clearly knew the answer as well as Pinocchio, but she couldn't bring herself to admit this terrible truth.

Cinnabar, however, had no problem saying it. "His Immortal Lordship was only using you as a hiding place, puppet. He sent the Ancientmost Pearl with you, because Geppetto was the only human in the empire he could trust. And Prester John hasn't been dying because the doge shackled him in lead. He's been dying because he no longer has the Pearl of Immortality."

The words were like stabs in Pinocchio's heart.

"And now," Cinnabar continued, "we have to return the Pearl to His Immortal Lordship before it's too late."

"But what will happen to me?" Pinocchio asked.

Mezmer put a hand over her mouth. "Oh, my darling boy . . ."

"You'll return to the way you're supposed to be," Cinnabar snapped. "Back to being an automa."

"I . . . I don't want to be an automa again," he said. "I want to be alive. I want to be with my father."

Cinnabar showed a mouthful of fangs. "It doesn't matter what you want, you detestable pu—"

"SHUT UP!" Lazuli shrieked.

Cinnabar flinched. "But Your Highness—"

Lazuli struggled to compose herself, but her distress only seemed to mount as she put her trembling hands to her temples and looked around, wild-eyed. "Just . . . just be quiet, Cinnabar, until we figure this out!"

"There's nothing to figure out, Your Highness," Cinnabar said, crouching submissively. "We've nearly reached your father. We've brought the Ancientmost Pearl to him. We can save His Immortal Lordship and he can free us from the Deep One so we can return to Abaton. It's that simple."

"It's not that simple," Lazuli uttered. "Not for Pinocchio."

Pinocchio took a shuddering breath. "Yes, it is."

He knew what he had to do. He hated it more than anything. Hated it with a white-hot fury. He wished with every trembling molecule of his body that he didn't have to do this. But there was only one way now to save his father. There was only one way for them all to reach Abaton.

Pinocchio pointed into the darkness. "We came here to save them. They're that way. Let's go."

Pinocchio walked in stony silence. Mezmer looped her furry arm through his and walked by his side. Sop slumped along behind them, as melancholy as Pinocchio had ever seen the cat. In front, Lazuli walked beside Cinnabar, the djinni lighting their path with the handful of flame. Lazuli looked back from time to time at Pinocchio, casting her dimly lit, bleary eyes toward him and seeming to want to say something, but unable to find the words.

She didn't need to say anything. He understood.

Pinocchio was struck by a memory now, back when he was in Geppetto's wife's villa and Maestro was trying to explain about Geppetto's grief. The cricket had told him how all the living feel pain at the loss of what they love. *It can't be helped, Pinocchio,* Maestro had said. *It's part of life.* Pinocchio remembered how he had told Maestro that he was glad he wasn't alive.

Now he wasn't sure what he felt.

Being alive was full of such joy. But would it have been better if he'd never had to feel the heartbreak of leaving Wiq or the terror of battle in Al Mi'raj's theater or missing his father so desperately, even if it meant never having all the happy moments too? He couldn't say. Right now it just felt so unfair. So cruel that he had to give up living when he finally knew what it meant to be alive. And although they weren't saying it, Pinocchio knew that Maestro and Mezmer, Lazuli, and Sop were thinking the same thing.

Step by terrible step, they journeyed farther into the Deep One. Each step brought them inevitably closer to Prester John, closer to the dreadful moment when he would have to give back what rightfully belonged to the king of Abaton. Pinocchio tried not to think about it as they trudged on.

A distant light appeared that seemed higher than the marshy floor, as if it was hovering in the darkness.

"How do we know it's not another dirt-born settlement?" Sop asked.

"The Hunter's Glass shows my father up there," Lazuli said. "But we'll be cautious."

As they drew closer, Pinocchio could tell they weren't reaching cliffs like the barnacle people's homes or the crude fortresses of the dirt-born. Whatever lay ahead was towering up from the flatness.

"What is that, Sop?" Mezmer asked. "Your eye is the best."

"Bones," the cat said. "It looks like bones."

The others were reluctant to believe this—until they reached the structure. The bleached bones were enormous. The skeleton of a whale, or several whales, or possibly some other enormous leviathan of a creature that hadn't been too large for the Deep One to swallow whole, formed a tower, rising up to a massive skull crowning the top. Light flickered from within the hollow eye sockets far overhead.

Cinnabar cupped his hands around his mouth and shouted, "Prester John! Are you here?"

A silhouette appeared at one of the eyes. "Who is down there?" a voice called.

Pinocchio knew that voice! It felt like it had been ages, but he would recognize his father's voice anywhere, that gruff but rich, warm voice.

"Father!" he shouted.

All the fear and anguish that had filled up inside him drained away. He had finally found his father. Pinocchio's heart swelled with gladness that at least they would be reunited, even if it wasn't to last.

"Father!" he cried, running as fast as his legs would carry him. "Father, it's your son Pinocchio! I've found you, Father!"

He sprang halfway up the tower of bones on his seven-league boots—Father!—then climbed hand over hand, ascending with ferocious urgency—Father!—knowing the others must be following, but he couldn't wait for them, not when he was so close, not when he was nearly there. Father! He had to see him, had to know that he was truly all right.

When he reached the skull, Pinocchio rushed into the lofty domed interior. Geppetto stared at him, openmouthed. Even as Pinocchio flung his arms around him, his father looked down, disbelieving.

"No! Why have you come here?" Geppetto gasped.

"To save you," Pinocchio replied.

Geppetto's mouth trembled. His eyes searched Pinocchio's face with wonderment. Then he clasped Pinocchio by the arms and pulled him tight against his chest. "My boy. My boy. How I longed to see you again. But not here. Not in this place. But oh . . . look at you!" He let him go and stared. "You are . . . No, you're not . . . Are you . . . ?"

"I'm no longer an automa," Pinocchio said. He turned around and pointed to the back of his neck, where the keyhole mark was all that showed from his former self. Then he spun around and pulled back the collar of his shirt to show the smooth flesh of his chest. "I'm human like you now! I'm alive, Father."

"I can see," Geppetto said. But his smile faded as his gaze drifted over to the figure resting on the far side of the skull chamber.

Bundled in a heavy cloak and propped upon a makeshift bed of vertebrae and blankets, Prester John was an ashen husk of a man. He wore a delicate golden crown, but dark gray skin clung to the bones of his bald head. If it hadn't been for the brightness of his eyes, Pinocchio would have believed him dead.

As the others reached the top, one by one, Mezmer, Sop, and Cinnabar fell to their knees reverently. Last to appear was Lazuli. She ran to her father but stopped short a few paces, giving an awkward curtsy.

"Your Majesty," Lazuli breathed. "My . . . my lord."

Prester John wheezed a few moments before saying, "Who is that? Who is there?"

"It is me, Lazuli. Your daughter."

"Lazuli," he said. "Yes, you are my daughter. I thought you were dead. I thought I had lost you, child."

Geppetto was staring, amazed, at Lazuli. She gave him a

little smile and then slowly approached her father, taking his shriveled hand. "I'm here, my lord."

Pinocchio was happy for Lazuli, glad that, like him, she'd been reunited with her father. He smiled at his father, but Geppetto was looking back with worry.

Cinnabar stood suddenly. "Your Immortal Lordship, we have brought you the Ancientmost Pearl. You hid it from the doge in this automa. The Pearl has been safe and now we have delivered it to you."

Prester John winced. "Who are you, djinni?"

"Cinnabar, my lord. I am one of your subjects, freed now by your daughter from the vile humanlands of the Venetian Empire. My companions and I are here to return your powers and accompany you to Abaton."

"No," Prester John wheezed.

Cinnabar blinked. "But . . . my lord. I did not serve the empire willingly. I was enslaved, and now I serve you—"

"I do not wish to be served anymore," Prester John said. "Too long have I ruled. I have returned to the Mother. Here I will remain until my death."

Cinnabar looked too shocked to speak.

Lazuli clutched her father's hand. "What about Abaton, my lord?"

"Do not call me that, my child," he said. "I am your father. Although, I fear, I have not been a very good father. I realize that now. Once I gave up the powers of the Ancientmost Pearl, an unforeseen clarity found me. I realized . . ." He wheezed for breath. "Too long have I clung to the throne of Abaton, Lazuli. Too long have I tried to shape the world with its wonders. And for what? Look what sickness has been unleashed on the world of men by Abaton's magic. It is time for another to rule."

"But who?" Lazuli asked.

He patted her hand warmly. "You, child. My youngest child. My last child. You shall rule. Take the Ancientmost Pearl. Go home and be my successor."

Lazuli was shaking her head. She pulled back from him, her whole body trembling. "No. I don't want to rule."

"If not you, then who?" he said. "Be strong, my daughter. You have always been the best of my children. That you do not want to rule is what makes you the most fitting heir."

"Prester John, please!" Cinnabar said. "You are our Immortal Lordship. Princess Lazuli does not want to rule. She is young. Too young. We need you! Come back with us. Take the Pearl and lead us to Abaton."

When Prester John didn't reply, Cinnabar rounded on Pinocchio, pointing at him venomously. "You agreed you would return the Pearl to His Immortal Lordship. Give it to him!"

Pinocchio looked helplessly around at them. "I don't know how. I thought he would know—"

"You said you would save him!" Cinnabar shouted. "If His Immortal Lordship won't take it, then give it to Princess Lazuli. She needs it. We need it. All of Abaton needs it! It is the only way for us to get out of this beast and go home."

"But I'm not an automa any longer," Pinocchio said. "The panel is gone. There's no way to get the Pearl out."

"There is," Cinnabar spat. He spun around and snatched Sop's sword from his belt. "I will cut it out of you if I must!"

Geppetto stepped in front of Pinocchio while Mezmer flashed out with her spear, knocking the blade from Cinnabar's hands.

"You would play the traitor when our lord Prester John is dying before our feet?" Cinnabar snarled at Mezmer.

"This is not the way, Cinnabar," Mezmer said.

"Then how else?" The djinni looked crazed and desperate as he stared around at the others for support.

Pinocchio realized Cinnabar was right. But what was he to do?

"Father," Lazuli said, "Pinocchio should not die so that we have the Pearl. It's not worth this. Please, is there a way to take it out and let Pinocchio live?"

Prester John breathed noisily, as if each breath was excruciating. His glazed eyes flickered from Pinocchio to Geppetto. "I am sorry. I do not have this power. I cannot give life. Only the Ancientmost Pearl gives life."

Cinnabar showed his gleaming fangs. "Then it is settled. You are holding the blade, Mezmer."

Mezmer's fox ears flattened against her head. She looked at the spear in her hands and at Pinocchio. "No!" She let the spear clatter to the floor. "You know I cannot. Not Pinocchio."

Pinocchio gave Mezmer a grateful nod. "I am sorry. If I was only an automa again, I could give it to you. But it is trapped inside me."

"True," Cinnabar said, his voice going calm and quiet. The djinni slipped a hand beneath his cloak. "There is still a way."

Before anyone realized what was happening, Cinnabar pulled out the handheld crossbow and aimed it at Geppetto. In that instant, only Lazuli reacted. She leaped at Geppetto as the bowstring twanged. She knocked Geppetto to the ground.

Sop and Mezmer tackled Cinnabar. "It was the only way!" Cinnabar shrieked. "The only way to get back the Pearl!"

"Father!" Pinocchio screamed.

Geppetto lay across Lazuli. As Pinocchio rolled him over, he saw to his relief that his father was not hurt. But Lazuli lay on her back. Blood soaked her tunic. The crossbow bolt was lodged by her heart.

Geppetto gasped. "No, child!"

Lazuli gulped hopelessly for breath. Pinocchio could hardly fathom what he was seeing, the shock and horror of it all was so intense. It was as if the world had gone suddenly silent except for the thundering of blood in his ears. Mezmer's mouth was open with anguish. Sop was spitting and hissing in fury at Cinnabar, while the djinni pleaded. But Pinocchio could hear none of this.

He fell to his knees beside her. "Lazuli . . . you can't . . ."

The blue light was fading from her eyes. He could plainly see that any moment the wound would prove fatal. . . .

But for now, there was still time. If he hurried.

Pinocchio wiped the back of his hand across his eyes to clear his vision. He grabbed the crossbow bolt with both hands, and without hesitating, without letting the fear of what lay ahead give him any pause, he tugged. The barbed tip caught, and Lazuli lurched forward in pain.

He was hurting her, but what else could he do? He had to get the bolt out if he was going to save her life.

"I'm sorry, Lazuli," Pinocchio said. Once more he pulled. The bolt came loose. The tip had broken off, but it was out.

Lazuli's eyes rolled. She groaned and arched her back in pain. Blood spilled faster. Pinocchio pressed both his hands over the wound.

"Hold on, Lazuli," he begged. "Just a moment more."

"What are you doing?" Geppetto said, pulling at his shoulder.

Pinocchio could not explain. There was no time. He pressed his hands over the wound and closed his eyes. When Pinocchio had saved Mezmer, he had still been partially an automa. The sensation then had been as if his gearworks were melting, as if steam were coming from the valves in the cavity of his wooden body. But now, as flesh and blood, the sensation was something worse. It was as if every nerve in his body were being singed.

Pinocchio grew dizzy with the pain, but he held his hands tightly to Lazuli's chest. He couldn't stop. Her life depended on him.

The burning feeling disappeared, replaced by something dull and cold. Looking down at his forearms and hands, Pinocchio watched as his fingernails vanished. The tiny hairs on his arms disappeared. The wrinkles upon his knuckles and the slight lines etching his skin deepened into grooves of wood grain once more.

Blood stopped spilling from Lazuli's chest.

Pinocchio felt his thoughts thickening. In a moment, this Pinocchio—the living, feeling, thinking Pinocchio—would be gone. The mindless automa Pinocchio would return. Although he couldn't see it, he knew the keyhole had opened up on the back of his neck. The panel in his chest was accessible once more.

Lazuli would live—would be able to take the Pearl. Abaton would be safe. His father, all his friends, they would be saved.

This life, he accepted in those fading moments, had always been a temporary gift. Nothing more than an accident. A wonderful accident . . . Pinocchio smiled as Lazuli's eyes began to regain focus, light returning to them.

Geppetto pulled Pinocchio into his arms. He held him like a child. Tears spilled down his whiskered cheeks.

Pinocchio whispered, "I'm glad I had the chance to see what it was like to be alive, Father. I only wish . . ." His thoughts were fading fast, cooling like molten lead into something dense and impenetrable.

"I . . . I . . . just wish . . ."

But there was no use wishing. He knew this was what had to happen. If only he could have seen Abaton too. It sounded like such a wonderful—

Whatever he had been thinking vanished like the last wisp of smoke from an extinguished candle. The automa Pinocchio clattered up stiffly from his master's arms, gears clicking into place.

He waited for the wide-eyed man, his master, to tell him what to do.

24.

The Battle Atop the Tower of Bones

Maestro sprang to Lazuli. "Are you all right, Your Highness?"

Lazuli touched her chest. Her fingers came back red, but the wound was closed. Something dull ached deep in her chest. Something painful lay lodged next to her heart. But for now, she was alive. Pinocchio had saved her. And the deep-down pain was nothing compared to the pain of realizing what Pinocchio's sacrifice now meant.

The blank-faced automa rose to his feet, oblivious to the stares of everyone around him.

"Master Geppetto," she said, reaching for him. "I'm . . . I'm so sorry."

Sop still held Cinnabar, his hooked claws snagged in the djinni's cloak. Cinnabar wriggled free, and Sop didn't try to stop him. Like the others, the cat was stunned, staring at Pinocchio with misery and disbelief.

"Now do you see?" Cinnabar said, climbing to his feet. "You all seemed to have forgotten, but see, it was nothing more than an automa."

Lazuli gave Cinnabar a vicious look. Her voice cracked as she spoke. "How could you do this?"

"I did not mean to shoot you, Your Highness." Cinnabar knelt before her, his head cupped in his hands. "Please forgive me. I meant to shoot the alchemist. I wasn't trying to kill him. I knew the automa would save him. But you live. And now we are all saved. Please, Princess Lazuli, take the Ancientmost Pearl."

When she did not move, Cinnabar rose and approached Prester John. "It was for Abaton, Your Majesty. Tell your daughter. Tell her to take the Pearl."

Prester John didn't seem to hear Cinnabar. He watched Pinocchio and the others. For the first time, the immortal king of Abaton looked perplexed.

"Why do you weep for this wooden boy?" he asked.

Lazuli wasn't sure how to explain this to her father—how Pinocchio had seen Gragl for what she truly was when the others hadn't, how he'd saved Mezmer's and even Captain Toro's lives, how he'd followed only his heart, wanting nothing more than the impossible dream of being a son to Geppetto.

"Can you not see, Father?" Lazuli said. "He was loved."

Cinnabar said, "It was just an automa, Your Majesty. How can they have loved a contraption? It is time to go to Abaton. Princess Lazuli, if you won't, then I will take the Pearl. I will give it to you, my lord."

But as he reached to pull open the front of Pinocchio's shirt, the automa grabbed Cinnabar's arms in a crushing grip.

The djinni howled. "Release me! You're breaking my arms."

"I cannot help it," Pinocchio said flatly.

Mezmer grabbed Pinocchio but couldn't pry his grasp from Cinnabar. Finally, Geppetto dug out the fealty key and, scowling, gave it a turn in the lock. Pinocchio let go and Cinnabar fell, gnashing his teeth in pain.

"You fool," Mezmer snapped at Cinnabar. "Don't you realize there's no way to get it from him? There's a protective charm. He can't let you take it."

"Then how are we to get it?" Cinnabar said.

"Allow me," a low voice said, filling the room like an icy wind.

Through the dark openings in the whale skull, red-armored Venetian soldiers charged in, muskets leveled. The doge entered slowly, a triumphant smile on his face. At his side stood Captain Toro.

"Clear them," he ordered his guards.

Mezmer and Sop sprang up, but too late. The soldiers knocked the weapons from their grasp and pinned them to the floor. Lazuli and Cinnabar charged forward as well. But it was hopeless. The doge had too many soldiers. They disarmed the two and forced them to the ground beside Sop and Mezmer. Swift blows from the stocks of their muskets stilled any resistance.

Pinocchio stood in front of Geppetto, the model of a good automa guarding his master.

The doge approached. "Naughty Geppetto Gazza, again you betrayed me for Prester John. After your capture, I showed you mercy. I took you back in to help me claim Abaton's throne. But you have shown you are not to be trusted. I will not make that mistake again. When I take the Ancientmost Pearl, when I use it to command the Deep One to free us, you will not be coming with me."

Geppetto scowled. "It is not for Prester John that I betrayed you."

The doge cast a scornful glance at the automa protecting Geppetto. "Oh, for that? Your wooden servant? It will not be able to protect you or the Ancientmost Pearl from me. And I have you to thank for that, my disreputable high alchemist."

The doge pulled off his glove, exposing his leaden hand.

He reached out for Pinocchio's chest. Pinocchio clutched the doge's hand to stop him, but the lead took effect immediately, and Pinocchio clattered limply to the floor like a dropped marionette.

"No!" Lazuli cried, struggling beneath the bootheel of the guard who had her pinned.

"You see?" the doge said, kneeling beside Pinocchio. "It is time for Venice to possess the jewel of immortality. It is time to expand our empire. No more monster kingdoms. With this, I will at last lay claim to Abaton for humans."

He ripped Pinocchio's shirtfront. With a snap of the latch, the doge opened the panel and stared in confusion. He put a hand to the pinecone. "What is this?"

The guard who was standing over Lazuli flew forward, almost as if he had been hit by a cannonball. His armor clanked as he hit the opposite wall and toppled to the floor, unconscious.

The doge spun, his bulging eyes wild with confusion. Gragl lifted her barnacle-encrusted head from where she had rammed the soldier. She stared fiercely at the doge. "You will not harm Pinocchio."

The doge sputtered in disbelief. "You nasty little crustacean!" He signaled to his guards. "Shoot her."

Several of the guards fired their muskets. Shells cracked and turned to powder as the shots thudded against Gragl. She fell back. But as the smoke from the musket blasts began to disperse, Gragl groaned and staggered to her feet.

"You will not harm me either," she said.

From behind her, more of the barnacle people emerged, their meekness now replaced by something dangerous, something angry, something menacing. Although the interior of the domed skull was large, the flood of barnacle people quickly filled the room as they charged at the guards. More shots boomed. Musket balls cracked against their ancient, crusted armor.

"Glorious battle!" Mezmer cried, grabbing her spear—and Sop—to join the horde of barnacle people clashing with the doge's soldiers. Lazuli crouched beside Geppetto, protecting him and her father.

An airman fell through the line of barnacle people and landed at Lazuli's feet. When he looked up dizzily, Lazuli saw that it was Captain Toro.

"Captain!" the doge cried from behind the wall of guards protecting him from the crushing onslaught of barnacle people. "Look! It is the Ancientmost Pearl! Take it. Take it before it's too late!"

Lazuli saw Captain Toro look over at Pinocchio, lying motionless on the ground. Pinocchio's chest panel lay open and empty. Lazuli was terrified that the Ancientmost Pearl had been lost, knocked loose and kicked away in the frenzy of battle, but no, there it was, lying on the floor.

It was no longer a pinecone. Her father's glamour, the spell that had transformed it to keep it hidden, along with the protective charms, had worn off. The Ancientmost Pearl, free of Pinocchio, showed itself in its true form. It indeed looked like a pearl, although more massive than any pearl Lazuli had ever seen. It swirled with a dazzling storm of color and pulsing light.

"Hurry, Toro!" the doge shouted. His forces were outnumbered. Gragl and her people were driving back the doge's men. At any moment, they would reach the doge himself.

"Now, Toro! Take it!"

Captain Toro locked eyes with Lazuli.

Lazuli felt weak from her wound, but she was not too weak to defend the Ancientmost Pearl from Captain Toro.

But Captain Toro wasn't looking at her anymore, or at the Pearl. He was staring at Pinocchio. For the briefest instant, a look, the strangest look, passed over the captain's face. She might almost have thought it was sadness.

Then Captain Toro leaped to his feet. Lazuli struggled to stand, struggled to raise her sword. But Toro didn't go for the Pearl. He spun around and gave a roar. His wings opened, and he flew across the heads of the barnacle people.

He grabbed the doge and pulled him off the ground. Captain Toro's wings flattened shut as he rocketed out one of the skull's massive eye sockets and snapped open once they were outside.

"No!" the doge screamed.

The remaining airmen, realizing that they were overwhelmed and their doge was safe, hurried after, escaping the barnacle people's grasps and vanishing one by one into the darkness.

The battle had all happened so fast. Once the guards were gone, the others looked at one another, breathless and astonished. Gragl inched her way past them to reach Pinocchio.

"What's happened to him?" she whispered.

Lazuli knelt beside her, putting a hand on Pinocchio's motionless one. The automa's eyes were open. But Pinocchio stared blank and sightless.

If the Ancientmost Pearl had remained in Pinocchio's chest, he might have eventually changed back into a human. But now that it was out, now that it had been taken from him, he was just an automa, an automa with an empty hole in his chest, an automa that would never again come to life.

Maestro crept onto Pinocchio's shoulder, his antennae drooping. "He's gone. And I never got to play 'Orpheus' for him again. It was his favorite song."

Geppetto knelt to brush a hand across Pinocchio's cheeks, closing his eyes. He gave Lazuli a sad, gentle smile and said, "It's all right, child. There was nothing you could do."

Lazuli brushed angrily at her eyes. There must have been more she could have done. And so much more Pinocchio would have done had he lived.

"My daughter," her father spoke behind her. "You . . . have done well. You will make a wonderful ruler."

She squeezed her eyes shut, unable to face him. Wasn't this what she had always wanted? For her father to see her as more than just another princess to greet guests at the Moonlit Court? So why did this not feel right?

"Lazuli," Prester John wheezed. "The powers of the Ancientmost Pearl make you the new prester . . . make you Abaton's protector. Take it. Lead your people home."

Lazuli opened her eyes, but she didn't look up. Her gaze fell on the jasmine vine twisted around Pinocchio's wrist. Pinocchio's promise to his friend Wiq.

What a friend Pinocchio was. What a friend he could have been. He cared nothing of impressing anyone, of doing what he was commanded to do or expected to do. He was driven simply by his concern for those he loved. This was how a good prester should lead.

Lazuli picked up the Pearl. It was surprisingly heavy. More dense than if it had been solid metal. As she held it, she felt the immense power of the object. Her body tingled from her toes to the tips of her cropped blue hair.

The others stared at her. Cinnabar smiled. "Our queen," he said.

"You will serve me?" she asked.

They all bowed their heads. "Yes," they each said in turn.

"Then the Pearl is mine to do with as I see fit."

Lazuli knelt down to Pinocchio and placed the Ancientmost Pearl back inside his chest. She slid it into place and closed the panel.

"I'll put it back where it belongs," she said.

Golden light filled Pinocchio's eyes, and he blinked.

25.

The Fate of Abaton

What a terrible sleep he'd fallen into. There hadn't been dreams that he could remember, but the sleep itself was so unsettling. A cold and empty nothingness. He was glad to be awake.

Pinocchio looked around. "Why is everyone staring at me?"

They didn't answer.

It came back to him with the force of a thunderclap. Cinnabar wanting the Ancientmost Pearl for Lazuli. Geppetto being shot with the crossbow, except that Lazuli took the bolt instead. She was dying. Then it was all lost.

He looked at his hands. They were still wooden, but he could feel something happening. Warmth was tingling at the fingertips. "I'm . . ."

"Alive, my boy," Geppetto said, pulling him into an embrace.

Pinocchio hugged him back hard, until his father grunted and said, "Careful, son. You've got the strength of an automa."

"Sorry." Pinocchio looked over his father's shoulder at Prester John. "Did you do this? Did you bring me to life?"

"No," Prester John said, frowning. "Lazuli did. Although I'm not sure exactly what she's done."

Pinocchio let go of Geppetto and faced Lazuli. "How did you do this?"

"I gave you the Pearl," Lazuli answered. "I have no need for immortality."

Pinocchio touched his chest, feeling the edges of the panel. "But . . . the Pearl belongs to the ruler of Abaton. That's you!"

Lazuli shook her head.

Cinnabar spat, "So you're handing over the rule of Abaton to . . . to a . . ." He seemed reluctant to insult Pinocchio if he was to be the new prester.

"Lazuli?" Geppetto said. "You can't honestly mean for Pinocchio to take possession of Abaton's throne. He's not even Abatonian."

"Neither was my father," Lazuli said.

Prester John was watching all this with a curious expression. "It is true," he wheezed. "But . . . this wooden boy? Would your subjects accept him as their prester?"

"You don't understand who he is, Father," Lazuli said. "Look at us here. We would not be here if it were not for Pinocchio. It is because of him that we've come this far."

The others, except for Cinnabar, were nodding. Even Gragl and her people.

"But your father's right," Pinocchio said. "They don't know me in Abaton. They know you! They respect you."

"So what would you suggest?" Lazuli said with a smirk. "Do you want me to take it back?"

"No, but—" Pinocchio stammered. "Lazuli, you can't be serious. King? Me? I'm . . . well, I'm just an . . ."

Lazuli cocked an eyebrow. "Just a what?"

Pinocchio bit his tongue and then said, "I'm just . . . Pinocchio."

"Yes, you are," Geppetto said. "And you are my son."

"And my friend, darling boy," Mezmer said. Sop purred in agreement.

"We will proudly serve you as prester," Maestro chirped.

Pinocchio sighed at Lazuli. "If I have to do this, then at least rule with me. I'll need your help."

"You'll need all of our help," Geppetto said.

Lazuli's mouth twisted apprehensively. "You would agree to be a court adviser, Master Geppetto?"

"Of course, Your Majesty," Geppetto said. "As you wish."

"And naturally, I'll be able to counsel you both, along with Geppetto," Maestro said, his antennae jutting proudly straight up. "The court of Abaton can be a tricky business, even for you, Princess . . . I mean Queen Lazuli. Fortunately, I know the ins and outs, having served your father as court musician."

"Naturally," Geppetto said. "You were in the Moonlit Court for—what was it?—two, three whole months before Prester John sent you to Venice."

Maestro fidgeted on Geppetto's palm. "It was the *quality* of my experience serving in court, not the quantity, you incorrigible alchemist."

"Of course," Geppetto said. "Prester John, will you agree to this?"

"I have no say in the matter," Prester John said. "The reign is out of my hands. I trust my daughter to make the decision. She has what I never did. Friends."

Lazuli smiled. "Then it's settled."

"All hail, King Pinocchio and Queen Lazuli!" Maestro proclaimed, bowing his antennae.

Mezmer and Sop dropped to their knees. Geppetto joined them, followed by a reluctant Cinnabar. "Hail, presters of Abaton!"

Pinocchio gave Lazuli a panicky look. "Make them stop, please."

"Now you see how I feel," she said from the corner of her mouth. She gestured for the others to stand.

Geppetto beamed with joy at Pinocchio as he got to his feet. Mezmer's orange fox eyes shone. Sop, like all cats, was incapable of smiling, but Pinocchio was sure his snaggletoothed snarl was meant to be a grin.

Pinocchio smiled back, the smile erupting into laughter. Was this all really true? Was this really happening? He had no idea how to be king. He was just glad to be alive, glad to be back with his friends again.

Lazuli slowly approached Prester John, kneeling by his side. "What will . . . become of you, Father?"

Prester John smiled. "I am dying, child. No, don't cry. It is all right. I do not mind."

Lazuli shook with sobs, and Pinocchio felt his heart lurch watching her. "I mind," Lazuli said. "I don't want you to die."

"Of course you don't," he said weakly. "But I have lived for so very long. And I feel peace now, knowing that you are safe . . . that Abaton is safe. . . . I have not felt so happy . . . in ages."

Geppetto said, "Prester John, we will say our good-byes now. Lazuli, stay with him. We will be waiting for you below."

Gragl's people walked past Prester John in a line, making gestures to the lights atop their heads that Pinocchio took as some sign of honor. Mezmer, Sop, and Cinnabar bowed before the dying king, long and low, before turning to climb down the tower. Pinocchio approached the prester with Geppetto and Maestro.

"Thank you, good Geppetto," Prester John said with a smile. Then he nodded to Maestro. "And you, my grand musician . . . I admit I had a poor ear for music, but you . . . were the finest . . ."

Maestro trembled on Pinocchio's shoulder. "Good-bye, my lord."

Prester John took Pinocchio by the hand and spoke softly. "You will discover how to use the Pearl. It . . . has many powers. The foremost is the power . . . to command the elemental forces of the world. The Deep One is but one of the four primal beings. The monster-queen of oceans . . . she will obey you."

"So for us to leave," Pinocchio asked, trying to wrap his head around all this, "I can tell her to . . . um, open her mouth?"

"With the Pearl . . . you command her," he said.

"Oh, good," Pinocchio said, still not quite sure how this commanding business was going to work but eager to try.

Prester John gave a soft smile. "I am beginning to grasp why you are so remarkable, lad. Yes . . . your friends are right. I believe . . . you will make a fine prester."

"Thank you, my lord." Pinocchio gave a deep bow.

Before he left, he looked back at Lazuli. Tears wet her face. But she smiled at Pinocchio.

He waited with the others at the bottom of the tower of

bones, not speaking or rejoicing that they were going home, but simply huddling together around the fire in Cinnabar's hand. Geppetto put his arm around Pinocchio, and he nestled against his father.

"We're finally together," Pinocchio whispered.

Geppetto smiled down at him. "Yes, we are. You were so brave, my son. I'm proud of you."

Pinocchio leaned closer into his father. "Do you think Lazuli's all right?"

"It'll be hard for her," Geppetto said softly. "She will need us. But she'll get through. When a loved one has reached the end of a rich, full life, no matter how much you might miss them, you know the time is right."

Pinocchio found himself thinking about Geppetto's son, Alberto. His life had been cut tragically short. And at the time, Pinocchio had imagined that death was a terrible thing. But he could see now that for someone like Prester John, death might not be something to be dreaded.

At last, the light in the top of the tower went out. Lazuli floated down to them, holding her father's crown.

"I'm ready," she said, wiping the back of her hand across her cheeks.

"So what now?" Mezmer said. "How do we get out of here?"

"The doge's ship," Pinocchio said. "We'll fly out."

"But how will we get out of the Deep One?" Sop asked.

"I'll command her to release us," Pinocchio said.

Sop's ears flickered. "What exactly does *release us* entail?"

Pinocchio shrugged. "I guess she'll just spit us out."

As Cinnabar followed the others, he looked like he was seriously considering moving in with Gragl's family.

They journeyed from the prester's tower of bones, back past the dirt-born settlements—which fortunately were quiet—while Lazuli told Pinocchio what had happened with the doge.

"Good ol' Gragl!" Pinocchio said proudly. Gragl flashed him a smile. "But why didn't Captain Toro take the Pearl when he had the chance?"

"Maybe he thought it was more important to save the doge?" Mezmer offered.

"Or," Sop said, narrowing his lone eye, "that cowardly airman was afraid the doge would make his escape without him."

"I don't think so," Pinocchio said. "Captain Toro wasn't cowardly. Maybe Mezmer was right."

Lazuli shook her head. "I'm just not sure. He had such an . . . odd look on his face. Like he couldn't bring himself to do that to you, Pinocchio."

"What does he care about me? As far as Toro was concerned, I was finished at that point."

"True," Lazuli said. "But I wonder if he thought he owed you something. You did bring him back to life at the river."

"Only after I drowned him first!" Pinocchio said.

"Still, you didn't have to save him." Lazuli shrugged. "But you did anyway."

Pinocchio blinked in wonderment. He supposed he'd never really know for sure why the captain hadn't followed the doge's orders and taken the Pearl.

"Who cares?" Sop said with a lash of his tail. "Toro will have all the time in the world to explain it to the doge as they get nice and cozy in their new home down here."

"We just have to hope they haven't taken back over their ship," Maestro chirped.

Pinocchio breathed a sigh of relief when they reached

the doge's grand ship and found it still empty. Gragl's people supplied them with food and water for the journey before clustering around to say their good-byes.

"Thank you, Gragl," Pinocchio said. He bent down to give her a hug, and she pulled him in tight, shells poking against him. He was glad he was still wood and endured it politely until she scampered shyly back to her family.

"I'll miss you," she called.

"I'll miss you, too," Pinocchio said, and realized with a grin that he really meant it.

One by one, the others boarded the ship.

"Well, King Pinocchio," Lazuli said with a smirk before they climbed the chain. "Are you ready to see your realm?"

"Don't call me that," he said. "I don't feel like a king."

"And I don't feel like a queen," she said. "Promise you won't treat me like one. Promise we'll be friends no matter what."

Lazuli was his friend. And he was glad for it. He gave her a nod.

He looked down at Wiq's loop of jasmine around his wrist. He would keep his promise to that friend too. When he got to Abaton, he would find a way to free Wiq and all the enslaved Abatonians. He silently swore he would do whatever it took to bring Wiq to Abaton.

Pinocchio clambered up the chain after Lazuli. Gragl's people unhooked the anchor and then hurried back toward their caves, waving enthusiastically. Pinocchio waved back as their ship slowly floated higher.

"Lady Mezmer, knight of the restored Celestial Brigade, will you sail our ship?" Lazuli asked.

Mezmer hurried to the helm, her tall ears flicking proudly. "All ready?"

"Ready!" Pinocchio and Lazuli said together, and then gave each other funny looks. Pinocchio chuckled. Having two presters in charge was going to take some getting used to.

Sop double-checked the sail lines and gave a salute.

Geppetto tapped the lid of a barrel. "Cinnabar is secured."

His muffled voice came through the lid, "You're sure I'll be dry in here?"

"The barrel is lined with naiad scales," Geppetto said. "Even if the wood cracks, there's a film that will keep water—"

"All right, all right," Lazuli said. "Yes, Cinnabar, you'll be dry."

Geppetto gave a laugh and nudged Pinocchio forward. "Lead us home, son."

Pinocchio swallowed hard. He stepped to the bow of the ship. How exactly was he going to command the colossal monster to spit them out? He touched his chest and felt his heart beating fast. He must already be transforming back into flesh, little by little. He wasn't sure exactly how long it would take, but he certainly hoped the wood would all be gone by the time they reached Abaton. He didn't want his subjects to know their new prester had ever been an automa.

Abaton. There was so much about the notion that scared him. He couldn't worry about that yet. He had to focus on getting them out of here.

He cleared his throat and said, "Maestro, some music, please."

"Of course," the cricket said, flexing his wings. He began playing Pinocchio's favorite part of "Orpheus."

Pinocchio held up his hands tentatively. "Um, Deep One . . . Mother, Queen of Oceans, I command you to release us!"

Nothing happened. The others gave him worried looks.

A cold chill ran through Pinocchio, and he began to lower his hands, worrying that—

A deep groan began, followed by the thunderous sound of the ocean rushing in. Blinding light filled the cavernous space. The mountain of water swirled around until it rose high enough to lift the floating ship. Briny, cyclonic wind blasted from the depths of the monster.

The wind hit the sails hard, pushing the boat forward so fast that they were all knocked off their feet. All except for Mezmer, who held the wheel and howled, "Hold on, my darlings!"

The rushing wave and bellowing wind shot the ship past the massive teeth of the Deep One, straight out into a tropical blue sky. The ship rocked side to side among the clouds until the sails billowed and caught the wind.

Pinocchio stood, facing the south with the warm sun in his face and the turquoise ocean stretching into the distance. Geppetto put his arm around him, giving him an excited squeeze. One by one, the others gathered around them, staring out to the horizon, each hoping to be the first to set eyes on the enchanted island realm.

What lay ahead? Pinocchio wasn't sure. But he was glad for his companions, glad for his family, glad they were going home.

"TO ABATON!" Pinocchio roared.

The others cheered, their voices together as one. "TO ABATON!"

GLOSSARY

ABATON. An island in the uncharted reaches of the southern Indian Ocean, ruled by the immortal magician-king **Prester John**. While legends circulated for many centuries prior, Abaton was not discovered until the late thirteenth century by the merchant Marco Polo, although how Polo passed the Deep One to reach Abaton is the subject of much historical debate. Abaton has no human inhabitants, and very few humans have ever set foot on the island. All magic now found around the known world originates from Abaton and its **elementals**.

ABATONIAN DIASPORA. Abatonians who emigrated to the **humanlands** after trade began with **Abaton**. Most of the Abatonian diaspora are **elementals** and **chimera**, but a few human kingdoms have allowed other species to enter, often with dangerous consequences.

ABATONIANS. The nonhuman races of creatures native to the island kingdom of **Abaton**. Many (e.g., **elementals** and **chimera**) are humanoid. Others include talking animals as well as a great menagerie of monstrous species. **Elemental** and **chimera** Abatonians now live in nearly all human kingdoms around the world (see **Abatonian diaspora**), although only in the **Venetian Empire** are Abatonians regarded as a slave class.

AIRMEN, IMPERIAL. A division of soldiers in the **Venetian Empire**'s military. In addition to long-range muskets and weightless armor, airmen are issued mechanical wings originally designed by the renowned **alchemist** Leonardo da Vinci.

ALCHEMIST. A practitioner of **alchemy**. As humans, alchemists possess no natural magical powers over the elements, so they must work with **elemental** assistants to manufacture their alchemical designs using the laws of **transmutation**. Alchemists are able to integrate the various **elemental** powers in order to give technology extraordinary new functions. A rare few of the most talented alchemists have learned to use minor **elemental** beings (e.g., **salamanders**) to perform alchemy without the assistance of a major **elemental**.

ALCHEMY. A branch of human science devoted to engineering and design based on the **transmutation** of materials into magical states using elemental powers. Alchemical technology is almost exclusively found in the **Venetian Empire**, which closely guards the secrets of its workings.

ANCIENTMOST PEARL, THE. The mysterious object that is **Prester John**'s source of immortality and magical power. In the **humanlands** it is also called the Philosopher's Stone, since Prester John is the great "philosopher" of **Abaton** whose magic is the foundation for Venice's **alchemy**.

AUTOMA. Alchemical machines, made of wood and gears, that look like humans, act with limited independence, and are used throughout the **Venetian Empire** as servants and guards, especially by the wealthy.

BASE METALS. Metals, including lead, iron, nickel, and zinc, that are not found in **Abaton**. **Abatonians** cannot stand contact with any base metals. The **alchemists** of the **Venetian Empire** discovered that these metals weaken **Abatonian** magic and thus disrupt alchemical technology. Only transmuted alloys of gold, silver, and copper are used in **alchemy**. The **Abatonian diaspora** living in the **humanlands** primarily use weapons and tools made of bronze.

CATCHFOOLS. A well-guarded district in the city of Venice where **Abatonian elemental** and **chimera** slaves are confined away from the human citizenry.

CHAMELEON CLOAK. A non-alchemical magical item more commonly found outside the **Venetian Empire** that allows the wearer to become nearly invisible, as the fabric of the cloak assumes the appearance of the adjacent surroundings. The cloaks were first brought to the **humanlands** by **gnomes** with the **Abatonian diaspora**.

CHIMERA. A nonmagical humanoid race of **Abatonians** who share both human and animal features. Generally called **half-beasts** by humans of the **Venetian Empire**, as well as in many other human kingdoms.

DEEP ONE, THE. The colossal sea monster that guards the waters of the Indian Ocean around **Abaton**. The Deep One is one of the four rumored primeval monsters that, according to legend, spawned the elemental races of Abaton, and the only one known to humans.

DJINNI (*PL.* **djinn**). One of the four races of humanoid **elementals** of **Abaton**. Djinn are fire **elementals** and exhibit magical powers over heat and flame. Like their lesser **elemental** cousins, **salamanders**, djinn can grow new limbs when they are severed; the process often takes months to years, however.

DOGE. The title of the ruler of the **Venetian Empire**. Although the doge was an elected leader when Venice was a republic, after the large influx of **Abatonians** into the empire during the fourteenth century, the doge became the crowned emperor and the highest leader of all military, political, and daily affairs in the empire. The doge's wife holds the title of dogaressa.

DONKEY CARTS. Wagons equipped with mechanical legs to maneuver over rough terrain—an inexpensive mode of transportation used in the **Venetian Empire**. The mechanical donkey heads attached at the front are often built by second-rate **alchemists** from the parts of out-of-use **automa**.

ELEMENTALS. Magical beings, originating from **Abaton,** that draw their powers from the elements: air, earth, fire, and water. The four major races are intelligent humanoids: **sylphs** (air), **gnomes** (earth), **djinn** (fire), and **undines** (water). Some minor, nonsentient species of elemental creatures also exhibit magical powers, including **pixies** (air), **pygmies** (earth), **salamanders** (fire), and **naiads** (water). Rumors state that there are also four primeval elemental monsters, although, aside from **the Deep One**, little is known about these creatures, even in Abaton.

ELIXIR. A potion, derived from the properties of a **fantom**, that extends life.

FAIRY. A disparaging term, along with *blue fairy*, used by humans in the **Venetian Empire** (and in other human kingdoms) to refer to a **sylph**.

FANTOM. The principal mechanism that animates an **automa**. The fantom was first designed by the **alchemist** Leonardo da Vinci in the late fifteenth century. Composed primarily of transmuted gold, fantoms are the only alchemical creations that require the assistance of all four **elemental** races.

FEALTY COLLAR. A collar of transmuted bronze that tightens to the point of strangulation if the wearer tries to pass certain alchemied barriers. The collars are placed upon many **Abatonian** slaves in the **Venetian Empire** to prevent escape.

FEALTY KEY. A specially designed key that allows one to activate an **automa**'s obedience functions by inserting the key in the **fealty lock**.

FEALTY LOCK. A mechanism found at the back of an **automa**'s neck. Once the **fealty key** is inserted and turned, the **automa** follows all orders presented by its master. If the **automa** has confusion about its orders or begins to malfunction, an elongated nose shows that the **automa** should be repaired or destroyed.

FEALTY PAPERS. Official documents issued by the **Venetian Empire** to all **Abatonian** slaves to prove ownership and identify to which citizen, family, alchemical workshop, or governmental branch the **elemental** or **chimera** belongs.

FIRE EATER. A disparaging term used by humans in the **Venetian Empire** (and in other human kingdoms) to refer to a **djinni**.

FLYING CARPET. A magical item banned throughout the **Venetian Empire**. Flying carpets were first introduced to the **humanlands** in the Arabian Sultanates by **sylph** immigrants.

FLYING LION. An alchemical war machine, in the form of a winged lion, used by the **Venetian Empire**'s military. The design is based on the emblem of Venice.

FORTEZZA DUCALE, THE. The floating fortress and imperial palace of the **doge** of the **Venetian Empire**. Originally the palace sat upon foundations in the lower city, adjacent to the cathedral of Saint Mark. After several attacks upon the city by **chimera** mercenaries serving the Habsburg Empire, Venice's **alchemists** had the masonry transmuted and added gearwork propellers (the largest ever built) to make the Fortezza hover and to better defend the city.

GNOME. One of the four races of humanoid **elementals** of **Abaton**. As earth **elementals**, gnomes exhibit magical powers over metal, rock, and other materials of the earth. Because their flesh has a consistency similar to clay, gnomes can split apart at will into smaller versions of themselves, as well as fuse back together.

HALF-BEAST. A derogatory term used by humans in the **Venetian Empire** (and in other human kingdoms) to refer to a **chimera**.

HUMANLANDS. All kingdoms and civilizations around the world, with the exception of **Abaton**.

HUNTER'S GLASS, THE. One of the four glass globes, each with unique magical properties, made by the ancient **undine** magi of **Abaton**. It shows in which direction a missing object is when the object is visualized in the mind of the one holding it.

LEAD. *See* **base metals**.

MECHANIPILLAR. A mode of transportation used in the **Venetian Empire**. The mechanipillar is an alchemical machine composed of carriages connected in a line and propelled by a number of mechanical legs.

MOONLIT COURT, THE. Prester John's palace in **Abaton**. The Moonlit Court contains many magical wonders, although most are unknown outside Abaton, as few humans have ever visited.

NAIAD. A long, serpentlike, nonsentient water **elemental** with hard, transparent scales. Their scales are often used to strengthen fabrics or create flexible frames for fabrics, such as for **airmen**'s wings, or for naiad curtains, which can hold back water to create indoor tanks for **undines**.

PIXIE. A minuscule, nonsentient air **elemental** that becomes luminous when it feeds on air.

PIXIE BULB. A type of lamp found throughout the **humanlands**, but originally designed by early **alchemists** in the **Venetian Empire**. The glass bulb is filled with **pixies**, which glow as they consume the air pumped into the bulbs.

PRESTER JOHN. The immortal magician-king of **Abaton**. Although little is known of Prester John's origins, the source of his long life and magical powers is credited to the **Ancientmost Pearl**. He is commonly referred to as His Immortal Lordship by his subjects.

PYGMY. An amorphous, nonsentient earth **elemental**. Pygmies are hard to distinguish individually as they often cluster together and even split apart into nearly featureless blobs.

SALAMANDER. A lizardlike, nonsentient fire **elemental** that feeds on burning wood and other flammable objects and can regrow severed limbs. Salamanders are used occasionally by highly gifted **alchemists** to perform **alchemy** without a humanoid **elemental** assistant.

SENTRIES. Large, armored **automa** that function as guards throughout the **Venetian Empire**.

SEVEN-LEAGUE BOOTS. Magical footwear, more commonly found outside the **Venetian Empire**, that allows the wearer to travel great distances with each step. Despite the name, such boots are rarely powerful enough to cover seven leagues, and easily malfunction with dangerous consequences. Seven-league boots were first introduced to the **humanlands** of northern Europe by **sylphs** belonging to the **Abatonian diaspora**.

SYLPH. One of the four races of humanoid **elementals** of **Abaton**. Sylphs are air **elementals** and exhibit magical powers over the air. Having no wings, sylphs cannot fly. Due to their weightlessness and control over wind, however, many sylphs are able to glide short distances.

TRANSMUTATION, THE LAWS OF. The process of integrating the various **elemental** powers to change something into a different state or to give an object qualities it did not possess before.

UNDINE. One of the four races of humanoid **elementals** of **Abaton**. Undines are water **elementals** and exhibit magical powers over water. Since they are unable to leave the water, they are rarely encountered away from bodies of water unless they are being held in tanks or chambers separated by **naiad** curtains.

VENETIAN EMPIRE, THE. Currently the foremost empire in the **humanlands**, Venice was historically overshadowed by its larger neighbors, including the Byzantine Empire and the pope's Holy Roman Empire. After trade began with **Abaton,** however, Venetian **alchemists** began designing war machines and **automa** technology using Abatonian **elemental** magic. The empire grew in wealth and military might, soon conquering the entire Italian peninsula and eventually coming to control nearly all the Mediterranean Sea. Many human kingdoms around the world (most prominently the Sultanate of Zanzibar and the Aztec Confederation) have pledged allegiance to Venice under threat of conquest. The Venetian Empire is ruled by an emperor who is given the title of **doge**.

ACKNOWLEDGMENTS

Just as my Pinocchio discovers that we are profoundly shaped by the people around us, so too was this story. My boundless gratitude goes out to many....

To my editor, Rotem Moscovich, whose amazing instincts and special alchemy brought out the beating heart of *The Wooden Prince*. Also to Julie Moody, Karen Sherman, Maria Elias, Dina Sherman, and the rest of my extraordinary team at Disney Hyperion.

To my agents, Josh and Tracey Adams, for their enduring support and unwavering enthusiasm.

To my first readers, who always guide my stories in ever better directions: Jennifer Harrod, J.J. Johnson, and Stephen Messer. Also to the writers, teachers, and friends who lent their creative advice and generous support: Tom Angleberger, Tom Carr, Andrew S. Chilton, Alan Gratz, Greg Hanson, Lois Pipkin, Carrie Ryan, Amy Kurtz Skelding, Sharon Wheeler, and the wonderful Carolinas kid lit community.

To my family—Bemises, Butchers, Bauldrees, Byes, and Gorelys—for being my best cheerleaders.

To all the loyal and passionate fans—you know who you are!—who have been clamoring for new books.

Most of all, thank you to my wife, Amy Gorely, and daughter, Rose. Whether we are wandering beside the canals of Venice or relaxing at home in Hillsborough, every day is a glorious adventure.